Praise for Jason V Brock:

"Bravo!"

—RAY BRADBURY

"A damn good writer; I enjoy [Brock's] work."

—DAN O'BANNON

"An excellent writer and natural storyteller."

—EARL HAMNER, JR.

". . . a clever young man, Jason Brock."

—HARLAN ELLISON®

"[Brock] makes the fantastic utterly believable. A fine writer indeed."

—GEORGE CLAYTON JOHNSON

"[Brock] takes characters and situations into places I would never have thought of . . ."

—RICHARD MATHESON

Books by Jason V Brock:

Totems and Taboos (Poetry)

The Bleeding Edge:
Dark Barriers, Dark Frontiers
(anthology; with William F. Nolan)

William F. Nolan: A Miscellany

The Devil's Coattails:
More Dispatches from the Dark Frontier
(anthology; with William F. Nolan)

Milton's Children

Simulacrum and Other Possible Realities

jason v brock

SIMULACRUM

and Other Possible Realities

foreword by william f. nolan

introduction by james robert smith

hippocampus press

new york

Acknowledgements: see p. 249.
Published by Hippocampus Press
P.O. Box 641, New York, NY 10156.
http://www.hippocampuspress.com

Cover art and design by Jason V Brock.
Cover production by Barbara Briggs Silbert.
Hippocampus Press logo designed by Anastasia Damianakos.

First Edition
1 3 5 7 9 8 6 4 2

ISBN13: 978-1-61498-055-1

Contents

Dedicated . . .

to Sunni, our creatures, all the animals of the world (past, present, and future), and our friends—William F. Nolan, Diane O'Bannon, George Clayton Johnson, John and Wilma Tomerlin, Jerad Walters, Les Barany, Rocky Wood, Frank M. Robinson, and S. T. Joshi (and Mary Krawczak Wilson)—for their kind support and advice.

Also . . .

Not to forget friends and family we have lost: Dan O'Bannon, Norman Corwin, Ray Bradbury, Charles E. Fritch, Adam Niswander, Forrest J Ackerman, and April Brock.

The author would like to extend a heartfelt personal *"Thank you"* to Richard Matheson and to the awesome specter of the late Charles Beaumont. And Hippocampus Press!

Ad mala patrata haec
sunt atra theatra . . .

Foreword:
Man of Many Talents

Who is Jason V Brock?

Well, I predict that one of these days, in the very near future, this question won't have to be asked, because Jason will be well-known for his multiplicity of talents: short story writer, novelist, essayist, poet, photographer, filmmaker, artist, designer, editor, musician, publisher, documentarian, performer, panelist—he's a dynamic force for all seasons, a brilliant, intense, fast-talking one-man band who excels in all these areas. Jason is a cyclone on two legs, with an encyclopedic mind that retains thousands of odd facts on literally dozens of subjects.

You don't *meet* Brock, you *experience* him.

An avowed reptile lover, Brock and his equally amazing wife (love ya, Sunni!) share their busy life with several "reptile children"—four diapered tortoises, two skinks, and a tough-minded iguana named Liz. Jason and Sunni are dedicated vegetarians who vigorously support animal rights while feeding flocks of local birds in their expansive back yard (officially designated a wildlife refuge). I find it nearly impossible to write an objective piece about them; they are much too close to my heart for objectivity.

Above all else, Jason is my closest friend, someone I can always count on, a caring, generous, sensitive, hard-working collaborator with a devastating sense of humor who never fails to amuse and amaze me. I've never met anyone remotely like him. Well, that's not entirely true, since he shares many virtues with my dear-departed pal Charles Beaumont. Chuck was a true phenomenon, but was not quite up to Brock's high level—which is why I call Jason "Super Beaumont." By way of explanation, a brief personal aside . . .

In the 1950s, I was a member of what is now known as "The Group" or "The Southern California School of Writers" (celebrated in my book *California Sorcery*). We were a diverse cluster of young scribes whose influence on popular literature (*Playboy, Esquire, Collier's Weekly, Rogue,* multiple acclaimed novels and collections), television, and film was (and still is) considered enormous.

Other members included my dear friends Ray Bradbury (*Fahrenheit 451; Dandelion Wine*), Richard Matheson (*I Am Legend; A Stir of Echoes*), George Clayton Johnson (*Ocean's 11;* and with whom I wrote *Logan's Run*), John Tomerlin (*Challenge the Wind*), Chad Oliver (*The Winds of Time*), and my best pal for a decade, Charles Beaumont (*The Twilight Zone; The Intruder*). Latter-day members included Harlan Ellison (*Deathbird Stories; I Have No Mouth and I Must Scream*), and Robert Bloch (*Psycho*).

We worked on many of the greatest shows of the time and beyond (*The Twilight Zone; Have Gun, Will Travel; Star Trek; Night Gallery*), and are responsible for some of the most well-known films also (*Duel; The Incredible Shrinking Man; The Raven; Somewhere in Time; What Dreams May Come; Burnt Offerings; Logan's Run; Trilogy of Terror*).

People that were touched by, or collaborated with, "The Group" (or who cite them as an influence), include Stephen King, Rod Serling, Steven Spielberg, Roger Corman, William Shatner, Jack Nicholson, Frank M. Robinson, Dennis Etchison, Dan Curtis, John Shirley, Joe R. Lansdale, and innumerable other writers and filmmakers.

To my mind, Jason V Brock belongs in this select category: in the 1950s, he would have been one of "The Group" along with Beaumont, Matheson, Oliver, Tomerlin, Johnson, and myself. Not just a follower or influenced by us, but part of the core: *one* of us. Allow me to elaborate . . .

Overall, Jason is a remarkable fellow and an awesome talent. This is not hyperbole; open up to any page in this book and you'll see what I mean. An award-winning artist and author, his latest verse—and a small complement of his drawings—supplement the fiction in this strong collection. A love of irony and a stinging social commentary permeate Jason's work (for example in the poems "Pathologist's Roulette" and "Frac/tion," or the stories "Milton's Children," "The Underground," and the marvelously complex "Simulacrum"), as well as preoccupations with themes of inner turmoil, justice, and the human condition (as in the haunting "Where Everything That Is Lost Goes" or the disturbing "Red-Wat-Shod").

To that end, he can be honest and direct to a startling degree. Witness this line from his story "What the Dead's Eyes Behold": "None of the drugs—pot, xtc, Klonopin—insulated her against herself: Her wounded psyche was content to itch her insides, and she was content to rub herself raw." This is a man who deals with absolute truths, abhorring deception and artifice.

He is a deep-thinking individual, even a provocateur, and his work is sometimes extreme, dark, and gruesome. Violence in his writing—some of it quite brutal—always serves a purpose; he uses it to expose some flaw or weakness in a character or scenario, never as merely an end in and of itself, as in this quotation from "P.O.V.": "So I closed my fingers around her throat . . . like a god or something. And once I had my hands on her, she was just—a ragdoll. She fought me, but it only hardened my resolve. Then, her face sort of . . . puffed up, started turning blue. Her body relaxed, but I kept on squeezing," or this one from the frightening "Dream Poem #00":"To rot in vermin amidst blood-spattered walls / And the only answer to the screams / Are the echoes of the end of / Hope." Fortunately, he is also blessed with an ever-present sense of humor and a plentitude of wit. To that end, a quick glance at "The Hex Factor" had me laughing aloud.

Just as it can be blunt, forceful, and firm-minded, Jason's work can also be tender, emotional, and beautiful. Near completion of his first novel, called *(UnSub)*, his ear for dialogue, deft characterization, and sharp prose is here on clear display. The deeply moving "Object Lesson" (my personal favorite, and one of the best stories I've ever read in any genre, by *any* author) bears this out. The lovely poem "Story of a Blade" brought tears to my eyes. I like every story and poem in this book; frequently innovative and original, each has a special power, and they cover an amazing range—from horror to science fiction to comedy to literary.

Suffice it to say, in this remarkable collection you will encounter a powerful new creative voice. There is much to savor in these pages. To rework a prediction regarding a young Richard Matheson: You may be in at the birth of a legend.

Welcome to the fictional worlds of Jason V Brock: Go, Jason!

He's amazing. So be amazed.

—WILLIAM F. NOLAN

Vancouver, WA

Preface

Welcome to my first short story collection. In no particular order, the writing contained herein spans all periods of my life—good times and bad—from early works to some of the most recent. I am not one to stick to a certain type of story, and I abhor what passes for most horror and science fiction these days, so there are very few "straight-on" treatments of the standard tropes that seem have taken over the post–King/Koontz/Barker era (nothing against them in particular, but I grow weary of their laborious, massive texts, and even more weary of their slow-witted, plodding imitators). My perspective is more informed by Borges, García Marquez, Serling, surrealism/fantastic realism (as in the art movements), Lovecraft, Poe, and Bradbury's early works (there are others, but that's a good start). Also cinema of all kinds. And music: One must have music in one's life.

This means I am terribly bored with gore, torture-porn, zombies, slashers, Hell/Heaven (in other words, monotheistic notions of an afterlife), vampires, and just staid thinking or conceptualizations in general. Do I ever write about any of the above? Certainly. Nothing is off-limits, but it must compel me *mightily* for me to pursue it, or at least be what *I* consider a fresh approach for me to write it. On the other end of this spectrum (especially as a fairly seasoned editor), I am also fatigued of "high and twee" self-consciously bookish navel-gazing and cuteness, and too many stories (even from different authors) striking the same "note." It's analogous to listening exclusively to one or two musical acts, or admiring the output of one visual artist and shirking the whole wide world of voices and expressions that are available. It's also a bit cliquish, I feel, and will be the undoing of the field in the long run as the audience we are interested in cultivating grows away from us. It appears that most writers these days seem to have run out of interesting ideas (or just stick to a formula) and have little grasp of how to write an effective tale (or how to edit their own work even if they have ability and can write well) in other styles. Am I the world's greatest writer, or the most original thinker in genre fiction? (And believe me, it's *all* genre, from porn to co-called chick-lit to horror to literary fiction, so if there are those reading this who eschew labels and the like, I have this to say: Please get over it!) No, I'm sure I'm not, but I do have eclectic tastes, some talent, and a strange worldview, so I figure I'm ahead of the game, at least to some degree. (On a side note, it also helps to have these other qualities: a sense of humor, good editing skills/instincts, a love for rewriting/revision, and a keen proofing eye. Just FYI!) I'm sure there are people who will hate some of the things that I feel are hallmarks of my work: intensive characterizations, experimentation with format, cinematic presentation. I can appreciate that, and that's OK. But enough of the theory and observations for now (the postscripts to each story will also illuminate the outlook, I believe, at work in each piece).

Like most folks, I love being productive. Often, I wind up drawing or painting my ideas—or composing songs—instead of (sometimes in addition to) writing stories. Wherever the drive to create originates from, it is more profound than religion or politics, more merciless than love or hate, and more pleasurable than money or fame. It is what pushes us onward as a species to ask questions, and to tease out the answers to the mystery of existence in any form that we can, be it the visual and performing arts, science, music, film, or writing, from the first hominid to the present.

I have always been a writer: poetry, short stories, nonfiction, and so on. I hope that the content within these covers is thought-provoking, moving, frightening, perhaps even a little humorous—but never forced, boring, or contrived. It is my sincere wish that you like reading these stories as much as I liked creating them. The whole reason, after all, for any creative endeavor is to *share* an experience—a moment in space and time—and to come away with a fresh, novel, or changed perspective.

That has certainly been the case with my wife and me: We both feel quite lucky to be able to have had such great mentors as the ones I mention on the dedication page to alter our mindsets, challenge our preconceptions, inspire us. In all cases, they touched us in ways that we grasped immediately, and in other ways that we only realized later, with their insightful critiques, extreme kindness, and gentle guidance.

For all that—and more—we are very grateful.

—JASON V BROCK

Vancouver, WA

Introduction

I met Jason V Brock when he was just a kid. I was running a comic book shop at the time and he ended up working in the store for a while. Even then I realized that Jason had an unusual mind and was creative on a level far exceeding his years. He was not only precocious, but very intelligent.

Also, he laughed like Peter Lorre, which I thought added to his charm.

Over the years, though, I lost touch with Jason. I stayed in Charlotte, North Carolina, treading water and trying to edge my way into publishing as a full-time writer. I sold stories and articles and review columns and, eventually, novels. And every so often I would wonder where Jason was and how he'd ended up as an adult. I always figured the bright kid I had known would end up doing all right for himself and make a mark creatively as a writer or an artist.

Finally, one day, I did get an e-mail from Jason. Although I'd tried to find him several times via the Internet, I had not succeeded. However, he had found me first. He was much the same as I had remembered him:

Intelligent, funny, creative, dangerously irreverent, and self-assured. Also, he still laughed like Peter Lorre. (Cue Weevil from Bobby London's *Dirty Duck*.)

As Jason and I reintroduced ourselves after so many years, I learned that he had traveled far and wide while I had remained in my adopted hometown of Charlotte. Jason had journeyed to points west and north in the US, had visited nations on the other side of the Pacific, and had been to Europe. As for his creative side, he had been busy with poetry and graphic arts, and I soon learned that he had no less than three film documentaries in production.

And, more, he had met and befriended some of the great artists and authors whose work I had long admired.

Jason Brock had not been treading any water.

With this collection, *Simulacrum,* we get to see Jason Brock as a full creator. On display here are not just his well-crafted short stories, but also poems, script-as-story, and illustrations. I am impressed, as you will be. Jason has not spent his years idly. He didn't just meet those authors and artists and screenwriters; Jason shows here that he has learned much from them, has absorbed the things of worth that they have to offer, and displays his own additions of skill to the various forms.

When I was reading "Black Box," a story he wrote as homage to the great Richard Matheson, I was impressed with Jason's ability to achieve true tension within the brevity of a short story. This is something that is not easy to do and something that some writers who have many years of experience are unable to duplicate.

In stories like "Simulacrum" and "The Central Coast" you'll see that Jason knows the world. He has not lived an insular life sitting in one place, meeting few, knowing fewer. His fiction illustrates vividly that he has absorbed the world in which he has moved and that he has understood—or tried to understand—everyone he has met.

He amazed me with "P.O.V." How detailed a story can an author tell within the confines of 4400 words? You'll discover how with this exceptional tale illustrated in a way that I found not only unique, but ingenious. Someday I hope to write something like that!

Simulacrum as a collection is something you will not forget. It is not—as so much is, these days—an amusing gossamer thing to be experienced and then dismissed forever. This collection is, like the anthologies that Jason Brock has edited, like the graphic art that he has brought to vision, like the sparkling and haunting documentaries that he has directed, a thing of permanence.

Jason V Brock was a talented and unique boy when I first met him. Now, he has proven that the precocious kid has become a skilled creator as a man. We always hope that the promising youths we knew will bear out that promise in later years. Jason has multiplied that promise. The bright boy is now golden.

And he still laughs like Peter Lorre.

—JAMES ROBERT SMITH

Matthews, NC

Simulacrum and Other Possible Realities

What the Dead's Eyes Behold

"Look at that."

It was not the pendulous, ripe globes of her breasts—decorated by dark, erect areolas—which captured his interest.

"Something's going on there."

It was not even the way the skin of the ribcage and flat, lightly toned belly—covered by the faintest down of hair above the mons—still responded with gooseflesh at his touch that intrigued him.

"Amazing . . ."

It was not the tuft of pubic hair—just a neatly cropped, teasing strip—nor the creamy round hips, curving into the supple thighs . . . Not the full calves, tapering into tiny ankles and ending in the demure feet that was so captivating.

"But what does it mean?"

Neither was it the fleshy, enticingly round, tight and smooth buttocks, sloping in at the narrow waist along a muscular back to form a graceful hourglass, dimpled on both sides just above the *gluteus maximus,* that he found so compelling. Though he knew her body would make a fantastic mold; her addition would be one of his greatest pieces.

"Uncanny . . . same as all the others . . ."

It was not the delicate scapulae, the fragile, nearly hairless arms, or even the fine clavicle indentations, like kilned porcelain—all so very beautiful. None of these things held his gaze: the lustrous shock of onyx hair, the petite, completely feminine voluptuousness; the pale, resplendent face; the lush, swollen lips—ready, wet, inviting . . .

No: it's those dark, dark eyes . . . Haunting. Knowing. Mysterious.

"What do you see?"

Her silence frustrated him: Already her eyes were glassing, the pupils fixed, dilated. *It's as though the dying suddenly "get it" at the last minute, and they can't turn their gaze away from whatever "it" is . . . Little boys. Policemen. Goth chicks. Bikers. Lawyers. Street people. Prostitutes. All the same . . .*

As he looked into the snuffed orbs of this exquisite corpse, as beautiful a carcass as he had ever seen, he felt a chill—not from the autumn cold—but from the dawning recognition of what he must now do; trapped in the moment like an insect in amber.

Calliope—that was her name . . .

Calliope.

"Yeah, I'll tell you what I see, all right."

Calliope laughed to herself, studying her nails, not sure if they needed a repaint as she waited for his reply. Chatting online gave her a way to express her pent-up, Sagittarian fury, her exhibitionistic streak, her creeping nihilism. She was getting impatient.

Some people . . .

The IM window popped up: **Where?**

None of the drugs—pot, xtc, Klonopin—insulated her against herself: Her wounded psyche was content to itch her insides, and she was content to rub herself raw.

The wharf, she typed, tilting her head slightly.

She was alone now. With herself, her thoughts and fears. She hated it. After Ryan, she had tried girls: they bored her. Fucking them supplied no element of *danger;* it was like masturbating with a friend.

Ryan, her junky ex-boyfriend, but the only one she loved, used to strangle her during sex; it turned her on. After he overdosed, she discovered that she wanted it that way all the time. She was hooked on the *taboo-ness* of it: she craved bigger thrills, higher highs, closer brushes with death to get off after him.

Good choice, the chat window chimed. **When?**

She looked at the clock: *12:45 A.M.*

Her nails clacked across the keys: **About an hour?**

Cool. C U there :-) His avatar dimmed as he logged off.

She stared at the monitor a moment, feeling suddenly weepy. She figured this guy was worth meeting once. At least he was interesting; everybody else was too . . . *timid* for her liking. Maybe he was like Ryan.

She sighed, rubbing her forehead. As she sat in her squalid little room, awash in the sickly blue glow of her computer monitor, the MP3 player next to her bed pulsed *Personal Jesus.* She studied the faded scars on the insides of her arms. Mouthing the lyrics unconsciously, she traced the patterns on her skin, resisting the old impulse to lightly pull a razor—so delightfully painful, so deliciously relieving—across her delicate skin. She licked her lips in remembered anticipation of the thin lines of red that would open on her wrists, her forearms. She closed her eyes.

How has it come to this? Meeting strangers online . . . living hand-to-mouth in a studio apartment in a shitty part of town . . . shaking my ass for money . . .

Even though her body was strong, her routine honed by years of ballet and gymnastics, her face told another story.

She looked intently into the magnified makeup mirror on her nightstand, its fisheye distortion revealing every crow's foot, every spider vein, every single flaw and pore in unflinching detail.

Maybe this guy's the one . . . Maybe this'll be the night. Another sigh slipped from her black-lined lips, quiet as the rustle of a raven's wing.

"We'll see . . ."

Leaning back in her chair, Calliope lit another clove cigarette. She pulled the separating scrim next to her bed aside, peering into her miniscule closet: kitten heels, stilettos, hose, lingerie, mini-skirts, sheer blouses—her tools of the trade. She took a drag, blew it out, contemplating.

"What to wear?"

When he arrived, she was already there. He always liked to be a little late for these rendezvous; one could never tell where they would lead.

Across the inlet, blinking markers tolled mournfully in the water. The salt air was cutting: full of innuendo, fear, desperation.

For a moment he absorbed the scene: cold, misty harbor, choppy waves causing a late ferry to bob distantly on the horizon. Sleepy gulls peered at him from atop some burnt out streetlights, their feathers ruffled against the early morning chill. Far away, he heard the muted sounds of other nocturnal denizens in their cars; human flotsam moving through the mercury-vapor illuminated byways of the city. . . . He imagined that they were hurtling into the future, or perhaps fleeing the past, these self-aware collections of atoms . . . struggling in every living moment either to enact or to overcome their own personal inertia. He regarded the proscenium of the sky, their own personal theatre with its yellow, gibbous moon, where some drama would play out this very evening. The overcast, light-polluted sky, an otherworldly pink hue, was glowing above; the setting was exquisite, lonely, perfect. It was beautiful in its desolation.

He saw a figure under one of the lamps: a girl, her smoky breath trailing away at intervals like a wraith.

There she is . . .

Nice: fishnets, micro-skirt and garters, short jacket . . .

He walked closer, his heart beginning a familiar tattoo in his ears.

"Where *is* this guy?"

Calliope was cold: her nipples were like glasscutters under her corset. She took a long drag of her clove, shifting from foot to foot in an attempt to keep warm.

I hate it when people are late. She was a lot of things to a lot of people, but late was never one of them. She checked her cellphone. *Maybe he's lost. He said he was just passing through . . .*

"Fifteen minutes late," she muttered. *I'm giving him ten more minutes, then I'm going clubbing while it's still early. I just need to pull out of this funk I've been in.*

She leaned against the post, watching some buoys in the water. She closed her eyes, the lap of the surf soothing her mind; the saltwater smelled like sushi. She smiled.

I love sushi. She looked at her phone again, then lit another cigarette, its glowing orange tip making an arc in the night. "Five more minutes, dude."

Every night he tried to drum up something. A few magical experiences had stayed with him, though.

Like the ancient wino he had set on fire—the guy's breath had flared up like some organic flamethrower on his dying scream; or that tranny hooker whose wig flew off as he bashed her head in with a mallet—for a minute, he thought he had torn her head completely *off . . . Then there were the runaway identical twins. They had hitched a ride, then propositioned him for sex: "Sheryl" causing a distraction as "Shelly" tried to rob him. Unfortunately for them, he was hip to that game. Sometimes he felt a little twinge of remorse when reflecting on how the sisters had begged for one another's life, each volunteering to be his victim in exchange for letting the other go . . . That kind of loyalty is pretty rare these days, even in families.*

Of course, it did nothing to change their shared fate . . .

"PlayMisty4U?" he asked as he approached her.

She took another pull on the cigarette. "Diabolicus13?" she responded, stamping her cigarette out.

His eye fixation had begun around that time. His attitudes about life and death had been changing—evolving—based on medical texts he had read regarding advanced trauma care. After much research, he decided he wanted to tie the two sides of his personality together—his artistic impulse to create and his gnawing compulsion to annihilate and destroy.

"That's me. You look nice." He smiled at her. They shook hands under the flickering radiance of the streetlight.

To that end, he began collecting "souvenirs" from his conquests. In time he graduated to taking physical "trophies" from their bodies, which he started working into his art. Later this morphed into posing his victims; then came recording the scenarios.

His art took off at that point: after years of obscurity, he finally began to garner attention for his increasingly outrageous sculptures. The more visceral and realistic his dioramas became, the more successful his shows were. Even the most debauched subjects of his latest works—necrophilia, cannibalism—were readily accepted by an increasingly eager public. It brought him a perverse pleasure that no one realized the scenarios were based on actual incidents: his own crimes—rape, torture, mayhem . . .

The more outré his sculptures became, the more in demand he was as an artist, the better attended his exhibitions were.

Lately, though, he yearned for more. He was growing bored with killing, and his art needed something else. That was when he started to incorporate the insights and thoughts of his victims, to give it more—ever more—of an edge . . .

"Thanks. So do you. Call me Calliope," she said, brushing hair from her face.

As he had gotten older, he sought understanding of his darker motivations, beyond the whining of pop-psych, or the high-minded self-serving condescension of the

FBI's Behavioral Sciences Unit.

He pulled his lapels around his throat. "Aren't you cold? It's chilly out here!"

He actually longed to know the architecture of the fantastic—the bridge between life and death; the dynamics of physiology, consciousness, and the '21 grams.'

For him, at this particular moment in his life, it went beyond sex and murder: it was the purest form of research—a quest for the soul itself. He had grown bored of divining the future from scads of entrails—he wanted empirical proof from the victims themselves.

"I am a little. It won't matter soon," she said, staring at him. She was intense, her eyes piercing.

Some people, confronted with the end, were too afraid to follow through; others lied in a feeble attempt to placate him, his demands. These were the lost souls, the broken, the weak.

They needed him . . .

And he needed them.

Once a few more platitudes were exchanged, the typical scenario unfurled under the dock: tongue thrusting; squeezing of ample breasts freed from the bondage of faux leather; the stroking of slim fingers over the stiffness of his crotch.

Now she was squatting, naked skin flushed in the cool night air. Oblivious to the chill, she sucked him with audible zeal as she fondled and rubbed herself. Her moans made the shaft of his penis vibrate.

"Oh God!"

"That's it!" he exclaimed in response, sweat breaking over his body. He felt a rush of blood from his pelvis as he emptied his testicles into her mouth. She stroked his body as she licked him clean.

At last she stood, and they kissed deeply.

Looking at each other—their cold breath falling away in the November air—it suddenly seemed as if they were occupying a vacuum: there was no sound, no movement, nothing but the moment.

"Remember what you said in the chat," she whispered, her tiny voice like a tornado breaking the silence.

He regarded her wordlessly, then: "I do. Don't forget your part . . . you promised you'd tell me before you died what you see, hear, feel."

She nodded, and her liquid green irises were huge in the half-light, darting from his cold eyes to his grimly set mouth. She was shivering now, her nude body striped by the moonlight between the boardwalk slats.

Relaxing as he clasped his strong hands around her neck, she never reached up during the entire process. As the pressure gradually increased, her eyes popped out slightly, her lips became more pronounced, her skin reddened. Then her eyelids began to droop, and petechiae blossomed on her face.

"What are you seeing?" he demanded, intensifying his clutch on her throat.

Briefly, this caused her to refocus on him and she half smiled, like his personal Mona Lisa. Her tongue, congested and thick, struggled, and she stammered through distressed vocal cords: "It's . . . it's . . . bright—sun! It's . . . it's . . ."

Then, in a millisecond, she was gone, eyes an emotionless desert. She went limp in his hands.

"Come *back! Calliope!"* Relinquishing his grip, he gently lowered her naked body to the shore, glancing around as they crumpled to the sand.

"Was Calliope a part of the 'Goth' scene, Mr. Manfred?" the young blonde reporter asked, thrusting the microphone into the distraught old man's face. The camera operator made a sharp, poorly focused frame of the tired man's red-eyed countenance.

"No. No, she was—" Mr. Manfred stopped for a moment, the camera steadying as he collected his thoughts. Images of Calliope Manfred—her childhood, the prom, dance recitals—panned by on a remote broadcast monitor. He continued: "She was a sweet girl growing up. Loved dancing . . . And animals—took to being vegetarian as a little girl."

The blonde reporter was back: "Such a tragedy." She flipped her hair from her face, pouting her lips.

The jumble of words mixed together . . . sounds, images overlapping, layering one atop another . . . There would be much attention for a few agonizing weeks, then a gradual fraying into static; yesterday's news blown down the street. To the media, it was just another story; to the survivors it was their new reality—a life that death forced them to occupy day in and day out like some ill-fitting skin.

Calliope's parents were devastated, but—strangely—unsurprised. She had never been "right"; not like her brother, the short-haired, God-fearing Republican.

"Now she's gone. The marriage, the kids, the SUV, and the big house in the suburbs—her list was left undone," Mr. Manfred said, looking directly into the camera. He suddenly walked off, then got into the car with his wife and son; they drove away together, alone.

"This is Veronica Boyd, KPXZ News, reporting from the wharf. Back to you, Steve."

He sat with Calliope for a long time, listening to the hypnotic wash of the surf on the shore.

We all want to know what's next, don't we? There's got to be something more than just . . . this.

He studied the harbor without really seeing it, trapped in the web of his thoughts. The slowly brightening horizon indicated that it would be dawn soon.

Life comes down to a few instances: Do it or not, left or right, yes or no.

He rose to his feet, rigidly moving toward the black water. *Time to decide . . .*

My whole life has been one big attempt at delaying the unavoidable. . . . If I could understand death—the why *it happens, the* how *it's different from life . . .*

He glanced back at Calliope's still form under the dock.

"It's all a matter of *will*." His throat was tight, dry.

The answers he needed required comprehension: the antithesis of the modern approach to the study of death and dying. Scientists, he knew, loved to shine light on process, leaving the metaphysical facets completely enveloped in darkness. To them, it was all just a personally removed analysis of the suffering of others: overzealous cells multiplying out of control; syncopated hearts collapsing on themselves; overtaxed axons drifting into the void.

Then death arrived: demanding, implacable—like Beethoven's Fifth Symphony. Then quiet. Then quietus. That was where art could complete the loop of understanding.

It was the work of a life, now: his own.

Slow lingering death. Naturalistic death. Torture. Instantaneous death . . .

He had tried nearly every type of victim, human or otherwise, and every conceivable methodology as well. Studying and documenting the ways they acted and reacted to death and the dying process gave his rage and fear a focus. Sometimes he cursed himself at the lost opportunities and experiments from his youth, which he now regarded as valuable research opportunities that he had squandered on sheer hedonism.

Of course, he had come a long way; that was obvious the times that he flipped through his meticulously organized notes or studied his fading Polaroids: a scrapbook of serial murder.

"If I'm completely honest, it's all to one end: to avoid fate by way of destiny . . ."

He had tried to leverage his intellect to take the sting out of the sharp terror he felt about his own mortality. Perhaps if he possessed greater understanding he could live forever through sheer willpower; then these deaths would not have been in vain, but noble sacrifices. Necessary offerings surrendered for the worthiest of causes: his continued renewal.

Paradoxically, the more he learned, the more his fear diminished. In fact, he grew increasingly curious about going through the whole process himself. The act of dying bothered him less and less. He did worry about pain.

"What's it like?"

That was when he began to ask them what they saw—the eye fixation: their observations, his insights.

He walked to the edge of the beach, cold water soaking his shoes.

Life comes down to a few important instances. This is one of those times, I think.

He felt no pain as he walked into the icy water. He inhaled deeply, the savory fragrance of Calliope's hair suddenly fresh in his nose, the tang of bitter almond sharp on his tongue.

"If I really want answers, there's no time like the present to find out."

Trembling in the frigid dark, once the freezing water was at his chin he turned away from the blackness and looked to the shore a final time, his head floating like a flame on the water's surface. The lights onshore resembled stars to him.

He put his face under at last, deeply breathing in the cold saltwater. Reflexively, he propelled himself up from the sea, coughing and gagging. In the back of his mind, he was astonished at how far he had drifted. Already he could not feel the bottom. In the dim sunrise, the dock was a tiny blob to his salt-stung eyes.

Once more he dove under, inhaling the briny liquid through his nose and mouth.

Looking up from under the ocean, the water had a frothy green glow from the early morning sun. As his lungs filled with fluid, he relaxed—numb ragdoll arms drifting lazily overhead, trailing air bubbles.

The current turned his body, pulling him in an ever further spiral from the light and shore . . . his hair waved in and out of view like seaweed.

During his silent, slow-motion descent, he saw what he had been so very curious about all this time: gently gripped in a final embrace, it was just as Calliope had described.

Bright. White. Overwhelming.

No time like . . .
the present . . .
to . . .

Author's Note

Stories sometimes write themselves, especially if you have so much knowledge about a topic that the plot just presents itself. This is one of those times; I imagined what a character such as this would be going through, and though I find the behavior repellent, it is oddly compelling to reflect upon whatever humanity may lie under all that insanity. By way of explanation: I did massive amounts of research on serial homicide because of a desire to become a behavioral sciences candidate for the FBI, something that intrigues me, but I was unable to afford to pursue; I will instead pour all my research and observations into my fiction (my first novel centers on this subject).

Pathologist's Roulette

My friend and I have a little game we play
Over coffee and chai:
It involves sitting at the local café
And guessing everyone's demise.

He is a pathologist,
And I—well, does it matter?;
No doubt you have spied us somewhere—
Impolitely hiding our laughter.

Who will yield first to the Reaper?
How about the old guy, the nanny,
or the priest?
We take turns judging folks—
The waif, the idiot, perhaps the grossly obese?

And how will they succumb,
These random bits of DNA?
Heart attack, stroke, suicide bomb?
One can never be certain
These ever-shortening days . . .

It's a fun game, to be sure,
And I try never to miss it;
The more we play,
the stronger the allure:
Now I dare not dismiss it.

Smug in repose,
As we empty our cups,
Does he ever ponder,

I sometimes muse,
How I *might wind up?*

He seems to sense this,
Evinced by a Cheshire Cat smile:
One cannot help, I suppose,
wanting to go out in style . . .

But as we bid adieu and finally depart,
Embraced by the clutch of eve's frozen ire,
Each of us is sure of the other's prospects
In his own murky heart;
Know this: I'll never talk;
After all,
He doesn't offer to tell *me*—

and I *never* inquire . . .

The Central Coast

Alex was cold.

Wistfully observing the now silent ambulances and police cars pull away in the darkness, red and blue lights painting the black grass with glowing streaks, he thought: *Man, I* hate *that yellow crime scene tape . . .*

He swallowed hard, head buzzing, and turned around. A warm breeze caused the palm trees to rustle, but it did little to change the icy mercury of dread creeping up his back as he stood on the sidewalk facing his house. Staring ahead, blood crusting on his shirt, sticky on his hands, his thoughts were confused, jangled. He felt removed from life—a dreamless somnambulant.

Entering the living room, Alex paused in the shattered doorway, a strange metallic tang on his tongue. He heard women quietly weeping: some of the last remaining guests, they looked up at him from blood-drenched seats, coated with gore and bile themselves. Slowly shaking his head, he shrugged imperceptibly, at a loss as to what to say.

Surveying the demolished remnants of his home, he regarded his visitors, mute with astonishment. *Hell of a party,* he mused. *Damn crime lab left the place more of a wreck than before they arrived.*

And those police interviews . . . those really killed the mood.

The migraine pulsing in the center of his head made him grimace. Stumbling toward the kitchen, Alex contemplated what he should say to the survivors.

Maybe 'Thanks for coming—I'm relieved the rest of you are going home in one piece . . .'

He paused near the threshold of the closed kitchen door, head pounding, face warm. *No, too direct . . .*

Mentally bracing himself, he slowly pushed on the door. His breath was shallow: he was afraid of what might still be on the other side.

Perhaps, 'Glad you could make it—that was quite the dessert course . . .'

He closed his eyes as he inched the door open. *That's no good,* he reflected. *Too morbid.* Sweat caused his shirt to cling to his body. His heartbeat grew louder in his ears, drowning out whispers emanating from the living room.

How about: 'Next time, let's just play Twister and forget the drinks . . .'

Eyes closed, he smiled half-heartedly at the thought that anyone on earth would ever play another party game—or even *go* to a party—after what had happened tonight. His legs were unsteady; the door felt as though it weighted a thousand pounds.

Probably best not to say anything . . . pretend it didn't happen . . .

Thank God *someone cut off the stereo.*

The door was fully open at last; Alex reluctantly opened his eyes, his face twitching involuntarily.

"Jesus . . ." His voice was constricted, weak. Stomach lurching, eyes watering, he sagged against the doorframe, fighting vertigo. Unconsciously holding his breath, he exhaled with a sob.

At least the paramedics took the bodies away . . .

The room was coated in a thick syrup of coagulating blood. The coppery smell of carnage was nauseating. Broken platefuls of ripe cheese, overturned bottles of alcohol and shattered wine glasses—all covered in the fine black grit of fingerprint powder—completed the surreal montage. Distantly, he felt more than heard the scurrying departure of the former revelers leaving him alone to clean up his destroyed residence.

Guess it's not every day you see people slaughter each other at a social gathering . . .

Something slid under his shoe. Pulling his foot up, Alex realized the popping sound he had heard was Jordan's eyeball.

He screamed.

"I'm tired."

Alex's eyelid twitched at the sound of Jordan's whining.

"So am I," he said, glancing at the gas gauge. "We're making good time." Changing the subject, he continued: "We should be hitting Paso Robles in about fifteen minutes, and you know what that means."

"Wine tasting!" Jordan exclaimed, squirming in the passenger seat. He smiled at her childish clapping.

"Olives, too," Alex reminded her.

"Yes! Mmmm . . ." she said, smacking her lips.

The drive from L.A. was long, but they needed to get to San Francisco the following day for an industry seminar. He was annoyed that the *en route* visit to her mother's had kept them so late; ever since reading that creepy Etchison story, Alex found stopping at rest areas disturbing—especially after sundown.

Upon returning, they were scheduled to finish some pickups for the movie: reaction shots and a scene with Jordan's erstwhile best friend, Krystal. Afterward, the plan was to have a nice week or two of vacation on Kauai. In spite of all the traveling, it would be fun to get out of the rat race: *No helicopters, no high-speed police chases, no junk mail from realtors, no credit card offers . . .*

At least temporarily.

"I think we should re-fi the house," Alex said, breaking out of his thoughts.

"Yeah—I was thinking that, too. We could get a better rate and use some of the equity to remodel the guest bath," Jordan said, squeezing his hand.

He looked at her. She was tan, healthy. Her skin was clear, eyes alert. He had always liked her hair, which she kept shoulder-length these days, and more blonde than when they first met. She also seemed more confident, more relaxed. *I have to admit: the increase from B cup to DD was a good move.*

Alex had first met Jordan on the set of one of her early films. He was dating Krystal at the time, and it was she who had suggested him as a replacement for the prima-donna European director who had bogged the whole production down. Alex's first feature film break after too many commercials, endless numbers of music videos, and a good deal of episodic television, the movie's success catapulted him into a lucrative new career: the go-to director able to bring a tough project in on time and under budget. Jordan—a rising starlet at the time—was very personable and pleasant: not the sneering, preening monster some of these people could be.

For Alex and Jordan it was love at first sight, and he had to end his two-year romance with the fiery Krystal. Unfortunately, Krystal had been unable to come to terms with the dissolution of their relationship. Even after all this time there was tension between the two women on-set, although they were always consummate professionals once the cameras started rolling. Alex secretly felt that the animosity and competition only added to their performances, especially during spanking, or girl-on-girl action.

Jordan's intense performances had interested Alex from the beginning, and he had been glad to get the chance to work with her. Even when being pounded in that bare vagina after five other positions, Jordan was still top-notch: the hottest breasts, ass, and legs in porn.

Some actors popped practically the second they started doing her: that face; those eyes; the sweaty hourglass body—it all just worked. She obviously relished her ability to milk the studs dry and was game for new challenges: DP, anal, even strapping on to teach the guys a thing or two.

Fortunately for Alex, she was familiar with his work. He had especially enjoyed getting to know her after hours. It was a slow process, as she was cautious about dating people "from the industry." He found her to be a down-to-earth girl, very liberal, and fascinated by insects.

Everything was going well: married for nearly two years, they were prepping Jordan for "retirement."

"I want to go out on top!" she always joked. He was glad for her; soon he would have her just to himself.

The signpost up ahead read: 'Entering Paso Robles.'

"We're here!" she squealed. "Let's find some wine and get buzzed!"

Alex felt wobbly; perhaps it was the long drive—or the fact that the heat was more than he expected for late September on California's Central Coast—but it was probably due more to overindulgence during their wine-tasting odyssey.

"You're drunk!" Jordan teased, tickling his side. "You're supposed to taste, then spit—not drink it all. You'll get hammered!"

"I'm a swallower," he slurred, crooked grin on his unshaven face. Both of them laughed as they got into the car.

"Are you OK to drive?" she asked, looking at the map.

"I'll be fine. . . . We picked up some killer wine, huh? Let's do one more for the road; how about that Spanish-sounding place?" Alex pulled the car onto Highway 101, which was strangely deserted.

"Oh yeah! They were closed last time." She glanced at her watch, then toward the sky as the vehicle jostled down the road. The scent of wet earth was strong, fresh, comforting; the landscape was rustic, romantic: sunlight dappled cypress trees, gently rolling hills, the sky fading into a gorgeous rust and blue mélange in the early twilight.

"Doesn't this place remind you of Tuscany? Kind of near Firenze?" Jordan asked at last.

Alex nodded. "I was just noticing that. It's the quality of the light, I think."

She smiled, looking down to study the atlas once again. "Here it is: *Sotanos Negros del Diablo.* It's about three miles north."

"Let's hit it, then on to San Francisco," he said, gently touching her thigh.

In the distance, lightning flashed.

"You see," the vintner stated, "my grandfather came from the Old Country to South America on a steamship as a young man. Who knows why, eh? Adventure? Women? All the things that make life worth living, no?" He winked at Jordan. She blushed, giggling as she inhaled the full, sensuous aroma of her first taste: a Nebbiolo.

His gentle brown eyes glinting, the old man continued: "Later, Grandpapa moved up here, but only after a long apprenticeship with a master winemaker—Señor Azura—and began our family vineyard on a small plot of land with old vines from France and Chile."

The proprietor gave a sweep of his arm toward the windows.

"As you can see, we have grown! We have our own lines of Merlot . . . Chardonnay . . . Petite Syrah, and this huge Zinfandel Port—as good as any you'll find in Napa or Sonoma, we feel. Try it." He pushed a glass toward Alex, then poured Jordan another sample.

Swirling the taste of Port in his glass, Alex savored its sweet, dark, cinnamon fragrance. *Look at the legs on that! The nose is phenomenal . . .* He took a sip, relishing the lush velvet spreading over his tongue—liquid divinity. While they conversed, Alex studied the luxurious mahogany counter top.

The tour of the vineyard had been educational. Alex loved the process of planting, tending, harvesting: the nurturing aspect appealed to him; perhaps that was why he preferred directing to performing.

The elderly winemaker was full of stories: about the vineyards, the history of the area, his family, and viticulture in general—the whole process of winemaking. He seemed to be a nice man, but something about him made Alex just a little . . . uneasy.

"Awesome! Chocolate!" Jordan chirped, remarking on the Port. "Wonderful bouquet." She cleansed her palate with a slice of ciabatta dipped in extra virgin olive oil, pouring the remaining sample into a reservoir on the table. The old man nodded his approval, the smile under his mustache causing his dark, weathered skin to crease.

They were the only patrons; as Jordan continued to try other varietals, Alex wandered over to the exhibition area. The prices escalated the higher the bottles, all resting sideways, were placed in the cabinet shelving. The furnishings, which were deeply carved and artfully arranged, also showcased several winemaker's medals, framed sepia-toned photographs, and various other spirits, from 125-year-old French wormwood Absinthe and dessert liqueurs to the present vintage of the estate's Meritage. Behind him, Jordan mumbled to the owner about taking a couple of Ports, the Nebbiolo, a Baco Noir, and a Pinot Grigio. Just then, Alex noticed a lone ornate bottle, cloaked in shadow, at the top of a huge tiered shelf.

"What about that one?" he asked, transfixed.

The wizened merchant stepped from behind the wine bar, wiping his hands on his apron, looking to where Alex pointed. As the light slowly faded outside, the room was getting dimmer. There was a sudden chill; the thin old glass of the huge bay windows overlooking the vineyards no match for the cool air from the approaching storm.

"That, *señor,* is the last bottle we have of our special *Estate Reserva.* It was depleted years ago, except for a few we kept as . . . mementos. It is highly prized by collectors."

"Must be good," Alex replied, curiosity piqued.

"Of course . . . the best! It is one of the first wines vinted by the Manor, grown from the original old-world vines."

The aged man paused, looking up at the bottle. "It . . . We only made it one year. Grandfather said we should only make more once the last bottle was gone. We call it *'Absentia Anima.'* It's a wonderful 1917 vintage: truly beautiful—so I have been told. We have so few that

I've never even tried it myself! Right before the great wine reviewer Pierre Cocteau disappeared, he gave it a Platinum Medal and Five-Star critique in his prestigious *Wine Connoisseur* magazine."

Alex's gaze locked momentarily with the winemaker's. "So it's for sale?" Alex asked, mentally calculating the funds in his wallet. Glancing at Jordan, he pursed his lips. Her eyes were wide with excitement: she loved wine and was always after him to beef up their modest cellar.

The old man looked again at the bottle. He made a face as if tasting something bitter, then straightened.

"Yes, yes it is. *Sí* . . . it's quite expensive, *señor.* To be sure, it's no ordinary bottle of wine; at a hundred years old, it can remain bottled for many more years."

"I understand: it's extraordinary. That's what we're looking for. How much?" Lightning flashed, but there was no thunder. As the proprietor stared at him, eyes narrow, Alex could swear—if only for an instant—that something changed on the man's countenance. It was strange. *Macabre.* It seemed almost—subliminal. *Probably just a trick of the lightning,* Alex thought.

"Promise me," the owner said finally, "that you will share it with your friends, *señor*? This exceptional wine—it is *meant* to be shared."

Alex nodded, hypnotized by the intensity of the old man. They were practically whispering.

"Let me get it for you, *por favor.* Wine is truly a gift to be enjoyed by all."

The vendor stepped away. Alex and Jordan watched him retreat into a curtained doorway behind the bar. From the back room, there was faint clanging and thudding. Alex strained to hear.

"How exciting!" Jordan quietly mouthed, softly clapping her hands.

"It is . . ." he agreed. The exchange with the owner had Alex a bit spooked. *That guy is* strange, he thought. More noise from the back, followed by swearing in Spanish, then silence.

"At last!" the old man exclaimed, appearing in the doorway with a rickety wooden ladder. He waddled across the cavernous room, propped the ladder against the dust-covered shelves, and began his slow ascent, breath wheezing. The ladder groaned under his weight. Reaching the top, the proprietor hesitated. Lightning flashed again, brilliantly illuminating the room for a split-second. Thunder growled in the distance as rain began to tap at the windows. It was nearly dark, and the storm seemed to have settled in for the evening.

"You're sure you want this, *señor*? It's *very* expensive." His hand was on the bottle as the winemaker peered down at them, his eyes like pits.

"Yes, we want it—we're looking forward to it," Alex replied, voice tight. *Bet he thinks I can't afford it.* The vintner nodded, pulling the container from its housing.

Once back on the ground, he handed the bottle to Jordan, beaming proudly, his forehead dewed with sweat. Alex gazed over her shoulder, admiring the engraved image on the cobalt glass. Wiping away the dust and cobwebs, they turned the bottle to read the back label:

Aged in the finest American and French barriques,
this unique vintage is nearly impossible to grow in
North America.

Potent, powerful and specially crafted
from only the finest and rarest of ingredients,
an ancient recipe and exacting standards imbue it with
wonderful color, intense aroma, and piquant taste.

These characteristics give us our name:
Sotanos Negros del Diablo.
Enjoy with friends and family.

Vintage 1917
Absentia Anima
Estate Reserva

"Nice bottle," Alex said, looking at the vintner. The man seemed mentally preoccupied, pensively staring from the rain-streaked windows into the darkening yard. Thunder rattled the old windowpanes. The owner turned to face them.

"Let me wrap it for you, *señor*."

"That guy was a little odd, huh?" Alex said as they pulled away from the winery.

"You think? He seemed pretty nice to me," Jordan replied.

Alex frowned in response, watching for cars as he pulled onto the rain-slicked road. The downpour nearly overwhelmed the robotic synching of the wipers.

"Acted to me like he thought we couldn't afford his precious wine—"

"Don't be silly! Maybe he just wanted to keep it for old time's sake. . . . You know—kind of like you and your books even though you never read them," Jordan said.

Lightening up, Alex smiled. "I suppose. . . . I just get tired of being—judged."

"Well, doesn't everybody judge everybody all the time? Anyway, you pushed him—you made your point and got what you wanted, so be happy about that."

This practical, laid-back aspect was one of the things he found so endearing about his wife. *That, and she's hot.* "You're right—I'm being a jerk. Guess I'm just ready to get to Frisco and chill."

Jordan caressed his thigh. "Maybe we can do some stress relief later," she said, smiling impishly.

As rain daggered the ground, the runny red sunset smeared the horizon.

The stopper was obstinate.

The last thing I need to do is break the fucking cork off in it . . .

Alex had—finally—retrieved the cherished, dusty bottle from the basement. Resisting the temptation to imbibe the special *Estate Reserva* for over three years, it seemed the perfect choice for Jordan's "retirement" party.

The time has arrived . . .

Alex patiently worked the corkscrew, slowly pulling the plug. At last, there was a satisfying 'pop.'

The strong aroma from the bottle made him smile. *Excellent: needs to breathe a little.* From the living room, he could hear the festivities getting lively: toasts being given, music thumping, laughter.

Jordan came up behind him, encircling his waist.

"Oh—this is wonderful," she said, sniffing the cork. Alex poured several glasses for their guests; he was still working on his first glass of the Baco Noir.

Estate Special
1917
Sótanos Negros
Absentia

"Could you finish pouring the rest of the *Reserva* for everyone while I take these out?" he asked Jordan as he took a tray of the wine to the living room.

She kissed his cheek as he passed. "Of course! How yummy looking . . ." She took a sip of the *Reserva.* "Wonderful—I *love* it!"

As he was about to exit through the kitchen door, Krystal walked in.

"Jordan, darling, do you need any help?" she asked. Alex smiled at her on his way out, pleased that they all got along again.

"Krystal!" Jordan exclaimed, still pouring. "Do come in . . ."

Vino rosso: the blood of the vine.

Alex relaxed for a moment in the living room, delighting in the last of his Baco Noir. He was looking forward to his share of the *Absentia Anima* when he heard a demented cacophony erupt from the kitchen. The party was suddenly quiet, except for the stereo. Again, another anguished howl from the kitchen. Rushing into the room, Alex was dumbfounded by the gruesome spectacle unfolding there beyond the door:

Jordan was hunched over on the ground, stabbing Krystal repeatedly in the crotch with a huge knife. In the corner, Krystal's surprised face stared up from the floor; she seemed to observe the mêlée with detached reserve, vertebrae sticking out of the ragged ruin of her neck, bloody lips twitching, before her eyes finally fluttered closed.

"Jordan!" was all Alex could exclaim. Yowling in response, she turned to kick and slash at the bewildered Randy, Krystal's husband, who had suddenly appeared. As Alex remained frozen in shock, Randy attempted to disarm Jordan, but it all seemed to be in agonizing slow-motion, like some dreamy, gore-streaked ballet. Behind him, a chorus of screams rang out from the living room. . . . It was then that Alex realized his friend Terrence was lying next to the stove, swimming in a virtual ocean of hemoglobin and lymph. Though his vision had tapered to a blurry tunnel, Alex could still comprehend: *Jordan had eviscerated Terrence as he was returning from the bathroom. . . .* Vomit and blood slicked Terrence's chin as he held his sanguineous intestines, which looped in his shaky hands; after a few dry heaves, he collapsed, his face drained to the color of a sheet of paper.

"What the fuck?" Alex screamed, hoarse with disbelief, cold sweat breaking on his body.

As if in the grip of some demented chorea, Jordan leapt forward, nearly severing Randy's upraised hand. He regarded his new injury—which swung impossibly from the meaty, spurting stump—in silent amazement, paying no heed to Jordan as she descended on him. Biting his throat, she tore out a great chunk, the carotid artery spraying the room in a grisly red mist. Randy blurted out a final gargling scream as he fell to the ground, eyes bulging.

Now everything seemed impossibly fast: finished with Randy, Jordan turned her attention to Alex, blade flashing in her bloody, athetotic fist.

Everyone in the living room had panicked by now, but the front door refused to budge; a few of the guests began to jabber, some wailing like Jordan. Just prior to turning on one another, they were afflicted by the same weird facial contortions, the identical outlandish dyskinesia.

In the kitchen, Alex dodged Jordan's knife, observing that she was no longer clothed: just stained head to foot in offal and excrement.

"Jordan! Stop! Jesus!"

His spouse lurched toward him in a spastic St. Vitus's dance, slicing the fetid air. Her discolored, twisted face was writhing, covered in what looked like small blisters.

"Stop, please!"

The commotion in the den was now fever pitch: a riot exploding the small confines of the house.

Far away, Alex thought he heard sirens.

Still screeching, Jordan pulled her eyes out. She threw the orbs and the bloody knife at Alex: her mushy, gaping sockets streamed garnet tears.

In a burst of adrenaline, Alex grabbed the nearest object at hand and beat her; grunting like a wild beast, he bashed Jordan's head until it was an unrecognizable mass of pulp, hair, teeth. At long last her congested whimpering stopped; Alex was hyperventilating, blood warm and salty on his lips.

As he sank to the floor, the police kicked the front door in—their stunned demands immediately swallowed by the crush of screaming and noise. Once the assaults started on them, their warnings yielded to a barrage of gunfire. In the end, there was only a smoky, expanding silence, attended by the reek of sulfur.

"Yeah, we got it now," a young black cop said into his walkie-talkie, out of breath. He lowered his weapon, sweat beading on his bald head as he surveyed the tableau: "Holy shit . . ."

Alex slumped in the entryway of his destroyed kitchen. Oblivious to who might be left alive, he barely acknowledged the reinforcements asking if he was okay. He waved at them without looking, then picked up the object that he had used to murder his wife: an empty wine bottle. He focused his eyes on the back: *Estate Reserva, Vintage 1917, Sotanos Negros del Diablo, Absentia Anima.*

Great, I never even got to fucking try it.

So this is what the French mean by "terroir," I guess . . .

More like "terroir-ism" . . .

In the distance, Alex heard more sirens. Growing in intensity, they seeped under the wash of crying, then drowned out the pulse of *Sympathy for the Devil* playing on the stereo in the living room. He was afraid to look, knowing what he would see, and continued to study the bottle.

Nice artwork. Alex admired anew the shape and dark color of the clot-encrusted receptacle; the front image—a graven bas-relief of an orange-irised eye weeping a single red tear—gave him pause. He turned the vessel upside-down; its last claret trickle fell to the floor, blossoming in the blood.

It's like egg-drop soup . . .

Many years later, Alex was a saggy old man.

Giving up the movie business long ago, he had semi-retired to Europe on Jordan's life insurance after leaving the mental institution. He picked up part-time work here and there as a waiter; it was enough with Disability and Social Security to meet his meager day-to-day existence, and was really all he could muster psychologically.

Alex enjoyed the human contact, and the work could be fun; it offered relaxed schedules, free meals, and nocturnal diversions to keep his mind busy. Between the medicine and lifestyle, it almost permitted him a respite from that horrible night, now so many years ago. He never remarried.

During the weeks—and the interminable police interrogations—that had followed, Alex explained that there must have been something about the wine. To his way of thinking, the alcohol and the violence had to be linked—though the toxicology reports were all negative for ergot poisoning or anything else.

He spent several years trying to find the winery again, to no avail. The place seemed to have vanished—almost as if it had never existed. Of course, Alex knew better.

On his final stay in Rome, he served a young American couple a fine Tuscan Chianti with their dinner. He smiled at them, knowing heartbreak was probably inevitable.

"*Buona sera!* Join us for a sip, *signore*?" the young man asked. "We just got married, and we're touring Europe on our honeymoon. It's wonderful here!" He hoisted his glass in a gesture of salutation.

Alex only gave him the same melancholy look he gave all newlyweds.

"Wine?" he asked, then shivered. He looked at the fading sunset, rheumy eyes shining as though remembering something from long ago. "Sorry, son—I can't drink it anymore . . ."

Author's Note

I love wine. My wife and I were driving through the California wine country (Sonoma and Napa) on a fine Saturday a few years ago on our way down to L.A., and I thought of this story. I told it to her, and she loved it. I think it raises some interesting points about personal responsibility and the repercussions of wish-fulfillment (specifically its unintended consequences). I also like the novel structure: Start in the present, return to the past, end in the future.

Passage

Begin:

Shrouded by mists of antiquity.

Emerge:

Onto an overgrown road of gravel.

For quite some time
This avenue has not been travelled;—
Small wonder,
as its path is rocky and
torturous
as far as can be seen . . .

Ahead:

Some spots look easier—
fewer hills and puddles;
flowers appear.

Ignore:

Bodies in the ditches
along the way;
Try to focus on the here,
the now.

After all:

It's not the destination that really matters,
but the jaunt . . .

One for the Road

Three A.M.

Elizabeth was tired: bones heavy, neck stiff, eyes burning. The rhythm of the white dashed line reflecting off the interstate made her feel so

very . . .

drowsy . . .

"Gotta stay awake!" She reached over to the dashboard and cranked up the radio. For a moment—as she belted out a few lyrics of choice metal—she was more alert. Even with that shot of adrenaline, though, Elizabeth could barely fend off the highway hypnosis: her energy ebbed quickly. In the mirror, her eyelids were droopy, whites bloodshot in the dim luminance of the speedometer. She cracked the glass for some fresh, cold air.

"Jesus, that's *too* cold!" She rolled the window back up, shivering. Mid-January in the Pacific Northwest was no time to be cruising around with the window down, especially on a night like this.

"What I *really* need is to get to Seattle." She had known better than to start the trip from Eugene so late, but the argument with Derrick had taken her off-guard: she had no idea that he was so jealous about her taking the new management position. She now regretted snubbing his offer to accompany her.

He should be happy for me! For us! *More money, better benefits . . . There's no reason for him to be so insecure after all this time.*

Just thinking about it made her anger flare.

I should have stopped over in Portland—but they said the orientation meeting was supposed to start at eight-thirty sharp. . . . If I can just get to Seattle, maybe I can snag a couple hours' sleep . . .

Before . . .

Before sun . . . rise . . .

Elizabeth jerked the tiny car back onto the Interstate, roused by the roar of the tires on the wake-up strip next to the shoulder. She was scared wide-awake now, heart in her throat, mouth like cotton. The blasting radio seemed distant. Around her—hurtling through darkened space—there was nothing: it was as if she was the only human alive on the planet.

Three-thirty. Meeting at eight-thirty . . . Seattle's still at least another hour and a half out.

Elizabeth settled into the seat with renewed resolve, taking a swig of diet cola from the can between her legs.

"I read somewhere even a twenty-minute catnap can help when you're tired. Maybe I'll just do that. Set the cellphone for thirty minutes, then keep on grinding. Stay over in Seattle tonight before I go back; Derrick'll understand." Checking the fuel gauge, she saw that she had more than enough gasoline to get to the Emerald City. In the yellow glow of the headlights, a sign came into view:

Rest Area: 2 Miles
Next Rest Area: 63 Miles
Safety Break: Free Coffee
Wi-Fi Hotspot

She smiled to herself. "Perfect."

The pale sodium-arc lamps cast eerie pink illumination on the empty asphalt of the parking lot.

Creepy . . .

She parked under one of the light posts, double-checking that all the doors were locked. She sat for a minute with the engine idling, the radio off, and took in the surroundings. It was drizzling now, mixed with a few flurries of large wet snowflakes.

Directly in front and to the left of her was the entrance to the ladies' room, and opposite that was the men's lavatory. In addition to housing the restrooms, there was a tiny, dark Plexiglas-encased building where elderly volunteers normally offered free coffee, tea, cookies. A halo of moths threw themselves at the sputtering fluorescent lights of the small complex.

Many times Elizabeth had seen different older couples at this very rest station, which was a lot more inviting in the daytime, chatting jovially with travelers who would stop to stretch their legs or make use of the facilities.

"Nobody home tonight, though . . ." She cut the engine. *I'll just use the bathroom, get back in the car, lock up, and nap for a few minutes . . . then head on up to Seattle.*

A sudden gust made the trees rustle. The place was strangely forbidding, draining her normal moxie; she swallowed, throat parched.

Better make it quick.

It felt good to empty her bladder: Elizabeth had not realized that she had been holding it for so long. As she cleaned up, she heard the door creak open. Her blood pressure spiked: *Just another woman needing to pee . . .*

The person was walking quite slowly, the reverberation of the steps on the tile very measured, as though they had difficulty moving.

I won't flush; I'll just excuse mys—

Dark shoes shuffled into view under the door of Elizabeth's stall as she buttoned her pants. The person on the other side said something in a hoarse voice, then loudly rattled the handle.

"Coming out—I'm done!" Elizabeth yelped, mentally reflecting on how rude it was that this person would not use one of the other unoccupied commodes. She threw the door open.

Time ballooned: for how long, it was impossible to discern. The old woman in front of Elizabeth was staring with huge, runny eyes, blood pumping from a ragged gash under her jaw.

The injured woman reached out with a gory hand, rasping: "H-h-help m-me pl-*please.*"

Elizabeth stifled a shriek, dodging the old woman's outstretched arm, never taking her eyes from the blood-soaked vision. The woman, shirt saturated with red, tracked her—watching as Elizabeth backed toward the door.

"H-h-hel p! No!" Blood foamed in the raw wound as she collapsed, her strangled pleas bouncing off the tile floor.

Suddenly Elizabeth was outside, sweat pouring down her back, stomach roiling as the noxious scents of urine and oily wet pavement collected in her nose. The wind stung her face, but she was too shocked to react. Looking down, she noticed a trail of bloody footprints.

"Oh God, oh God, oh *GOD!*" she screamed, now fully comprehending the reality of what she had seen.

"God," a husky male voice said, "ain't got nothin' to do with it, lady." The voice was emanating from a silhouette sitting on the hood of her car. The glowing, orange tip of a cigarette was the only visible detail of the hulking figure.

Glancing around the parking lot, Elizabeth could see that it was still deserted: there were no other cars. She froze, watching the cigarette burn brighter, then dimmer as the man took a drag in the darkness.

"Shame about Grandma, huh? She's been stumblin' around for ten minutes." The man stood, flicked the cigarette to the ground, then began walking toward Elizabeth.

Another scream blossomed in her throat. She looked around, her knees starting to buckle. The car was only thirty feet away at most—but between it and her was . . . *him.* It may as well have been the distance between the sun and Pluto. She could always retreat to the bathroom—but then she would have to deal with the old woman, and there was no way to lock the only entrance . . . or exit.

Immediately to her left was the door to the little room where the volunteers resided when dispensing coffee and snacks: she noted that the door had a keyed lock.

As the man closed the gap between them with his colossal strides, Elizabeth leapt to the door.

"Oh, God!" She turned the knob and pushed, seeing stars as hyperventilation brought her close to passing out.

Miraculously, the door opened. She fell into the comforting blackness of the small room, whimpering involuntarily. She kicked the door closed just as the stranger was upon it, pushing the button lock in, then—

Nothing.

Elizabeth huddled on the floor, regarding the hard lines of the utilitarian furnishings: a wooden, stiff-backed chair; a miniscule sink; the built-in countertop, which served as a desk. The unhealthy cast of the greenish fluorescents outside was the sole illumination. The terrifying man was nowhere to be seen; her ragged breathing was loud in the cramped space as her heartbeat began to slow. She felt better as her muscles relaxed. It was a very 'dead' room acoustically, compared to the resonant bathroom: every noise seemed clipped off the instant it was completed, as though the gloomy air itself was consuming the sound waves.

She was shaking as she grabbed the edge of the counter and peered through the scratched Lucite windows. The only thing she saw were some snowflakes swirling among the naked trees just past the parking lot.

Who was that poor old lady? And that guy—did he do that to her? Christ! She closed her eyes, imagining the woman dying in the toilet.

The little room was still: she heard the muffled whistle of wind, the patter of falling rain and snow. If she held her breath, she thought that she could just make out the sound of icy grass and leaves crunching as the man stalked outside. Her ears tightened on her scalp.

He's out there!

"You come on out," he proclaimed, out of sight. "No sense prolonging this."

Just then, the doorknob shook violently, punctuating his demands. Elizabeth's chest ached from the pounding of her heart. She scuttled farther from the doorway, scanning the tiny chamber for another place of entry: there was none. It was a claustrophobic room, with high, bare ceilings—like a tomb or mausoleum. She hated tight spaces normally, but, under the circumstances, she was grateful that it was no larger than it was: she could view the entire room at once.

"We ain't got all night for these games, bitch!"

Abruptly, the rattling and banging ceased. She strained to look out of the dirty windows, trying to be as inconspicuous as possible: nothing, just her snow-dusted old sedan in the gradually whitening lot.

My car! If I could just get to it . . . I'm sure I could make it if I ran . . . She felt for the keys in her pocket: still there. She moved quietly over to the door of the little room, watching for any movement outside.

Wait—Derrick! I'll call Derrick; he might be able to meet me, even if I have to wait till morning in here. No—911 first, then *Derrick*. Elizabeth patted her pockets for her cellphone.

Damn! I left it charging in the car.

A shape materialized in the corner of her eye. It scared her to realize that only a couple of inches of wooden door separated her from this man. She crouched down, but her eyes were riveted on him: he walked over to her car once more, smoking another cigarette. The rain and snow had subsided for the moment. He was large and seemed in decent shape, but otherwise she could make out no real details.

If I can just hold on till daylight, maybe he'll leave. But I'm so tired . . . and the meeting . . . damn it!

He was sitting on the hood again, vapor trailing from his silhouette. After a few moments, he stood up, trolling around her vehicle like a shark.

If he leaves I'll break for it . . . but what if he's waiting for me on the other side of the door, or behind the room? Her hand moved instinctively to her throat as gruesome images of the old woman crowded her mind.

Who knows how many times he's done this before? I guess I'd better just wait it out.

As she watched, he strolled up to the shack; she tried to make herself small again.

"Who are you kidding? We both know you're in there," he said, backlit by the streetlights. "I can see you! Think you're gonna wait me out, huh? Well, that little lock ain't enough to stop *me*."

With that, he stormed out of sight: Elizabeth thought her heart must have stopped as she waited on him to pound the door in. She sat there in a ball, breath shallow in the darkness.

Nothing. She strained to hear over her own pulse. She was miserable: legs tingling from lack of circulation, fingers stiff from the cold as it permeated her shelter. Her coat was in the car along with her purse and phone: her intention had been to use the toilet and get back into the car as quickly as possible.

The best laid plans . . .

A shadow crossed her vision and she recoiled: it was a car.

As Elizabeth watched, the powerful beam of a searchlight washed over her vehicle: *The police!*

"Thank God!"

A finger of illumination probed the area around her car, then slowly moved away, bathing the surroundings with bright light, like an artificial sun in miniature.

Elizabeth jumped up in the dark room. She was reacting, her numb body moving automatically, as if gripped by some out-of-body experience. She began clawing at the window, her gaze never leaving the police car. She went to the door: it was sticky, but after a few hard yanks it gave way, just as the cop doused the lamp and started to pull off.

"*NO!* Don't leave me here!" She screamed, barreling out of the tiny room with all of her might.

All she could think of now . . .

absur d int er val of time passing

was narrowing the gap . . .

DistanceGrowingTheCloserSheGets

between herself and the patrol car . . . Finally: the cold wet metal and glass of the doorframe.

The officer flipped on the blue emergency lights, swinging the searchlight in Elizabeth's direction.

"Thank God! Thank God!" Elizabeth could see the whites of the cop's eyes through the moisture-beaded driver's side window: a woman in her mid-forties, hair pulled back in a tight bun.

"Help me! Please—he killed the old woman! *Oh God,* help me!"

"Hold on! *Who,* lady? What's the problem?" the officer demanded. As the police scanner blared, the entire place was now splashed with sapphire from the twirling lights on the roof of the vehicle.

"I don't know! I—I've been trapped in the visitor's reception room for a while—*he's out here!* Please, let's go! *Please!"*

"Wait—you're fine—I'm here. I'm not gonna to let anything happen to you, okay? Catch your breath."

Elizabeth was shaking uncontrollably in the cold. Stepping from the car, the officer unholstered her weapon as she placed a hand on the other woman's shoulder. Gradually Elizabeth calmed down, her hysterical yells dissolving into sobs of relief.

"Wait here—I've already called for backup. Where did you see this dead woman?" the cop asked, looking into Elizabeth's eyes. Elizabeth studied her, slightly dazed as her body began to unwind, to relax; she pointed a shaky finger at the building near her car. It began snowing again, harder.

"In there," she whispered. "In the women's restroom . . ."

"Okay—stay here. If you see or hear anything unusual, scream, run; don't worry about me. I've got this." The officer brandished her gun, then stroked Elizabeth's hair. "It's going be all right, honey."

She watched the woman move cautiously toward the restroom. The officer carefully opened the rusty door and disappeared inside. Once she was out of sight, Elizabeth's anxiety slowly resurfaced. She sat down on the edge of the driver's seat, mesmerized, waiting on the woman to reappear, to tell her that she had imagined it all . . .

The radio suddenly broke the hypnotic silence, startling her. Elizabeth realized that her hands were numb and stiff from the wind blowing through the desolate parking lot, driving an icy mix of sleet and flurries into eddies under the revolving blue lights. The hackles on her neck rose as she stood up in the doorframe of the police car, looking at the women's restroom.

"Think that bitch is gonna help you?" His hoarse, guttural voice was the last thing Elizabeth heard—a scream stillborn in her chest—before whiteness exploded behind her eyes: fighting the slide into unconsciousness, she crumpled to the unyielding pavement. The world receded—cold, wet snowflakes pelting her face and hissing distantly in the trees, swirling away as she stared into a dark, mournful sky . . .

Far away, she heard voices in the gloom.

"Took you long enough to get here—"

"There was an accident on I-5."

"We've got a problem—"

"I know, I saw . . ."

"Yeah, things got a little out of hand. Thankfully you got here when you did."

Elizabeth opened her eyes: she was in a squad car, lying in the backseat. She sat up quickly with a sharp intake of breath.

"Look who decided to show up—sleeping beauty!"

In the rearview, she saw the dark eyes of the female officer looking back at her.

"Wh- Where are we going?" Elizabeth asked, bewildered and aching from where she had been struck on the head.

"To Olympia," the officer in the passenger seat replied. He peeked back through the partition, then lit a cigarette. "But we got a quick stop to make first."

"You . . ." Elizabeth whispered. He resembled the horrible man from the parking lot, but it was hard to be certain. It sounded like him, though. She screamed, frantically kicking at the door.

"Hey! Relax, lady!" the male officer shouted, exhaling smoke. "You were being watched the whole time; that rest area has been under surveillance for a few weeks. The old lady was one of the perps we were after—"

Elizabeth stared at him in disbelief, shocked into silence: "Wh- what are you talking about?"

The female cop spoke first: "She was part of a ring that's been shaking people down. Their M.O. was to abduct people and rob them—pretend there was some sort of 'medical emergency.'"

"Wh- where is she? Is she alive?"

"Oh yeah; my partner's got her in custody back at the rest stop," the man replied, stubbing out his cigarette. "Along with her buddy, the guy that knocked you out. Good thing I showed up when I did."

"Yes," the other officer seconded. "You were very lucky."

Elizabeth was confused.

"Where are we going, then? You said we had another stop to make . . . Oh, God! My orientation!—can I go back?"

"As soon as we take a statement. We're headed to the hospital first, then the police station."

Elizabeth sank back into the seat of the patrol car.

So much for my new job . . .

The male officer lit up again, taking a long draw; the smoke made the air in the car dry and sharp. The woman glanced over at him. They exchanged a brief, knowing smile, then both of them started to laugh. The woman cut off the blue lights, which Elizabeth realized had been going without the siren. The rainy highway—vast and bleak—yawned before them in the dark.

The hairs stood on Elizabeth's arms: she suddenly realized that she was cuffed. Her face felt flushed, hot, and her stomach plummeted. Something isn't right! Her throat began to hurt: her scalp was taut on her skull, as if someone was pulling her hair out by the roots . . .

The last thing Elizabeth heard, his ragged breath hot on her ear:

"Told you that bitch wouldn't save you . . ."

The last things Elizabeth felt:

The rain, snow and wind chilling her damp face; a tangy congestion in her sinuses; a searing pain in her throat; the sensation of weightlessness in her extremities . . .

The last thing Elizabeth glimpsed as her eyes closed a final time:

The body of the dead female officer, soundlessly caressed by the spinning blue lights of her cruiser—face crushed. Next to her, propped against the blood-sprayed patrol car, was another carcass—this one decapitated.

Before the light faded forever, the last thing Elizabeth thought:

What is . . .

is he going to . . .

do with my . . . *head?*

Author's Note

My wife and I frequently make this very trip. On one occasion, this scenario presented itself, and it got me to thinking "What if . . . ?" I love the idea of disorienting readers in a way that makes them think, or is even uncomfortable. I think most people like to be challenged (not coddled), and I hope to provide that to some degree in my work. I'm sure I don't always succeed, but I do like to try, and to experiment with new ideas, different ways of telling a story, and other properties of narrative.

Palindrome Syndrome

"May you live in interesting times . . ."

So goes the curse:
It pales at the slow dawning
that all conspiracies are true;
In fact, they are all a part
of the one huge conspiracy:
Reality.

Unknown to most
(except you and me),
There exists a tiny, storm-swept island
In the grim grip of the North Atlantic . . .

Its solemn inhabitants are
the twisted progeny of
thousands of years of
Inbreeding.

Although this spit of land has only
been discovered in the
Astral Projections of convicted
murderers and parasitic twins,
If washed up
on its blustery, cobbled beaches
as a solitary shipwreck survivor,
One would behold a strange sight
before being consumed:
The bellowing and mewling of
these ghastly half-beings—
Shuffling, wild-eyed, toward an uncertain

future;
their smell fetid,
their sounds frightening.

Perhaps, at such a point, death could be
embraced;
Or suffer the fate of
Napoleon, who remarked:
"Able was I, ere I saw Elba."

Your fate: the same.
Your epitaph:
Lewd did I live, evil I did dwel.

Finally:
Assimilation.

The Hex Factor

"That girl ain't stealin' ma thunder no more! That's why I hired *you,* Mr. Blackwood."

Rupert Blackwood winced on hearing this; he leaned forward over the conference table, too aware of the clock ticking on the far wall of the small office.

The old hag speaking across the desk leered at him from her disastrously large left eye, wiping tears from her cheek where the unblinking orb continually watered. Her face was stern and gaunt, sprouting hairs in places usually reserved for the male of the species; her mouth smacked when she spoke, as though she were thirsty. Rupert gulped hard, rubbing his own eyes sympathetically as he shouldered the weight of her gaze.

Tugging his tie, he could sense heat rising in his face; he wanted to speak, but his throat felt as if it were packed with fungus. Finally:

"Mrs.—"

"*Ms.,* please Mr. Blackwood."

"Pardon me, of course: *Ms.* Stonecipher, this could be a hard case to prove at trial." His smile was wan, fragile.

The aged woman's face wrinkled further; she now seemed even *less* happy than before. Rupert glanced at the clock—which in his mind was *booming, booming*—but no one else appeared to notice. Another entreaty:

"Look—you said that you keep all this stuff written down, right?"

"Indeed I do." She wiped her cheek again and adjusted her jet-black shawl.

"Well, I have to see it. For goodn—for Pete's sake, how can I take on a case as your lawyer if you won't even let *me* see the evidence?" Rupert let this nugget sink in a moment; he hoped that her reluctance to part with her information would be daunting enough to get her to leave and give up this crazy scheme.

Cockles, Ms. Stonecipher's black cat, glared at him with great yellow eyes, perched in her mistress's lap. Once more, the old woman blotted at her bloodshot eye, at last turning her head away. Rupert added, exasperated:

"You can bet that won't play with a judge, either."

The elder gasped, looking at him again, her face softer. He blinked in response, thinking: *That changes things, huh?*

Rupert's newly found clientele sometimes gave him pause; he was in great demand ever since he won the class-action lawsuit brought about by the vampires. They had deemed it necessary to have special darkened areas in all restaurants so that they could integrate more fully into society. Exclusion violated their civil rights; it was a form of discrimination, no doubt. Whether the public—or the kitchen—was entirely ready to accommodate their rather *peculiar* dietary needs, well, that was another issue . . .

Overall, he was pleased at the resurgence in his career: it was one of the reasons he had been made partner. *After all,* he reasoned, *monsters had rights, just like anybody else.*

Like all jobs, his had its challenges as well as its benefits. For example, zombies tended to go to pieces on him over embalming practices and land-use rights, and often did not make it to the trial phase. In spite of their reputation as slow to act, they could be remarkably decisive, preferring to settle rather than get into some protracted mess. In addition, despite his best efforts, Rupert had to recuse himself from the werewolf depilatory cream allergy settlement offer—the guy was just too moody and emotional.

Regardless, his acumen and intensity—not to mention his success on behalf of the vampire contingent, his assault on the death tax as unconstitutional, and his work *pro bono* for The Flying Monkey Society—were well acknowledged in the field of law for all matters pertaining to "outsider" needs and issues. Whether undead, recently departed, infected, or reanimated, he treated all claims—even the more offbeat ones—with dignity and discretion. He no longer needed to advertise his services; he was overloaded from the word-of-mouth business alone.

And now this . . .

Ms. Stonecipher smacked her mouth dryly, sitting up as straight as her crooked frame allowed.

"But, Mr. Blackwood, I assure you that I'm a-tellin' the *truth.*" Her voice was cracked crystal.

Rupert raised his eyebrow. The old woman continued:

"I mean, you wouldn't understand most o' ma chicken scratch anyhow—"

"See here, Ms. Stonecipher—I'll be blunt." Rupert got up from the desk, walking to a window overlooking the parking lot. "We have to be able to substantiate your claims; you're making some pretty wild boasts about lost wages and trade secret violation."

The old crone muttered something, pulling a toad from the tattered overcoat under her wrap. She rubbed its head gently, meditatively. Cockles meowed. "Okay, Mr. Blackwood. Okay . . ."

Gingerly she perched the bewildered amphibian on the table, fetching something from another pocket in her rumpled dress. The toad sat there—fat, throat pulsing—staring at the lawyer, almost accusing him of some imaginary crime against his owner.

"Belvedere! Don't think such things about our friend Mr. Blackwood!" Ms. Stonecipher exclaimed, chiding the herptile. Belvedere waddled to the edge of the table, as though appalled by the whole affair. Cockles squeezed her eyes shut; the overly loud clock-tick assailed Rupert's head again; the air smelled suddenly like rain.

This is all a bit weird, Rupert thought.

At last, Ms. Stonecipher produced the small, threadbare notebook in question: it was the rough dimensions of a paperback, half as thick and bound in split brown leather.

How does one handle this type of intellectual property? Rupert mused as he looked at the manuscript.

"Here it is, Mr. Blackwood. Like I say, you prob'ly can't read ma writin' an' all too good." She offered the booklet to him, gnarled hand shaky.

Rupert took the small treatise. In the quiet of the room, he heard Cockles purring. Belvedere let a loud "ribbit!" fly. The law offices beyond the conference room door were churning dully as usual. He took a seat next to the woman, who was now looking from the window. He opened to a random page in the recipe section:

> April ninth, 1746—
>
> Hand rub the mixture of eleven herbs and spices onto the cleansed chicken, then roll in flour.

> Deep fry for ten minutes . . .

“That’s the one she sold to that damn chicken place—”

“You mean Kentucky Fried Chicken?”

“That’s it! Way back when; I’d been doin’ it that way for years, an’ she up an’ sells it to that ol’ Col. Sanders; *Harland,* that was him—Harland Sanders . . .”

The complete list of the eleven herbs and spices—and their correct proportions—was noted in the margin. Rupert flipped through the miniature tome again; Cockles and Belvedere watched closely.

> November twelfth, 1839—
>
> The elixir is greatly enhanced by a pinch of cocaine added during the cooling stage and dissolved completely . . .
>
> As for the other compounds, the most important would be—

“*Merchandise 7X?* I recall that from my patent days: that’s the secret ingredient in Coca-Cola, right?” Rupert glanced up at the old lady; her giant eye was fixed on his features.

“It is now!” she blustered. “That damn girl sold most o’ ma best recipes and made a dadblame fortune!”

Rupert was puzzled. *How can this be true? Some of the stuff in here is dated years before it appeared as any consumer product!*

Yet there it was, all written down in fountain ink on crumbling yellow parchment in Ms. Stonecipher’s handwriting. He leafed through more of the text: *Astrological Ephemerides; Raising of the Dead; Spirit Invocation; Use of Poppets . . .*

“I can tell by your aura that you’re a-doubtin’ ma claims, Mr. Blackwood.”

Rupert looked up, startled. “Oh—it’s, I mean, Ms. Stonecipher, let’s be candid. Between you, me,” he looked at the toad, “Belvedere and Cockles, here—”

“Don’t forget Sir Oberon,” she chimed, pointing to the owl on his chair back. Rupert had indeed forgotten the raptor, which had flown in upon her arrival and promptly went to sleep.

Forcing a smile, he said: “Hello there, Sir Oberon. Yes, well, what I’m saying is that these records don’t really mean *any*thing without some type of empirical data or an eyewitness that can verify what you are putting forth—" Rupert glanced at the book again, still going through its delicate pages:

Contacts—

Aleister Crowley; Leonardo da Vinci; Merlin . . .

"With all due respect, I don't think that you'll be getting any of your 'friends' here to come to your defense at the present."

She cackled at this. "Oh, really? To be sure, Mr. Blackwood, necromancy is one part o' the craft I done got down cold!"

Rupert gulped hard, staring at the old woman. "I see. . . . What you're saying is that—that you can . . . *produce*," he paused, glancing from Sir Oberon to Cockles and back to his client. "You can produce people to add veracity to your claims."

She nodded approvingly: "Precisely, Mr. Blackwood, precisely."

Rupert closed the strange old document, leaning back in his seat. Sir Oberon opened a sleepy eyelid and closed it again at the sound of his movement.

He looked at Ms. Stonecipher: she was gently smiling, her withered face relaxed, magnificently strange eye peering at him, brimming with expectancy. She dabbed at her cheek once more.

"Okay, Ms. Stonecipher: I'll try to help you, but on one condition."

She leaned forward, Cockles growling at the disturbance, her hand like a cold feather on his trouser leg. "Just tell me what you require, my sweet."

"I—I need you to prove to me that you really *are* a witch."

After a moment, the little old woman sank back in her seat, still smiling like a sphinx. The phone rang. Rang again. Rang a third time.

"Aren't you gonna answer it, Mr. Blackwood?"

Rupert picked up the receiver: "H-hello?"

"Darling!" his wife replied.

Rupert hung up the phone, his gut curdling. Ms. Stonecipher said nothing, just opened the door to his office and departed down the corridor to the main entrance, followed by Sir Oberon and Cockles.

I asked for it . . .

He watched his client as she stealthily left the building, then stood up and walked shakily over to his assistant's desk. Pale and sweaty as he leaned on the table for support, Rupert found his voice at last: "Ms. Reinhold, no more appointments today, please." He staggered back into his office, slamming the door.

"What the hell is going on here? What's gotten into Rupert?" Mr. Lawford asked, hobbling from his office over to Ms. Reinhold's desk. She seemed baffled.

"I—I don't know, sir," the young woman replied, shaking her head. Lawford squinted at the secretary, his wizened face crinkled in annoyance. He rapped his cane on the floor with impatience, regarding Rupert's closed door.

"Ever since he made partner, he's had a damned *attitude*. Better *before* it became Lawford, Jenkins . . . and *Blackwood*."

"Mr. Lawford!" Ms. Reinhold stared reproachfully at the senior attorney. He reddened under her gaze, then looked to the floor, muttering.

"Now, Mr. Lawford, you know he's been under a lot of strain since his wife, Ellen, passed on."

The old man huffed. He glanced up at Rupert's door again, then to his watch. At that moment, Rupert barreled from his office, clutching Ms. Stonecipher's volume in his hand, still donning his coat, face drained of color. A startled Mr. Lawford inquired: "Rupert, are you feeling okay? You look like you've just seen a ghost."

Rupert grasped the front doorknob. "No, sir. More like *heard* one."

"Mr. Blackwood?"

Rupert broke out of his thoughts. Pressing the intercom button on his telephone, a feeling of dread fingered his bowels.

"Yes, Ms. Reinhold?"

"Ms. Pettibone is here."

"Send her in, please. Thank you."

There was a moment's pause before the door opened, and Rupert caught the tiniest hint of perfume in the air. A throaty saxophone melody played in the center of his mind: sultry, dreamy.

The case of *Stonecipher v. Pettibone* was nearly ready to proceed to trial. All negotiations had soured into acrimony over the largest sticking point: "Hex Infringement."

While Ms. Stonecipher was willing to settle regarding lost wages and the other salient items for the good of the Coven, the infringement aspect was something that really bothered her; it was not only a position of pride, but an ethical question . . .

"I took the girl in, showed her the Art. She was a sharp learner an' had th' skills . . ."

"Then what happened?" Rupert asked, taking notes as he sat on her couch.

Sir Oberon—the lethargic owl—"who-*whoo*"-ed, staring at him, suddenly alert as the evening fell. Ms. Stonecipher's small residence was cozy and dark, decorated in black, crimson, and earth tones. The furnishings were modest, with comfortable—if threadbare—chairs, wrought iron and timber accoutrements, and many huge, well-used candles for illumination. Nearly every cranny and shelf in the place seemed to have some tiny figurine, Hummel or wooden cutout of fruits, vegetables, or farm animals. Framed cross-stitch consisting of simple aphorisms hung from the walls, giving a warm, homey touch to the dim interior. The smell of the woodstove and incense was breathtaking, with the entire place giving the semblance more of a cave than a mobile home. Rupert liked to think of it as Country Gothic. Cockles rubbed her ebon body against the attorney's leg, while Belvedere squatted on the living room table, the old woman calmly stroking his knobby head.

"She got too blame big for her britches. Started b'lievin' all that garbage them warlocks talk. You know how young girls is, Mr. Blackwood, nice-lookin' fella as yourself—females crave all that attention an' such. They start a-carryin' on with boys; doin' all manner o' stupid antics . . . comin' under th' influence of folks what ain't got their best int'rests ta heart . . ."

Rupert continued to jot down information.

How to play this?

"So . . . so Ms. Pettibone was living with you, correct?"

"Yessir, that's right." The ancient woman wiped her cheek, a cascade of impossibly long and thick blue-black tresses framing her petite shoulders in the soft warm ambience of the candlelight.

"And how long was she in your custody?"

Ms. Stonecipher tilted her diminutive head. "Prob'ly 'bout 150, 160 years or so, I reckon—"

"What?"

The old woman jumped a little, obviously surprised. Gibber, Thomas, Ivan, and Doodle, her pet rats, squealed in unison; Midori, the huge male iguana sitting on a rock next to the space heater, slowly closed his bottom eyelid, as if trying to make the whole scene disappear. Every creature in the house was looking at the surprised attorney.

"Uh—I'm sorry, Ms. Stonecipher. You kind of threw me with how long you've known Ms. Pettibone. Please proceed," Rupert said at last, dabbing his forehead with a kerchief.

The old lady chuckled. "We are old souls, Mr. Blackwood . . . this shell is but a temp'rary manifestation o' our eternal life energy. Anyhow, once she graduated to her first skyclad meetin' o' the Coven—"

"Skyclad?" Rupert inquired, writing furiously.

"You know . . . *nekkid,* Mr. Blackwood. Stark nekkid." Ms. Stonecipher smiled at the lawyer, good eye beaming. Rupert felt himself blush, and blotted his forehead again.

"Who was there?" he asked.

The elderly woman paused, counting silently on knotty fingers. "Let's see . . . me, Wilma, Ms. Pettibone, Sammi, Alice, Lucretia, uh, who else? Sinthya, Greta, Morgana, Marti, Darla, Mary . . . I b'lieve that's all."

Rupert wrote the names down. "Any chance of getting them to testify about what happened between you and Ms. Pettibone?"

"Pos'bly. Some o' the girls've taken on other, shall we say *aspects* at this juncture."

"You mean they've passed on?"

"No, now I wouldn't say that." She touched her collar, pulling it closed at the throat as a draft crept through the candlelit abode. "Just changed a bit. . . . I reckon you can still get hold o' Marti, Alice, Sammi, and Sinthya pretty easy."

Sir Oberon hooted loudly, turning his head almost completely around to groom his tail feathers. Midori licked the chilly air; Rupert's breath suddenly fogged. Ms. Stonecipher wiped her cheek with a bundled napkin, over-sized orb glaring.

That eye never blinks, Rupert mused.

"Fair enough," he said. "Your main concern is the infringement—you feel betrayed by Ms. Pettibone taking the Grimoire, selling the recipes and—"

"I'm mainly upset at that Jezebel stealin' ma spells."

"I was just going to say 'stealing your spells.'" Rupert wrote something else down. "Can you explain what spells and hexes are, and why you feel that she stole them?"

The hunched elder stirred in her seat, looking first to Belvedere, then at Midori; the reptile appeared to be sleeping. Sir Oberon whooped again. "Spells an' such is highly personal things, Mr. Blackwood. Takes a long time—a *mighty* long time—to build up a good spell book. Takes a lot o' effort, trial an' error an' the like."

Rupert kept writing. "I see." The old woman dropped a bit of cornhusk on the incense burner on her end table.

"Ms. Pettibone wanted a shortcut. Instead o' getting' ta work practicin' the Craft, she'd rather get into trouble with them boys an' whatnot . . . always showin' herself off, doin' other things . . . When she took ma book, I didn't notice at first; then she kept appearin' to have nicer an' nicer finery, more makeup an' all. I found out the truth from the girls in the Coven."

"What prompted you to take her in to begin with?"

"That's a long story. It was a favor," Ms. Stonecipher replied. "She's ma niece, an' when her father was killed, I knew somebody needed to raise the lass."

"What about her mother?"

"Died in childbirth."

"I see," Rupert said, continuing to make notes. He checked his watch. "Well, I appreciate your candor, Ms. Stonecipher, and everything looks right on track for—"

". . . the trial?" Ms. Pettibone asked. Rupert was momentarily confused.

"I'm sorry, Ms. Pettibone—could you please ask that again?" he replied, standing as she entered the room.

Goodness . . .

She crossed over to his desk with short strides, hips rotating languorously, spiked heels clacking in time to her steps. A grey microminiskirt hugged the curvaceous flesh of her thighs like a sausage casing. A patent leather belt cinched her hourglass waist; the filmy blouse—a clingy, neck plunging affair—left little to the imagination.

"I said that I wanted to know if there was some way that we could avoid the trial?" Her voice was smoky, her lips like ripe cherries. Scarlet hair framed her radiant, perfect face.

She's . . . bewitching!

The woman's intense lavender eyes pierced through him. Rupert felt lightheaded.

"I think your aunt has her mind made up, Ms. Pettibone." Rupert felt sluggish, drugged. He sank down into his chair once she was seated.

"There must be *some*thing that she'll agree to, Mr. Blackwood . . . some *settlement?* After all, I *did* return the book. It was never personal; I *love* Auntie. It's just business, plain and simple. Tell you what: suppose I give her some of the proceeds, or perhaps *promise* to straighten up and fly right, or *both*."

Ms. Pettibone—coquette that she was—languidly crossed her stockinged legs. Rupert just glimpsed that she was wearing dark purple lace garters—and nothing else. He felt his face grow warm and fixed his eyes on his notebook. "Uh—gee, I—I really don't think, um . . ."

The young woman leaned forward, toying with the pearl necklace she wore, mouth slightly open. Ample cleavage spilled out of her shirt, just revealing a hint of dark areola skin.

Damn! Sweat dewed his forehead.

"I—I'll ask again, Ms. Pettibone, but you know how she is . . . she can be—*determined*."

The girl was still slanted over his desk, caressing her exposed clavicle like a piece of fine, milky ceramic. She coyly turned her head to the side, holding Rupert's gaze. He felt something pass through the room.

"I *know* you can get her to rethink this, Mr. Bla—*Rupert*." She placed her hand on his; it was cold, icy. Rupert smiled thinly at her.

"We'll see," he said.

"I *knew* I should've settled this in the Old Ways! Now that hussy's a-usin' *ma own magic* agin me!" Ms. Stonecipher thundered, voice ragged. Her intense stare was burning through the lawyer.

"She seemed perfectly nice to me, and more than willing to settle out of court—"

"Pshaw! She's a-workin' th' *daylights* out o' you, Mr. Blackwood! That child's got her charms o'er th' menfolk, to be sure! *Damn her!* I'd take matters into ma own hands, but she up an' knows all ma secrets." The antique woman was breathing hard, weathered face frowning underneath the pointed black hat. She wiped her bulging, bloodshot eye.

Rupert felt like a fool, especially under the scornful gaze of Belvedere. The amphibian observed him with mute mockery and disgust, like some dumpy little god from the forgotten past.

This is nuts . . .

"Okay. I'm sorry I even brought it up, Ms. Stonecipher. Let's proceed as if—"

"Just hold on, Mr. Blackwood. I took a notion . . . you say she's a-willin' to bargain. She good'n well knows I can't be beat when ma dander's up. . . . Well, all right, I'll take her up on her offer. But *I* want some things in return."

Rupert brightened. He had not been looking forward to the trial. *Sanity prevails at last.* "Go ahead." He readied his pen.

"I want a cut o' that money—she's made out dang fine, and I aim to partake. That hussy *owes me.*"

"Got it. What else?"

"I want *all* ma spells back, an' she has to promise not to practice *my* hexes, chants, incantations, potions, or necromancy parti'clars *evermore.* She's gotta get her own, just like the rest of us has."

"Sounds reasonable. Is that everything?"

"No, sir." The old woman leaned in closer. Whispering: "I want her to expend some o' that magic she took an' fix me up; you know, purdy skin an' hair, big boobs, nice figure. . . . I might want ta take a dip in that pool o' men she's been a-swimmin' in!" Ms. Stonecipher winked her good eye at the attorney. He shuddered: *Gonna take a* lot *of magic for that . . .*

"Okay. What else?" The phone rang. Rupert swallowed. *I told Ms. Reinhold no calls.*

"Hello, Rupert Blackwood. Yes . . . Ah—I *see.* Excellent! Okay; I will. Thank *you.* Bye-bye." Rupert returned the handset to its cradle.

"That was Ms. Pettibone; she said that she agrees with your demands and would like to set things right as soon as possible. How did she—?"

Ms. Stonecipher's face thawed. "Zounds! I'm glad this all worked out; guess that meetin' o' the Coven helped after all. Or maybe she's finally a-practicin' weavin' them *mindwaves.* Oh, and of *course* my wonderful lawyer's persuasion helped a bunch." The old lady reached over and pinched Rupert's cheek. Belvedere grunted noisily.

"It was nothing, really; just a little mediation," Rupert responded, blushing.

Ms. Stonecipher stood to leave. Sir Oberon flapped nervously as he lit onto her shoulder, sleepy eyes fluttering.

"Can I call you a cab or give you a ride home Ms.—oh, wait; I guess you've got your own 'mode of transportation,' right?" Rupert asked, laughing dryly and winking at her. She seemed perplexed.

"Whatever do you mean, Mr. Blackwood?"

"You *know*—I get it. The broom, all that," he said, still grinning. Belvedere emitted a muffled croak from her coat pocket. She drew her cape up around her body.

"Mr. Blackwood," she said, and started laughing, "I don't know what you're a-talkin' about. My advice: don't b'lieve ever'thin' you read about witches. We *still* have ta obey the laws o' physics an' whatnot."

Rupert's laughter died in his throat. "I—I'm terribly sorry, Ms. Stonecipher! Please accept my apologies."

Offering his arm, he asked: "Can I give you a ride home?"

She accepted, slipping her dainty hand through the crook of his elbow: already her skin was smooth, healthy, and soft. As she crossed the room, Ms. Stonecipher's stooped shoulders straightened, and she grew taller with each step. Rupert opened the door to his office, glancing at her face. Night-black hair tumbled luxuriously across winsome features, magnetic blue eyes peering shyly from a creamy complexion. The demure nose was pert and perfectly proportioned above the full mouth.

My word! She's beautiful!

"Thank you, Mr. Blackwood," she said, her voice like honey. He grasped her warm palm in his own, smiling at this immaculate jewel.

"Rupert," he said, "please—call me Rupert."

Author's Note

Sometimes a preposterous notion makes an interesting tale. That's my feeling about this little number. It has a strange attraction for me, as the characters feel like people I know! In fact, they are based on a few of my relatives: That's all I'll relate about this!

Valve:
The Heart as a Metaphor for Postmodern Blight

("We were created in His image . . ."—so all the insects, whales, bats, et cetera tell their children. Dedicated to **Hector**: *murdered so oblivious urbanites could indulge in artificial rustication.)*

The pig's valves keep **you** alive—
Pumping away in your chest . . .

I wonder:
Have **you** ever given thanks
To *this marvel of engineered DNA*—
Forced to die—
So that **you** could live another day?

Let me be blunt, not obtuse:
Never one to do your best,
Does it occur to **you**
that these years of willful ignorance and
abuse
have made **you** the butt of a humorless
cosmic jest?

Do **you** convince yourself that it's your
"Dominion"
to take *someone else's* life
so selfishly,
After giving yours away to
Workplace demands, Marlboro, and Burger King?

We all succumb to something at some point,
Beings—so far—of only
Flesh, blood, and bone;
But what about these *other* parts of *Others—*
the dreams, the thoughts, the goals?
Did **you** bother to think of *their*
rights?
The answer, in a word:
"No."
(**You** may have *traded arteries*,
but cannot *trade souls* . . .)

I am reminded that—not so long ago—
Women were considered "beasts," devoid of any *essence*—"divine" or otherwise—they were just Property, for use or abuse; just a fixture in a man's home . . .

And have we already forgotten the terrible lessons—
the brutal and inhumane legacies—
of anguish, bitterness and pain,
that are splashed across the musty pages of History
regarding the genocide of the *Jews* in extermination camps
(where "God" wore jackboots);
the destruction of the *Native Americans*
(where the "Great Spirit" provided firewater);
the obliteration of Australia's *Aborigines*?
(Not to disregard:
The living deaths of *countless other beings* for the absurdities of "science,"
"fashion," "religion," or "Manifest Destiny,"
And the heinous evils perpetrated against *Asians* and *Africans* due to the global stain of *slavery* . . .)

The *creatures* of today are in the throes of *their own Holocaust:*
Enslaved in Factory Farms by the (c)Ru(e)ling Class
In an unending pursuit of cheap clothing and unsustainable goods,
Their perpetual annihilation expands with the populations and waist-lines of a World hungering for the things they think they want . . .

You: Xenotransplant > Industrial Mutant.
Less than Swine, but more than Man:
Reaping the benefit of the 21st Century's
Modern Pharmacopeia and Medical Advances;
You contribute nothing,
Yet gorge on *all;*
Oblivious to what is left to—or even *of—the rest,*
so long as **you** can remain unchanged, and forestall your own quietus . . .

I am done, but still I ask:
Now that **you** are truly *heartless,*
Do the *cannibalistic* overtones occur to **you**—
growing fatter and happier as **you** snack on your
sandwich of ham and turkey breast?
Keep ignoring me, please:
enjoy your thoughtless, monstrous
repast . . .

Honestly, how can *anyone* be "pro-life"
in the midst of such
waste, heartbreak, and death?

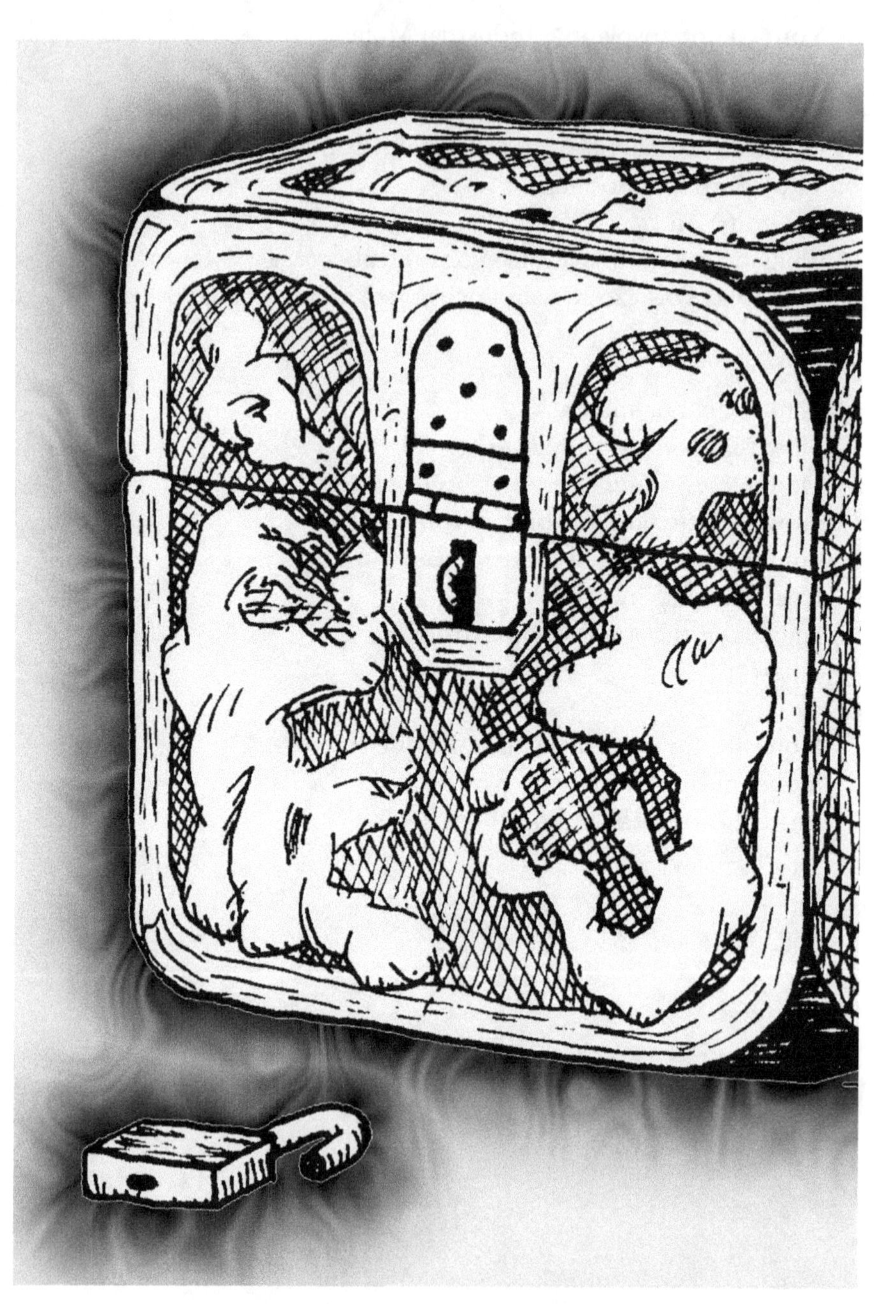

Valor: A Fable

"Still it rages . . ."

Weary, the king stood poised at the edge of his cot at the end of the world. In another time, he might have been declared an avenging angel—perhaps even a savior.

Not now . . .

Outside, the stalemate on the devastated heath held fast: the frenzied yelping of berserkers, punctuated by the insensible nattering of the dying drew closer by the moment.

"How has it all come down to this?"

Pacing anxiously in the confines of his tent, the king realized this final skirmish would decide the future, and he knew that his role in particular was the reason.

Finally, as he sat down on his tattered cot, he understood he should rest but resisted the call of sleep. After a few more moments, he lay down at last and closed his burning eyes, terrible visions painting the insides of his eyelids with gruesome tableaux.

"If we are vanquished, all will be lost forevermore."

An orange and yellow vortex blinded the boy.

Blotting the horizon away, its burning intensity scorched his face. Sweat and blood flecked his body, matted his hair. Delirious, he was hypnotized by this brilliant, shimmering maelstrom: the afterworld beckoned.

How great, how grand death will be.

Far off there were sounds; he struggled to focus. After a time he tried to stand, but realized he could not feel his legs. As he reached down with a shaky hand, the extent of his injuries became evident: a slowly beating heart throbbed through his shattered ribcage; further down, gentle loops of pulsing intestine pushed through a tight, ragged hole in his gut.

"By . . . the *gods* . . ."

Summoning all the energy he could muster, he resisted the celestial display and shoved his innards back into his abdominal cavity. Gritting his teeth, he flipped over, screaming the entire time. Calm at last, his exhausted body felt as if it were on fire, and he rested for perhaps a day; time was fluid: first molten, then crystalline, then molten again. The merciless sun stared down on his broken frame as he struggled to survive.

At last he began to crawl, taking an unconscious, grim assessment of his environs as he pushed forward: the charred ground sprouted with the bloody offal of destroyed men and animals like some alien flora. Pulling himself through the quagmire of flies, disease, bones, he sensed the battle was moving away—farther down the coast.

He crept onward for what seemed an eon, his breathing loud, sweat stinging his eyes. After several days of torment, he saw something through a cold morning mist: a cave.

"Your Excellency!"

BOOM

Boom

BOOM

"Your Excellency!"

BOOM

Boom

boom

In the dark, the king's eyes wavered open.

"Your Excellency! We *must* have an answer! Do we stand or retreat?"

As the fog of sleep lifted, the drowsy monarch gathered his thoughts: *Stand—or* retreat?

"*Please,* your Excellency!"

Rising from his makeshift bed, he observed the desperate general. The sounds of combat were closing in. He stroked several days' growth of graying beard, contemplating the question. *Unbelievable, this. How long have I slept? Too long, perhaps.*

"What is our situation, General?"

"We have lost our best—even though—"

"Then they were *not* our best!" the king roared. His dark eyes fumed in the dim candlelight from the general's lantern. There was a long, charged silence in the tent: the wails of the dying and ringing of armaments filled the space like the laughter of Thanatos.

"Yes, my Lord, you are right," the soldier said at last, looking to the ground as if it might spell out how to proceed.

"Now—what is our situation?" the regent asked, fully engaged in the moment.

"We are in need of supplies—there is no more pitch. The food and dressings are nearly gone." The general paused.

"Go on," the king advised, quiet, distant. The lamp's fire sputtered as though a ghost had entered the chamber.

"The enemy has advanced, my Lord. The men are showing signs of—*breaking,* Sire."

This was grave news indeed. The king turned from the commander. "We will fight," he said finally. "We must win. I did not come this far to retreat, General."

"But—*Your Highness!*"

"Enough!"

The king spun back to face the exhausted general, breath heavy in the half-light. After a moment, he walked past the soldier to a cabinet with an enormous lock, corroded by the years.

As he pulled a tarnished silver necklace from beneath his tunic, the king's expression seemed to change. Dangling from the delicate chain was a skeleton key, glinting softly in the lantern's yellow glow. "I have never shown this to anyone."

The general opened his eyes wide, looking up, his greasy hair plastered to his tired, filthy face. The hot, stale air was sharp with the fragrance of death.

"General, *this* is how we will overcome." With that, the sovereign unlocked the armoire. The rusty hinges creaked in the small void of the tent. "Bring the light, General."

The soldier quickly moved forward, raising the lantern.

The king hoisted out a small container: There were deep, fantastic carvings all over it, conveying a story of some sort. Once the heavy box was lowered to the ground, the king looked up at the general with eyes that were little more than bottomless ebony holes, dull and lifeless even as the terrible noise and stench of the battle drew closer, ever closer.

Dumbstruck, the officer could only stare at the strange, archaic chest. The king hesitated as he placed the key into its rusty lock.

After an agonizing pause: "General, is there any news of my son, the prince?"

Within the cavern, the darkness was almost a living being: heavy, wet, suffocating.

The young man collapsed against a jagged cave wall: *I made it.*

Awakening with a start, he drank water dripping from the ceiling, then fashioned dressings for his wounds from some moss and the remnants of his shirt.

Dawn was breaking; the mist was thick upon the moor. *So, this is home—for now.*

After another fitful nap, he awoke: hunger was on his heels. Looking around, he noticed something shining in the recesses of the grotto.

Perhaps it's a weapon or a tool . . . something of use.

With great effort, he reached the gleaming object: *A key . . .*

This silver key was what he had seen glimmering in the depths of the cave, next to an object that would forever change his destiny: a small, wooden, deeply etched coffer. For a long time he studied the wild collection of obscene figures adorning its surface, trying to comprehend the imagery; there were many beautiful panels, but the last was blank, smooth. A metal lock held the container shut.

There were several elaborate trunks like this in his father's home. His father—the king—had collected things such as this during his many bloody conquests. At last trying the key, the prince found that his luck was good: inside was an assortment of food, pitch, medicines. His sobs echoed loudly in the bowels of the lonely cavern.

"Thank the gods!" Tears spilled down his cheeks.

One of the things inside was a scrap of paper with some writing. He angled to where he could read it in the faint light of the cave:

Use what is needed,
Leave that which is not.
All Great Men know
Greed and lust are not answers
But the Soul's heavy locks—
Along with ceaseless woe

This is the spirit's final cost:
A True heart, forever lost . . .
Ignore this warning at grimmest peril:
To steal this cask bodes eternal failure.
Use what is needed,
Leave that which is not.

This caused the prince to laugh. He threw the note back in and began to eat.

He could hardly wait to go back home; though he detested his father's insatiable desire for battle and dominance, he knew that at some point—Fate willing—he would be king.

"I will be different. Just . . . merciful . . . kind . . ."

Contented, he moved himself and his spoils near the entrance, watching the sun set with tearful eyes. His fevered eyelids grew heavier as night descended, the murmur of crickets soothing his pain.

Drifting off, he thought: *One day, I shall make all things right with the world.*

"We have come to this because of me," the king whispered. It had been many years since he had opened the antique chest: dread had kept him from seeking out its infernal contents.

The anguished king's stare widened in the dimness of the tent: *It appears my reservations were not unfounded.* Peering into the wooden box after all this time, he saw that the only things in it were a furrowed, mushroom-like article—not unlike jerky—and a scrap of crumbling, yellowed paper with an inscription. The general grew more apprehensive. The king looked at the officer as the baleful lantern flickered.

"Your Excellency, how will—*this* help us?"

The startled king opened his mouth, but no sound would emerge. His eyes locked with his general's.

Boom

Boom

BOOM

The monarch's shaking hand darted under his shirt, to his obscenely scarred torso where fleshy keloid scars plotted his despair—daily reminders of what he had long ago traded. The atmosphere in the marquee was still—a stark contrast to the frenzied din outside. The enemy was nearly upon them.

"My *heart*—this is where I kept my spirit, General. My will . . . This was where I imprisoned my strong, beating heart for many years . . . inside this—this desolate box." The king reached down into the wooden coffer and pulled out the pathetic object: It was beating faintly in the lamp's dying flame, a subtle flexing in the shadowy confines of the Imperial tent.

The king looked to his general with sad eyes, saying at last, distantly, remorsefully: "After I . . . after I survived the Crusades, I recovered in a grotto. I vowed that I would keep my heart in here forever, so that it would remain pure, incorruptible . . . so unlike the heart of my tyrannical patriarch." A tear fell onto the failing organ in the once-mighty sovereign's palm. "My mistake was in not foreseeing that one cannot maintain justice and mercy without *feeling*—without *compassion.* My heart withered from lack of use, I realize now—precisely as my father's did so long ago. Willpower alone is not enough to sustain a soul. I . . . I thought that it was, but I was *wrong*—and here . . ." He looked to the horrified soldier, thrusting the gruesome object toward him: "*Here,* General, is the final cost."

He stared at the confused officer, eyes brimming with regret. "Gone is the queen . . . gone is the prince . . . for what? For—for the *vainglorious thrashings* of a man at loose ends. I—I have lost my . . . nay—*our* way, General." As the king gazed into the lantern's amber glow, the battle seemed just outside the tent. He continued: "It only left a lonely ache in an empty hole. Now—*look* at it! Look at *me! Behold the cost of vanity!"* Once more he thrust the desiccated thing at his terrified commander.

Finally, the general screamed in horror, crying out: "Sorcerer!" Drawing his sword as he leapt back in revulsion, he then plunged the weapon though the aged caliph's midsection to the hilt.

Still clutching his weakly pumping heart, the skewered king backed slowly off the blade, grunting with the effort, the crepitus of metal on bone loud in the tent.

"That . . . will do . . . no good, General. We are *all* dead now. . . . You, my wife, my son, I—*we are . . . damned souls.*" He chuckled bitterly, humorlessly.

The general, by now completely maddened with fear, ran screaming to his doom in the mêlée outside. The king regarded the leathery, atrophied muscle, still sadly pulsing in his hand; the outside world was of no consequence to him now.

"I let my true loves and beliefs get supplanted by petty concerns: revenge, lust, hatred, greed. . . . Much have I learned, but at too late a date. What good is a man without a heart? Without a direction? Without an heir? Without . . . without—*love?*"

Slowly, tentatively, the king raised the fragile, withered object to his lips, kissing it. The weak light glistened on his tear-tracked face, as a veil of sorrow descended over his mind.

Just then, an enemy warrior burst into the dank royal quarters; with a victorious howl, the soldier sought out his target, cleaving the humid air in a deadly arc as his gory blade flashed in the lantern's sooty flicker.

"The wise ancients believed," the conquered despot murmured in his last moments, "that the consumption of internal organs—especially the heart—imparted *bravery* . . . *strength* . . . in dire circumstances . . . *valor*."

In that long instant before the assassin's cutlass connected with his neck, the dispirited sovereign bit into his own heart's tough exterior. Black, syrupy blood—the color of a crow's eye—oozed down his bristly chin.

"Ego praevalebo."

As the king chewed, the sword found its mark.

As the king collapsed, the organ stopped pumping . . . his overturned lamp extinguishing itself at last.

And as the King died . . .

An Age of Darkness followed.

Author's Note

One can learn a lot from fables: I love re-reading them, so I thought I'd try to conjure some myself. I have a few more in the works. I especially like how the format allows such flexibility with social commentary. I feel all fiction should work on some subtextual level (the best stories and poems do, from Homer and Dante to García Marquez), and the forms of science fiction, magical realism, and horror are especially useful for this, freighted as they are with possibility and unreality (SF is better for political observation, I feel, whereas horror seems better suited for exploring personal anxiety).

Dragon

Once, I saw a Dragon:
(Reclining by the sea—)

Lifting his great, scaly head,
(He turned to look at me—)

Prismic pupils flashing in the autumn flaming light,
(Regarding my amazement with ennui and bemused delight—)

He opened his giant, toothy mouth and said:

"Some things are better left unseen . . ."

Then, he slipped beneath the waves,
(So languid, so serpentine!)

Vanishing.
(Under crashing surf in a dark and foaming sea.)

Object Lesson

First there is the darkness—deep and alien, it smothers all light, muffles all sound.

Eventually the ears detect something, as the heavy quiet is broken by the too-perfect, mechanized thump of a respirator.

Then there are the odors . . . like a pall over the world, the suffocating reek of sterility and talc blend sickly in the cold, stale air.

Walking closer, ghastly, xeric lips—quivering with artificial breath—come into view . . . followed by awareness of the faint rise and fall of the chest, as forced oxygen inflates failing lungs.

Finally, and most dreadful of all, the dead, unblinking eyes appear from the gloom.

Staring . . . vacant . . . endless . . .

Every beginning springs from an ending, he mused; today would be one of those times.

As he parked the car, he thought of her melancholy expression, just like the other million or so times it seemed he had been here. He cut the headlights and sat for a moment in the muted confines of the automobile, watching leaves scatter in eddies across the deserted parking lot. He pulled the keys from the ignition; he was tired, defeated, worn down. In front of him, the hospital loomed from atop a fog-shrouded hill, squat, sprawling, menacing. It seemed alive somehow; malevolent . . . as though it were waiting to consume him, like it consumed so many others every day: *They go in, and they never leave . . .*

At last he opened the car door and walked to the hospital entryway, pocketing his keys as he moved thought the crisp fall air. Once inside, hovering in the desolate lobby awaiting the elevator, he caught himself glancing too frequently at his watch but never noting the time.

Though uncertain about many things these days, this he knew: he loved her. She had always been there for him; she was a solid tether, even an anchor of sorts, as he navigated the ever more connected, paradoxically more insular world.

There was something else, though, that he had to admit: he also *hated* her. She was inexorable in her nebulousness, in her equivocation about living or dying; part of him resented her status as neither dead nor truly alive: she haunted his dreams mercilessly, and drifted through his every lucid moment like a phantom—

"Dr. Baker, please call the E.R. Dr. Baker." The intercom message jolted through him.

He hit the illuminated up arrow impatiently once again: "Come on."

The numbing ritual of coming to the hospital reminded him of the eerie calmness the day his father died. *That was so different from what I feel now, though. . . .* The elevator announced its arrival with a soft chime.

"Finally." He entered the polished metal crucible, doors sliding closed behind him. As usual, he was alone on his ride to her room. He pushed the fifth-floor button, drowned once more in the ocean of his thoughts and feelings.

He remembered that she was sobbing into the phone; it was late when she called with the news, and he had been sleeping: *"Heart attack . . . Daddy might not make it . . . Please come home . . . as soon as you can . . . Vegetative state . . . coma . . ."* He could only recall fragments of that time, like flashes of strobe light at a concert. He was certain she said more, but she sounded so very far away—tinny, distant. She could have been from any point in the trajectory of Time's pitiless arrow—another place, another era; perhaps the future, maybe the past. . . . Regrettably, she had been an unhappy emissary from an all too real present. The detachment that permeated everything from that point forward was still too easy to conjure; it pulled the color from the edges of his reality every time he came to see her.

Floor two.

He had not consciously understood much beyond her basic message, as his attention was unexpectedly flooded with mental calculations: planes to schedule, cars to rent, a sudden trip to plan. Dave Brubeck's "Strange Meadowlark," one of Dad's favorite tunes, had bloomed softly in his mind as a sort of mental soundtrack and played in his head daily for nearly a year after that. Fortunately, his new boss at the software company he had just started working for was understanding and gave him a generous amount of time to head home and get affairs in order.

He never spoke to his father again: Once the doctors informed her that the brain damage after his fifth consecutive heart attack was irreversible and profound, he instructed her to comply with Dad's wishes and sign the Do Not Resuscitate order, even if he was still en route. As he flew from one coast to the other, his father at last fully embraced the ultimate in digital expression—passing instantly from 1 to 0 in a matter of nanoseconds. The ring of a telephone late at night still made his hands clammy.

Surprisingly, he had been calm at the medical examiner's office as he stared through the glass: it looked for all the world as if Dad were just taking a nap. A day later, at the memorial service, he was still focused, the shock of it fresh. He had not cried, or even felt the need. He was adrift during the short eulogy and held it together fine as he kissed his father's face for the last time. Dad was so cold, smelling faintly of embalming fluid; the funerary makeup was a bit too heavy in the *memento mori.*

Visiting with her after the service, he saw the sad glass of water—half-empty—that was left unfinished, sitting on an end table near the couch.

"That's where he was sitting," she said, "right where you are now."

Then, unexpectedly, the tears came and would not stop. His own mortality had never loomed so large in his brain as during that fleeting instant. They talked, laughed, and cried until their throats closed and their eyes swelled shut. The full impact of his new reality finally caught up with him on the long flight home, as he traded the drone of cicadas for the pink noise of jet engines. Dad returned later in an urn: even after all this time it was still hard to believe . . .

Floor three.

In a way, it was as if Dad were just visiting some other place: After a few years his nonexistence solidified into an almost tangible "thing." Present became past, and the future washed by in a stream of daily obligations and new experiences. The bitter sadness of the whole episode was relegated to some half-remembered plateau, a forlorn amnesia lane as history receded from the confines of everyday life like a line retreating to a vanishing point of non-remembrance on the horizon.

After a while, they both came to grips with their mutually adjusted situations, learning each other's ways without his father's gentle filter. She was able to move forward as her own person; he found new friends and purpose, but neither of them totally forgot. Then came another fateful telephone call; though less urgent, it was no less ominous:

"Spots on the lungs . . . surgery . . . chemotherapy . . . prognosis uncertain."

He would mentally replay these scenes at the strangest times. While driving home, she hovered before him, her young and old selves morphing back and forth in the twilight; other times, images and remembrances would flash into his perception over dinner, or during a telephone call with a friend. Most disturbing was the quiet before falling asleep: Thoughts would gnaw at him, keeping him awake, causing the shadows on his ceiling to grow into menacing, crawling horrors, sometimes to the accompaniment of her strained voice reverberating through his anxious mind.

'I never see you anymore; when are you going to come visit me? Are you ashamed of me? Afraid? Don't you miss me?'

He tried to explain: He was building a life, a career, a self. He promised to visit more often.

The treatments went well at first; then the news that he had feared: while at the hospital for a test, she slipped into a coma. It happened when she was under general anesthesia for another biopsy. No one could explain why it had happened, and no one could say when she would come out of it . . . or if she would come out of it. He moved back to the city of his birth to be with her after that.

For support . . . out of obligation . . .

To wait.

Floor four.

That was eight years, three jobs, and a marriage ago for him.

"Can I do this?" The sound of his own clotted voice startled him in the tranquility of the elevator. He unzipped his coat, suddenly overheated.

Arriving at her floor, he wondered if this visit would end like all the others: mentally braced, but at the last instant looking into her face and breaking down, physically unable to bring himself to kill her. The doors slid open on the long dim corridor to her suite. A bead of sweat rolled the length of his spine.

Empty. Unexpectedly the story of the ancient Moirae popped into his mind, and he wondered if Clotho, Lachesis, and Atropos were watching him from some distant place in the universe, laughing perhaps.

Is this a ghost? I've never been given to believing in the supernatural, but maybe there is something else . . . something unknown, even unknowable. . . . What if poltergeists and spirits aren't ectoplasm and shadows, but flesh and blood—or flesh, blood, and the power company conspiring to postpone death? A sort of 'meta-ghost'!

He laughed quietly at the thought, then rubbed his eyes.

Besides, what's more haunting than the spectre of your parents hovering over your life anyway, dead or alive? Certainly not some metaphysical spook . . .

Exiting the elevator, he walked down the softly lit hallway, stiff, nearly insensible to anything but the entrance to her room. His footfalls seemed very loud to him, causing his face to twitch with each reverberation.

He paused just outside her door, heart pounding, feeling faint.

"Should I tell her—or just do it?" His mouth was papery, his hands damp.

He lingered there, the moment dilating into an hour before the mirror of his anguish was at last shattered by an announcement: "Good evening. It is now 8:55 P.M. Visiting hours will be over in five minutes."

Suddenly he was next to her bed in the darkened private room, swallowing against a lump in his throat, his chin quivering. He rubbed his face with a calloused hand as memories of all the times he was fortunate enough to spend with her flowed over him. They had shared every season of tears—anger, hope, bliss, remorse . . . If the eyes are the windows to the soul, then tears, he realized now, were the convex liquid embodiment of each individual moment, good or bad, refracting and reflecting reality into mortal lessons—bending insights into knowledge, prisming the rays of life's experiences into the spectrum of all emotion.

And in real time. Instant by instant, experience by experience . . . Never recognized as they happen, these moments combine in both tiny and profound ways through the lenses of love, trust, and implicit understanding to focus relationships and illuminate the cold darkness of a seemingly indifferent world with the radiance of shared familiarities.

Leaning close, he stroked the soft white tumble of her hair. *It's still easy to see how beautiful she used to be.*

"Remember our trips to the beach in the dog-days of summer? Or those cold sunrises at the mountains in October, watching the leaves change? How about when we had to deal with my meningitis? That was bad, huh? Or when I crashed the car? Remember when you hugged me at Dad's funeral?"

Tempus fugit, he reflected. *The tears come so easily now.* He paused there—half-smiling through his sorrow, one hand caressing her hair, the other poised on the plug that would stop the life-support system—oblivious. Although he was physically frozen in time and place for what seemed an eternity, his mind was frantic . . . reeling at what he was about to do.

Can I really go through with this?

A cramp burned whitely in his arm from holding the cord. A loud sob escaped him, reverberating as it exploded the silence of the room. He blinked hard, wiped his eyes, then looked around absurdly to be sure that he was still alone. His head cleared for an instant and his senses felt heightened. He tasted the warm air in the room—slightly acid, dry—like a corked red wine. And there was the smell of green soap and sickness—nauseatingly familiar, never comforting, and not quite succumbing to olfactory paralysis. The harsh streetlights outside cast stiletto shadows through his tunneled vision, and he looked to the tiny window, to the world without; it seemed to move on apart from him, as if he had been reduced from participant to spectator in his own existence. Every day seemed so removed from his inner experiences, his personal struggles—even from this very moment, this very instance of *now*.

"Professor Johnson," he began, studying the way her hair curled on the pillow as he spoke, "he once said he believed that darkness was faster than light. We all thought he was crazy—what did he mean? Everyone knows nothing is faster than light . . ."

Over the thump of the respirator and the whirring of life-support machinery, his heart seemed to synchronize with the beep of her pulse monitor, blipping in his ears. He felt blood in his face, throbbing, hot, paresthetic. Far away, a part of him tuned in to that other place again, the place outside: it was raining, and the wind seemed to whisper a sonnet beyond human comprehension. Everything was at once before and after, humongous and subatomic.

Maybe this is what becoming 'aware' is like when you're anesthetized. Burroughs's very definition of 'the naked lunch.'

He spoke once more: "Anyway, he just kind of stared at us—his face creased, with a twinkle in the eye, grinning—and then he said that 'the light only shows what the darkness already knows; think about it, that's all.'"

Again, and not for the last time, he wondered aloud if he were right in doing this. "Now I think I know what he meant. Who am I to judge? I'm not a doctor . . ."

Even at this late hour, he noticed that her hair was styled, her face made up—by some well-meaning nurse, no doubt. Flameless eyes, rimmed in black, stared at him. She seemed as though she were at peace—asleep with her eyelids open.

But I know the truth. Multiple useless therapies had kept her alive, but killed her in the process: not her body, but her essence.

Just because we can keep someone alive, should we? And for what reason? Because we love them or because we love the idea *of them? What's human—humanity—anyway?*

We've reduced dying from an art into a science: Dad's binary passage to a stretched-out analogue continuum of suffering and anguish. . . . How easily we kill the soul, yet don't even know where it resides. . . .

Medical science had beaten a microscopic Mephistopheles, obliterating her illness and prolonging her existence—but at a high cost. It had stolen her vigor; thinned her hair; bleached the color from her eyes. She lay there, not unlike a slab of meat: old, worn out—artificially carrying on processes that should have died long ago.

We have no right meddling in such things. We're just animals that pretend we can control our destiny, our reality. And just where does that reality begin . . . and end? Does it do either? Man isn't God—or is he? Maybe I'm just like the ones that want to keep you alive . . . selfish, deluded . . .

He glanced at his watch. *9:02 P.M.*

So will the real *God please come forward? I need some help here—Allah, Brahma, the Great Spirit, Yahweh, Odin, Zeus, the Kami . . . Maybe they're all right; maybe none of them are—*

"Attention. Visiting hours are now over. The lobby doors will be closing in five minutes. Please come back tomorrow. Thank you and good night."

And which messenger should I believe? Jesus, Moses, Muhammad, Buddha, the White Buffalo, the Dalai Lama, the Oracle of Delphi, Hugin and Munin?

Are they all just inventions of humankind? Just answers to our collective insecurity and a need to believe in something, anything? A fleeting hope that it all isn't just a black hole on the other side?

He tightened his grip on the electrical cord.

Some things aren't good or bad—they just are. *Accidents and illnesses are examples; they strike randomly and kill—or not—randomly. There is no malice, no evil intent, no grand design, although it might appear that way to those who are suffering and their families. Just errant cascades of events without thought, or hatred, or purpose . . .*

For the first time in more than a year, he looked into her eyes—and he knew what to do. "I love you," he said quietly. "Goodbye."

Just as he had envisioned a million or more times, he leaned down and kissed her pale, sunken cheek, surprised at how warm, how soft it was. When he could bear it no longer, he acted; the small room felt as though it were swelling beyond the confines of the present, beyond the constraints of the laws of the cosmos. With a shaking hand, he twisted the electrical plug, then yanked it from its wall socket, stunned at the racket blaring from the life-support machines before they finally lost power and the monitors winked into blackness.

"Code Blue! Room 527," an overhead voice droned in a mechanized imitation of life. As he fled, eyes filled with tears and the cacophony receding, he heard other voices on the system ring through the hallways. As the elevator doors snapped shut, he stifled a scream.

Once outside, running through the dark parking lot, he felt exaltation and revulsion, the terrible sounds still echoing in his head.

Convulsed by grief in his car, the rain pounding like the tears of Eros, he thought he might die soon.

It's done . . . no more pain, no more fear . . .

She and Daddy are together now . . .

It's the end of disappointment, the end of loneliness. She is beyond longing, beyond loss and uncertainty . . .

Isn't she?

He started the vehicle, catching a glimpse of the puffy-eyed stranger he had become in the rearview mirror: "Isn't she?"

He looked one last time to the modern cathedral that housed so much heartbreak and promise, so much life and death, vowing in his psyche never to return.

"There was no other recourse." His voice was rough, cottony.

Everything went almost as he had imagined all these years, except for one thing.

"It was the only reasonable thing to do—the only *right* thing . . ."

Wasn't it?

In the million or so times he had lived it before, never once did he envision the single, shining tear crawling down his mother's suddenly luminous face.

Author's Note

Some of the elements are true; some are an amalgam of the experiences of others. . . . I think this came out well: It was a work-in-progress for over twelve years.

Dream Poem #00

(*Taken word for word from a dream.*)

Unto this broken house of pain,
Where gallows from every ceiling fall,
In multiple cascades of rope;
Where on the floor the dead and dying
remain,
To rot in vermin amidst blood-spattered walls
And the only answer to the screams
Are the echoes of the end of
Hope.

Each room unfurls new horror
To the witness that dares tread
its seething corridors,
Of mirrors and darkness;
There is for those sentenced here no
tomorrow,
Only endless agony, suffering, shame, and
melancholia;
Unending heartache and bleakness.

There is no hope of escape
For those trapped in this house of anguish
Not even death;
to avoid the clutches of this fate,
One would do well to treat others with
Respect and abstain from malice,
Or wind up in this hell
where the chance of walking away is nil,
the chance of dying to escape is less . . .

Where Everything That Is Lost Goes

(Dedicated to April and Marti Brock)

Rod checked his watch.

3:18. Edith never can be anywhere on time . . .

"Late as usual." He looked up toward the entrance of the restaurant, both bemused and irritated at his wife's habit of running perpetually behind. In over fifty years of marriage, he was hard-pressed to recall more than a handful of instances that she had *ever* been on time. He took a sip from his water glass and dismissed the waiter with a wave of his hand.

Good thing she's so beguiling.

Unconsciously rubbing the face of his timepiece, Rod glanced at the door once again before he settled in for the duration. Waiting made him nervous. He was always *exactly* on time. Never early, never late: it was just his way. He closed his eyes, breathing deeply to calm his anxiety just as the doctor had instructed; the delicate perfume of the table's petite floral setting filled his consciousness as he focused his attention on the moment. The now. The present.

Opening his eyes, he felt better; the restaurant was comforting with its clinking glasses, its hushed discussions, its fine aromas from the kitchen. The linen tablecloth was a reassuring off-white, crisp, clean. The booth—their usual spot—was slightly out of the way, but within sight of the door. Inside the recesses of the bistro, sequestered in the mahogany confines of their table and the richly detailed wall decor, the two of them were free to indulge in their weekly rendezvous; meeting there had become, after several years, not only a personal tradition, but a way to keep their connection vibrant, romantic, sexy. It felt edgy—as though they were doing something deliciously taboo. The soft, dim lighting and few numbers of afternoon customers only added to the sensual ambience.

Turning his attention to the clientele, he found himself wondering about the other patrons. At the massive and beautifully stained wooden and brass bar, he saw an older man sitting alone, idly nursing a martini; his suit was lightly disheveled and he was staring wistfully into his glass, rotating it on the shiny countertop. His nose was large and red, his curly hair dark, but thinning.

Was he waiting on someone, too? Rod wondered.

Looking farther back into the establishment, he noticed an attractive young woman in a filmy, low-cut blouse; her chestnut hair cascaded down her shoulders, framing her luminous, fragile features. She seemed introspective, even lonely as she swirled a glass of red wine. He noticed the nervous kicking of her leg under the table, the flatware still enrobed in its cloth serviette.

Perhaps she's another one . . . waiting. It brought to his mind Beckett's existential classic *Waiting for Godot,* with its ceaseless expectation of arrival that never happens.

Sometimes I do *feel like Vladimir or Estragon. Luckily Edith does appear—eventually.* Waiting for Edith . . . *Has a ring to it, though, doesn't it?*

Rod smiled at the absurdity of the thought, scanning into the gloom at the back of the restaurant. In a booth next to the swinging door to the kitchen was another man. He was young, perhaps in his thirties, dressed in a sports coat and casual shirt, reading a book.

My God! *That looks almost exactly like Chuck!*

The resemblance to his old best friend was startling, even disturbing: similar jawline, the same quick mannerisms, a full head of dirty-blond hair—even the piercingly blue, intelligent eyes. The last time he had seen Chuck Berg was nearly forty years ago. They had gotten into a disagreement over something ridiculous that escaped his memory now and had not spoken since. Rod was not sure that Chuck was even alive.

Of course, there was no way that this was his old friend: they were nearly the same age—Chuck was a few months older, actually. So that would make him around seventy-nine; perhaps it was his grandson, or another relative.

Still, the resemblance was uncanny.

"*Bonjour, Monsieur*—are you dining alone today?" the waiter asked, jolting Rod from his thoughts. He blinked, looking up at the friendly server.

"*Bonjour.* You know, my wife . . . she's still on the way, so I haven't even opened the menu yet! Could you . . . could you bring me a glass of Cabernet Sauvignon? That would be wonderful."

"Of course. My pleasure." The attendant departed with a slight bow and disappeared into the interior of the café. Rod looked around the restaurant once more; the businessman at the bar had left, and the young woman was still waiting, toying with her necklace and scowling at the entrance to the place. She had another glass of wine lined up. He was hesitant to peer back at the table where the young man was sitting, and was relieved to see that he was gone when he dared glance back toward the kitchen. He looked at his watch again—it was 3:40.

Strange, that . . . I'll have to tell Edi—

"Rod?" The male voice was low, almost a whisper, but decidedly familiar.

Rod jerked his head toward the sound in disbelief. Standing near his table was the young man from the back of the restaurant. He was smiling.

For a long moment, Rod just stared at him, and he felt a touch of vertigo: the youth even had a mole on his cheek, just like Chuck. It was amazing, the likeness—and unnerving.

"I—I'm sorry! And forgive me for staring, it's just . . . Do we . . . do we know each other?" Rod asked.

The young man laughed.

"Quite all right, quite all right. It's me, Rod—it's Chuck Berg. From back in the day."

Rod felt as though he might faint. How could this be Chuck Berg? This fellow did look like his friend—very much, in fact—but Chuck would be an old man now, just like Rod. It was impossible that this was *the* Chuck Berg. Impossible.

"I'm sorry," Rod began, still shaken. "I think . . . I think you meant to say that you're his grandson."

"No, Rod—it's me. Don't you recognize me? I know—I look just like I did forty years ago. Don't you remember?"

Rod rubbed his eyes like a cartoon character. *This is impossible!*

"Look here, I did know Chuck Berg, and while you *do* bear a striking resemblance, you can't be the same person! I mean, Chuck was older than *I* am—"

"Oh, come on now, Rod! Just by a few months!" the young man exclaimed, a mischievous gleam in his eyes. Rod detected a sudden anger building in his stomach; his face felt hot, his mouth dry.

"Look, I don't know what your game is, or how you found me—or *why*—but I think you need to leave. This instant." Rod's speech was soft; he could barely contain his irritation as he held the man's gaze.

The younger man's smile faded, and after a pause he said: "Take it easy; I can prove who I am, Rod. Would you at least let me do that? I swear I can prove to you what I'm saying. Give me a few moments of your time, and if you aren't convinced I'll leave, okay? I promise. And you'll never see me again."

Rod considered the offer and checked his watch. "Fine. Sit. A couple of minutes—I want you *gone* before my wife arrives."

"And how is Edith?" the man asked, taking a seat opposite.

Rod sneered coldly. "I see you've done your homework. Remember, the clock is ticking."

"So it is, so it is," the man said. "I wasn't following you, by the way. I just happened to be in town and stopped in for a quick bite. I never thought that I'd run into any of the old gang . . ."

"I see." Rod took a sip of water. A bead of sweat trickled down the side of his forehead. "So—tell me something that will make the case. There's only so much one can research these kinds of things."

"True enough. Let me see . . ." The man looked at Rod, squinting his eyes in apparent recollection. "Okay, how about this: I remember the day that I introduced you to Edith. I even recall that the car radio was playing *A Nightingale Sang in Berkeley Square*."

Rod's breath caught in his throat. That was true. There was no way that someone could have guessed that. It was still one of their songs. The man continued:

"And I know that your *real* name isn't Rod: it's Franz—your parents changed it when they fled Europe after the war to hide you from the people that were trying to kill your father back in Prague. I remember Edith had a miscarriage when I was staying at your house that time. The time right after I lost Ruth to the plague . . . and I remember that—"

"Stop!" Rod was shaking: *no one* knew those things. Those were secrets that had haunted him his entire life. The only ones who knew them were Rod, Edith—and Chuck Berg, his best friend for over a decade before their rift. He could feel his pulse throbbing in the center of his head; his hands were cold now, jittery. "Okay, then—Chuck. Okay. I—I believe it's you."

Chuck leaned closer, his expression one of understanding and concern. "Look, Rod, I know this is a shock—"

"A shock! A shock, he says! Here we are, some forty years after we lost touch, and you look *exactly* as you did back then! I mean, look at me: I've lost my hair, my skin is wrinkled . . . Granted, I'm in fine shape for someone my age, but Jesus!" Rod was amused, shaking his head in bewilderment. "So—where's the painting stashed? Sure your real name isn't Dorian?"

Both men laughed.

"Your wine, *Monsieur.* Will your friend be joining you?" the waiter asked, placing the glass on the tabletop.

"No—I'm fine, *merci,*" Chuck said. Rod had drained the glass before Chuck finished the statement.

"Could you bring me another?" Rod asked, tilting his glass. "No, scratch that—bring me the whole damn bottle, please!"

The waiter was surprised. *"Oui, Monsieur."* He ducked away from the table, leaving the two men alone again.

"So tell me, Chuck: what gives? How did this happen? Or *not,* I guess, as the case may be!"

Chuck's jaw tightened visibly as he leaned back in the booth. He looked into the restaurant, then back at his old friend. "You wouldn't believe me . . ."

"No, no! You're not getting away with *that!* Trust me: I'll believe anything at this point!"

Chuck hesitated. "Well . . . After Ruth passed away, I felt directionless. I was hitting the bottle pretty hard; that's the period when we fell out, you'll recall."

"Oh, yes. It was a sad time for everyone."

"I know; I know that you guys were only trying to help, but I . . . I wasn't ready. So, anyway, I left town. I moved back to Washington for a while. I drifted around, doing odd jobs . . . writing . . . even a little local acting. Anyway, long story short, I got a job with the University there in the Physics Department and put my degree to work doing research in quantum mechanics."

Rod listened, but it was surreal hearing his friend after all these years. *The man has hardly aged!* He could sense that he was staring at Chuck, and was relieved when the waiter returned.

"Cabernet, as requested, *Monsieur.* Would you like to sample it first?" the server asked, displaying the ornately decorated bottle to Rod.

"No, that's fine. Chuck, please have a glass with me. For me."

"Okay . . . just a little."

The waiter nodded, placing another glass on the table. He uncorked the bottle and poured two glasses. "*Pour votre santé,* gentlemen. I'll check on you in a bit."

The men nodded as the server departed for another table.

After a taste, Rod leaned forward: "Continue."

Chuck looked askance at Rod. "This is where it gets weird, I'm warning you."

Rod laughed, uneasy, glancing around the establishment as he raised the glass to his lips. "Really, it *can't* get much weirder than it is now, Chuck." He smiled again.

"As I stated before, I was working at the University, getting my head back together, starting over. Things improved . . . but something was missing—Ruth. There was nothing I could do about that. Or so I thought. That's when I did it." He paused and took a drink. "Do you know about the thought experiment called *Schrödinger's Cat,* Rod? About the possibility of superposition in physics?"

Rod shook his head. "Sorry, no. I'm a mere mortal, I'm afraid."

Chuck nodded, continuing: "In a nutshell, it's the concept that reality can be changed by the intervention of what we call the Observer Effect. In the case of the cat, it's the notion that a cat is in a box, and depending on an earlier chain of events, the cat could be either dead or alive, so long as no one opens the box to find out. In other words, without empirical evidence to the contrary, the cat is—theoretically—dead *and* alive at the same time: that's the simple explanation of superposition, in which all states coexist potentially at the same instant in time. Once an observer sees the final state of the cat, then the cat is *either* dead or alive. So the cat can be a potential mixture of states, but an observer cannot, and thus influences the outcome to a certain degree."

Rod stroked his forehead, trying to conceal his bewilderment from his friend as Chuck persisted in his explanation. "I—I think I get it. So, what does this have to do with—*now?* Is this why you . . . don't appear to have gotten older? Did you create a time machine or something?" He laughed at the idea.

Chuck did not respond in kind. "Not quite; but these ideas opened my mind, let's say. I started thinking about how I could . . . change things with regard to Ruth." He took another sip.

Rod sat up straight. The room felt suddenly colder.

"So," Chuck began, "I did more research in my off-hours. The Observer Effect is powerful; and then new ideas about String Theory opened up other avenues about the way we interact and perceive history, about multiple universes. See, it seems that the universe we apparently occupy—I mean, it might not even exist at all, except that our observation of it appears to make it real! Anyway, our universe is most likely *cyclic;* the very fabric of space and time is not just expanding, but is part of a series of expansions and contractions just like the Hindus have posited for thousands of years."

The waiter started over, but Rod waved him away again. "Go on."

Chuck took another drink, then poured more wine into their glasses. "So it turns out that even history is not set in stone; it's possible we can only experience three to four dimensions out of maybe—*nine* or more, which are bent over onto themselves like an engine manifold. Imagine this: that space-time is comprised of membranes, like the skin on top of a soup. We live in one of these *'branes,* which are stacked one atop the other; *we* are stuck here." Chuck made a side-to-side motion on the tabletop. "But within our 'brane—what we call the third dimension—we can comprehend the dimension just above us, the fourth dimension, which we refer to as time—and all the others below us. Only gravity can escape to the other, higher dimensions . . . and maybe consciousness."

Chuck leaned in, his voice low, his gaze intense. "Now picture this, Rod—that every hour, every moment, every *second* likely exists *discretely,* in infinitesimally small increments that appear to us as the swift current of time's forward motion, but which are, in fact, frozen in space-time. That means that *all* time exists *all the time,* across all dimensions. Superposition again; all this is subject to the Observer Effect—and hypothetically able to be altered, the outcome changed. In other words, one might be able to create an alternative universe—just another out of an infinite profusion."

Rod took a long pull from his glass; it was smooth going down, but acidic on his empty stomach. "So, what does that all mean, Chuck? How does that explain your appearance? What's happening here?" he asked, pouring another glass of wine.

Chuck leaned back again. "Well," he said, "none of this is hard science—yet. So I . . . took a leap of faith, Rod. Life is about the choices we make on one level. Because life is short, we make haste; because life is long, we take our time. Seems like a paradox, but there's wisdom there. So I made a choice: I decided to stop aging."

Rod stared at his friend. "I—I don't understand. You just decided to—*stop* aging? That sounds crazy, Chuck. Come on: you can level with me. I'm not going to report you or something, for God's sake!" Rod checked his watch—4:02. *Where the Hell is Edith?*

"That's the first thing. No one would believe me, but it's the truth! I made up my mind, and that was it. I threw out my clocks, my watches, my calendars. I stopped reading the papers, watching the news, listening to the radio. I *believed*, Rod! I don't want to know what year it is, what day it is, what time it is. Nor do I need to know. I mean, I still read books, I still watch old shows on DVD, listen to music. I exist in a perpetual state of the *moment,* and I don't dwell on the past or the future: I blend them into a mélange of the *now*. I focus my energy on my primary goals—first, to stop aging. To freeze the . . . the *acceleration* of self. See, space and time are relative to each of us—we sort of carry them around, at least our comprehension of them, like a tortoise and its shell. My now is different from your now. Reality to some extent begins and ends here." He tapped the side of his head. "I have a rough idea of the passage of time, the years, the seasons and so on. I navigate by the world around me: the sun, the people in it. I don't have a need or desire to cut my life to ribbons with the second-hand of an expensive chronograph, no offense intended. I know you're the exact opposite, and always have been!"

Rod laughed. His friend knew him too well. "But Chuck, when you look in the mirror, you still see the same you that you've always been. When I look, I *like* what I see: my lines, my changes. It's like an external manifestation of my inner growth. Don't you miss the old group, what's left of us at least? How do you fit in with the youth of today? I mean, you aren't their peer—they don't know what *we* know, they don't have the same cultural references, and vice versa. Don't you feel—out of place?"

"Actually, no. Reason being is that most of the old group is either dead or I've lost touch with them, which is likely for the best. I mean, look at how you reacted, and you've always been one of the smart ones! And as for the kids today, well, they challenge me; they keep me young, mentally, emotionally. I still exercise, take my supplements. I'm not *immune* to the effects of the world, Rod. I could still be hurt in a fall, or killed by a disease. The longer I keep at it, the more I worry that something accidental might get to me, but the rest of it is my choice: I have decided that I *will* stay young, at least until I accomplish my goals."

"Yes. You said that there were two. One was to stop aging; what's the second?"

"I want to go back . . . to save Ruth. Then I *do* want us to grow old. But together. Even then, with what I know now, I think that we can forestall aging as a couple." Chuck took a sip of the wine, swishing the garnet liquid in its glass. "You'd be amazed what you can get used to, Rod. I learned a long time ago that anything can be endured if you take it moment by moment. You could do it. Throw that watch away! Don't miss out on any more of your life because of someone else's decision that *your* time is not your own, because it is, Rod. It is. Why be a slave to something that doesn't really exist unless you let it!"

Rod reflexively pulled his arm off the table, alarmed. "Are you serious? I couldn't do that! My watch keeps me on track—"

"Exactly your problem. Think of all the others that feel that way . . . as if they don't have a choice, or when they realize that they do they don't seize it, or it's too late. They lose their identity to a construct. Take the idea from Plutarch about the Ship of Theseus: Plutarch questioned whether a ship could remain the *same* ship if it were *entirely* replaced, plank by plank. Later, Thomas Hobbes presented another idea, wondering what would happen if those original boards were gathered up *after* they were all replaced and used to build a second ship. *Which ship is the real Ship of Theseus?* It's an interesting question: where do you end and I begin? Where do *I* begin and end? I mean, we replace all the cells in our body every ten years or so, so am I the same Chuck Berg as I was when I was five years old? I *believe* I'm the same, and have a sense of self that I'm the same, but am I really? Who can say? I feel that I am, so I am.

"You could ask the same question of the past, present, and future . . . if I replace each old moment with a new one, does that mean that I've reconstructed the past *in the present*—am I building the future *now?* Also, has that stopped bad things from happening, or helped the good things to become reality? Imagine everything that's been lost in the sinkhole of lost opportunity: wisdom, people, civilizations, souls, knowledge, traditions, youth, innocence, memories, even time itself. You can change not just the future; you could create a whole new past, too! Think about it. Think about it."

The room was getting darker. They had been talking quite a long time. Chuck got up from the table.

"Rod, it's been great seeing you. I need to go, but think about what I said. Best to Edith." After a handshake, Chuck walked to the front of the restaurant. At the entrance, he turned and waved goodbye before exiting into the night. Rod returned the gesture, then he was alone. He studied the rustic tableau of the empty wine bottle and their glasses.

Did that really just happen?

"*Monsieur,* will you be needing anything else?" It was the server again. Rod resisted the urge to check his watch.

"Yes, could you bring me one more menu? My wife should be here soon."

The waiter nodded and disappeared into the bistro.

Contemplating his old friend, Rod felt a twinge of sadness. Chuck was very much the same, yet quite different. He seemed both exhilarated, yet strangely unsettled, like a man unable to cope with his past or the way his life was now, though he claimed that it was his own choosing.

Rod could not imagine segregating his past from his present; even though he was afraid at times—of decay, of death—he was also wiser, more confident, more at ease than he'd ever been. He found comfort in his routines, his insights, his life as a whole. He did not want to revisit or relive the past, good or bad; he wanted to have a hopeful future, made better by learning from his missteps and rash decisions, not by trying to control or undo what could never really be undone. It was enough to remember, to reflect, to improve.

How would it be the same? An alternate universe is not this universe, and this is the one I know . . . the one I cherish.

He touched his face, gently feeling the creases along his brow, on his cheek, and he realized that he was crying. *How strange, and at the same time, how wonderful . . .*

"Hi! Oh, honey, I'm so sorry I'm late! The place was crazy, and then— What—what's wrong? Rod, are you okay?" Edith asked. She sat down next to him, an alarmed expression across her face. Rod regarded her silently for a moment, then kissed her deeply, luxuriating in her familiarity, her femininity.

He pulled away, then smiled at her. "Everything is fine. You finally made it! I'm so happy to see you!" He embraced her: she felt soft, warm, magnificent.

"Rod, are you okay? Have you had a stroke or something? Do you need a doctor?" Edith queried. She was getting more upset, he sensed. He pulled away again, then wiped his eyes.

"Everything is fine, I swear. I'm fine. I just want to know something."

Edith settled a little then, looking at him. She was still lovely, supple lips, nice skin. She could easily pass for a fifty-year-old.

"Do you ever want to go back to our past and change it? Are you pleased with us the way we are?" he asked, staring directly into her eyes.

She blinked in confusion. "I—I love how we are, honey. I mean, there are things that I wish had gone differently," she said, and looked at the table. "But, no—I wouldn't change it. I'm happy where we are now. Why are you asking me this?"

Rod looked away. "I was just wondering . . . I saw an old friend today—Chuck Berg."

"Wow! What a blast from the past! He's still around, huh? I thought he'd've passed away by now. He always struck me as old before his time, y'know? So, what did you talk about? How does he look? Dish!" Edith was squirming with delight in the booth; she loved gossip, Rod knew.

"Well, it's interesting that you'd ask that. The short version is this: he's fine. He actually looks good—*really* good, to be honest! Seems like he's retired, and was just passing through. He sent his regards. He's still pretty bad off about Ruth, though."

"Oh, such a shame. Sorry to hear that. I see you two had a little wine, huh?" Edith patted his thigh under the table.

"*Bonsoir, Madame.* Here is the menu. I'll return in a moment for your order. Would you like wine to begin?"

"I'll have the same thing that the gentlemen had, *merci!*"

Edith returned her attention to Rod. "So, is that it? Tell me more! And I'm so sorry I was late, dear. I promise to—"

Rod raised his hand. "One thing I learned talking with Chuck is how much I appreciate what I have," he said. "About what's important to me . . . and it's not this, I've decided." With one swift motion, he pulled the watch off and offered it to Edith. He had never let her touch it before: he even slept in it. She studied his face, her mouth agape.

"After the wine, let's go somewhere *new,*" he said, holding the watch up. "Take it! Get it away from me."

She complied, her astonished gaze going from the watch to her husband.

"After all," he said at last, "we don't want to get *old* . . ."

Author's Note

I think the problem of identity is always of interest. Who are we? Where do we come from? What makes us who we are? Is it our environs? Epigenetics? Our bloodline? I don't have the answers, but I do like the questions, the possibilities that can be explored, and that they could lead to (perhaps) personal insights or revelations. That's my intention, at least.

Godhead: How to Become a God / Goddess in Six (6) Steps

Note: Accompanied by the sounds of a heart monitor and the whirring and grinding of other Twentieth-Century machinery.

1. The mouse is in the maze; at the end she discovers a treat.
2. She is removed and placed at the beginning again, to time her progress in navigating to the reward.
3. This process continues, and each time her speed and accuracy improve.
4. Over time, she approaches Light Speed, and no longer occupies a place in *Time* or Space.
5. Eventually, she gets to the end of the maze before the food exists and starves to death *waiting* an infinity for it to arrive at a place that never existed.
6. [Analyze the Space/Time *Continuum* Rip.] Repeat from 1. as required.

The Underground

"We'll *never* make it on time now," the newest subway passenger, George, lamented as he checked his wristwatch.

Moving quickly past a razor-boned, nearly nude Goth couple osculating next to the entry, he walked by the requisite sleeping derelicts and a few other noisy individuals on his way to the rear of the ramshackle car. As he plopped onto a hard plastic seat, he made a muffled sound of irritation. George glanced around the foul, narrow compartment, his sallow expression approximating a grumpy hatchet fish. Finally settling in for the ride, his tall, thin frame protruded from the uncomfortable bench like a wire coat hanger.

After a lengthy pause there was a loud buzzing, followed by the sudden release of vapor, as though a pressure cooker was about to explode. The grimy doors closed with a shriek in the ripe air of the car; outside, he noticed a few latecomers milling on the platform as the train departed.

Impulsively looking at his watch once more, he purposely lit a cigarette in defiance of the tattered, pornographically defaced No Smoking sign.

These meetings at the Home Office are such a pain in the ass . . .

Studying the other riders as he took a long drag from his next-to-last smoke, he saw no one he recognized: the amorous Alternative couple; the gaggle of mephitic, fitfully napping winos; some old crone with a black veil staring out of the window, her gnarled hands stroking a large white rat; a dazed looking, finely dressed older man streaming blood from his temple.

"Quite the motley crew." His leg hopped nervously as he huffed a small cloud from the corner of his mouth. The old train lurched suddenly, causing the tunnel lamps to flicker. George stared from a barely open porthole near his head as the locomotive gathered speed, starting to daydream as graffiti adorned pillars and torn movie posters flashed by in mesmerizing smears of color.

"About time we were underway. Just my luck to catch an overdue train." Another startling jolt caused him to break away from his thoughts. Glancing around in annoyance, he noticed the reflection of a young man in ragged military regalia and dark sunglasses watching him from across the aisle.

He turned to face the man, voice edged as he spoke over the noise of the subway: "How goes it? The name's George."

The youth smiled cryptically. "Mm. They used to tease me about my coat, you know."

George was unfazed by the non sequitur. "Oh, really? Was I wondering about that?" He crushed out his cigarette, bemusedly peering through the bluish haze at the strange young man: *Takes all kinds, I s'pose.* "Who would do such a thing?"

"Pipe down!" one of the drunks shouted, looking at them with bloodshot eyes. "Got a long night comin' up!" His head dropped back onto the seat with a muted *clunk.*

"The other children," the young man said, not missing a beat, dreamily shaking his head. "I guess," he added as an afterthought, "it was because I was so different from all the other kids. Since I drank blood, I mean." He pulled his shades down, regarding George. "Oh, sorry, how rude of me. Timothy—my name's Timothy." The pointed redness of his tongue flicked from his mouth and was gone.

The next platform bell whizzed by; the whole car rocked as the subway barreled through the underground, metal wheels screeching. George checked his watch again. The stranger—Timothy—was still scrutinizing him over his sunglasses, a faint smile frosting his ruby lips.

After a couple few moments of noisy boredom, George finally asked: "So . . . how exactly did you *become*—what do you call it? 'Vampire'? 'Nosferatu'? What's the correct terminology these days?"

Timothy snorted, caught off guard. "Vampire is good, I guess!" There was a pause as he sorted through what to say next, or perhaps how to say it best. At last: "What I'm about to tell you is a mostly true story . . ."

The day was an interesting one, especially for twelve-year-old Timothy Lipscomb.

Timothy, apparently, was a vampire; though a well-known proclamation on his part, there were other, more concrete reasons that his friends regarded him with both enthrallment and foreboding.

Timothy did the strangest things—one day going to school with his hair standing on end, the next day shaved bald; sometimes painting his face half red and the other half black, much to the consternation of his teachers. Once, he brought a 'head' to school—it looked real, *very* real—but it was actually some sculpted piece of his own creation; its rotted 'flesh' constructed of colored tissues, string, and corn flakes held together with mortician's wax.

This monstrosity, and others like it, occupied his fancy far more than boring homework assignments or studying for tests. Whenever his parents confiscated such items, it only encouraged him to redouble their grotesque appearance upon reissue.

Other things stood out: He was the possessor of a peculiar "fashion sense"—sometimes wearing his shirts backwards, or one buttoned to another; there were instances of sundry bizarre hats, and even helmets being donned; one particularly strange bit of attire was an old blue Civil War–era military overcoat that extended beyond his knees.

Timothy was also an interesting physical specimen, all spooky eyes, veiny, pale skin, and spindly fingers. He took perverse pride in the fact that he was born with a complete set of teeth, so long that the very tips were visible even with his mouth closed. He would also gladly demonstrate, to the horrified squeals of all, that he had a *hollow* tongue—not unlike the proboscis of a butterfly.

People fainted . . . and not just females.

In spite of all, though, these attributes were not the reason that today was so different from the myriad other fine days that preceded it. Indeed, on this particularly crisp fall day, Timothy had at last decided to boldly assert what he knew to be the truth about his nature. Today, he would finally satiate his thirst for human blood. It was a momentous decision, and not the least bit casual. Unintentional, perhaps, but not without forethought; all he needed was a victim.

And here fate was to lend a hand.

Lilith Burgess, everyone agreed, was a demented old bat and should have stopped teaching the day she started, more than thirty-six years previous. Unfortunately, she was the only schoolteacher in rural

Kellen, North Carolina, and she would have to do.

Ms. Burgess was a superstitious woman: she did not like Timothy and made no bones about it. Frequently she punished him for looking at her crooked, reasoning that such a peculiar and strange-looking individual should be disciplined with more . . . *malice* than his comrades. Such was the case on this auspicious day.

"Timothy," Ms. Burgess had snapped, "dust these and be quick about it."

It came as no surprise to anyone, of course, that Timothy had to stay after school and dust the chalkboard erasers. She thrust the objects into his cold hands, scraping his overly long fingernails. The youngster made a low, hissing sound.

"See here, boy! That's enough of that!" She hobbled from the darkening room.

Timothy sneered after her in disgust. "Stupid old biddy . . ." After a few minutes of choking on chalk dust, his mind seized upon a novel idea, one that he was astounded had never occurred to him before.

Ms. Burgess! I'll get rid of her and satisfy my need for blood at the same time. He chortled to himself at the simplicity of his scheme, tossing the erasers and climbing a rickety bookcase. Secreting himself precariously on the topmost shelf, he waited, overjoyed at the prospect of terrorizing the old woman. . . . Just as he was getting bored, Ms. Burgess made a reappearance.

The room was very empty indeed when she tottered in.

"Timothy?"

Silence. The gathering nightfall spooked her; a growl of thunder vibrated the building. She pulled her shawl around her elbows as she scanned the dark room. "Are you here, boy? If you're tryin' to scare me, I'll tell your parents!"

The only response was a gust of wind as the storm drew closer. The old woman crept forward, leaning on her cane, eyes wide.

"I'm telling you, they will agree with me, young ruffian, when I say they need to *tan your hide!*"

Suddenly, directly above, there was a cracking sound, like a glacier thawing; some—*thing*—dropped from the ceiling like an obscene and uncoordinated spider, screaming as it fell.

Ms. Burgess shrieked, grabbing her breast as the creature landed on some desks.

"Lord! Timothy! Are you injured?" she warbled in a cracked, breathless voice.

The boy sprang up, lunging toward her as he held his bruised ribs beneath ripped coveralls.

"I'm a vampire!" he wheezed, chasing the old lady around in circles as she swatted at him with her cane.

"Lord, help me!" Ms. Burgess shrieked, whacking him on the head.

"Hey, that hurts! Stop it! I just need to drink *your blood."*

"Lord, help me away from this demon child!"

The old woman screamed as blackness finally engulfed the room. . . .

". . . I finally cornered her," Timothy continued. He paused dramatically.

"And?" George prodded, genuinely amused.

"And," the monster said, a grin starting on his pale features. "She kicked me in the crotch right when I was going to bite her." The banging of the subway absorbed their chuckles.

"That's when I *knew* I was a vampire for sure—"

One of the drunks made a muted screaming sound in his sleep. Another vagabond sat up quickly, his dirty face slick with sweat. He stared at them a moment, then blurted out: "Kid, who's not a vampire? A witch? An accountant? Whatever? Anyways, my advice: *SHUT! UP!"*

"Why don't you just mind your business, huh? You don't *own* this damned car," George responded, glaring at the rude man.

"Freak," the vagrant muttered as he turned over, drawing his filth-encrusted jacket over his head.

The other passengers found this noisy exchange mildly interesting; The old crone muttered a curse and gestured; the young couple looked up for a moment, then resumed their carnal activities; the finely dressed man with the bloody head wound slumped forward, as though listening.

Timothy studied his very long nails, anxiously glancing at George from beneath waxy eyebrows. Loud snoring now accompanied the rock of the train. After a few more strained moments he said, almost too loudly: "I know how it sounds, and I can understand why you wouldn't believe me. No one ever does." The passenger car shifted, its metal wheels clicking in a hypnotic rhythm.

"Oh, no," George said, shaking his head and smiling. "I believe you all right. You see, *I'm* different, too. Not a vampire, mind you—*ghoul* would be more appropriate, I suppose, since I eat flesh. Dead, alive—all goes to the same place." He smacked his belly, which grumbled in retort.

Timothy gasped, pulling his sunglasses from his face, his pale features reddening. "I—I'm sorry; here I've been prattling on like some know-it-all! I didn't realize. . . . Anyway, I guess we've all got something we have to deal with!"

George smiled, his leg hopping in time to the train's commotion. "That's quite all right—you can't really tell with me, everyone says so. . . . Boy, are *they* surprised come dinnertime!"

"No . . . no, you can't tell." Timothy eyed George with unspoken skepticism before putting his glasses back on. "Well, why don't you explain to me how you came to be one. Are you self-proclaimed like me, or . . . How does that happen, exactly?"

"Hmmm . . ." George checked his watch. Their train was not due to arrive at the Dis Terminal for another hour yet. Lighting his last cigarette, he sucked the smoke in deeply, eyes furtive, contemplative.

"What the hell? I guess I was about ten years old when I first began to feel—*different,* y'know?"

Timothy the vampire settled back in his seat, vaguely smiling, eyelids heavy behind his sunglasses. He seemed drowsy, as though he enjoyed the sound of the angular ghoul's clipped voice. As the passenger car swayed gently from side to side, they both relaxed as George detailed his own colorful childhood, his unusual job—shop steward for Gravediggers Union Local 1313—and his personal coming to terms with his odd—*condition.*

"Life is a strange thing, sometimes," George mused, checking his watch again. "You can never really anticipate how your actions will truly impact others . . . or even yourself, for that matter."

"Yes," Timothy agreed. "I am what I am. I was born this way, and it took me years to be able to really be comfortable with that truth . . . to fully accept it." The vampire smiled wistfully as the other man ground out his cigarette.

George the ghoul smirked, understanding the sentiment. "Yes. And not worry about whether *other people* can accept who—or *what*—you are. Like you, I learned a long time back that everyone has to be big enough to confront their own fears, deal with the consequences of their actions . . . and to know and understand their limitations and innate abilities." He checked his watch once more: *Not much longer until we reach the terminal.*

The lights in the compartment flashed, then went out.

The train compartment, rocking and silent, was getting hotter by the moment.

Author's Note

An older story that I find rather droll: I rewrote it after finding the bits of autobiography too interesting to ignore. . . . I guess everyone is horrified by his or her adolescence—right?

Frac/tion

I dreamt I walked in the
Marble halls of the sheeted
Dead;
My echoes followed quietly,
As—fearfully—I tread.

On those cold and barren slabs
Did the cadavers rest;
Some were poor and some were
Rich and several were recently deceased—
The ones that weren't,
However,
Inspired in me
the most terrible
Dread.

Death, I thought,
Is the last great frontier:
To conquer the worm
and destroy the nemesis
would do Man disservice—
For only in his reduction are we all truly equal—
He is the healer—
He is the destroyer—
and His treatment is the great
Denominator.

Van Helsing: His True Story

A few terrible cracks of the mallet finding its mark . . .

. . . cool gouts of blood on the face and hands . . .

. . . a final anguished outrush of breath . . .

At last, it is over . . .

"Rest now, *nosferatu.* Your unease is ended."

Hands folded, the old man kneeled on the cold hard stone of the dank mausoleum floor, staring at his gruesome handiwork. He was oblivious as the door gave way behind him, splintering asunder like the unfortunate creature's breastbone under the savage impacts of his sledge. Unexpectedly he felt a ripple of sadness looking into the pathetic beast's glazed, dead eyes . . . they were paradoxically alive with the yellow-orange glimmer of the belated search party's torches, and seemed to stare back at him from bottomless, shadowed sockets gouged into the pale mask of its blood-streaked visage—pleading, accusing.

"My Lord, Professor Van Helsing! *What have you* done *to her?*" Jonathan Harker screamed, throwing his light to the ground and rushing over to the crumpled form of his beloved Mina; he collapsed beside them, cradling her bloody, gamine figure in a sad caricature of the *pietà.* Considering her slack expression, the young man began to sob, the sharp echoes of his grief reverberating within the musty confines of the burial chamber. The other men at the entrance removed their hats, respectfully lowering their gazes to the floor of the crypt. Abraham Van Helsing stood, glaring at the assemblage blocking his exit from Mina's final resting place.

"Ja," Van Helsing began, "I did what had to be done, my boy. She had fornicated with the Evil One; she had become the concubine of Dracula. It is no life that she would want, *mein Gott.* Even without the fear of dying, she would be damned forever to search the Earth for

blood. An eternity of yearning . . . of craving . . . of never knowing peace, Jonathan."

Harker looked at Van Helsing, his blighted rose . . . his life . . . a bloody ragdoll in his arms. In the flickering torchlight, it was obvious that the bloom of death was transforming her face: the lush mouth had drawn into a rictus, the pallid skin was already faintly veined with decay.

"Who are you *to decide, Van Helsing?"* Harker shouted. "'Tis not for men such as you or I to mete out who lives, who dies! You and your—*obsession* with Count Dracula! You have just murdered an innocent! This is madness, Van Helsing!" The youth's stare, full of anguish and derision, seared into the old man.

The professor said nothing, just unbent his frame; his expression was a mixture of annoyance and sympathy. After a moment, he walked over to a shelf inside the vault where he had placed a candle and his attaché, returning the mallet to its rightful place within; his gait was stiff, his back rigid. He brushed the dirt of the tomb floor from his pants, then used a handkerchief to clean her blood from his face and hands. His back still turned to the coterie of men, he straightened his collar, running a weathered hand through his red locks.

"My dear boy, you are a naïf, no?" Van Helsing finally whispered. The elderly man paused, gently closing his case. The oily smell and sizzle of the burning torches and Harker's muted weeping filled the expansive silence. "Believe me, Jonathan, it was with a heavy heart that I put the poor thing from her misery; she was no longer the beautiful Mina that we once knew and adored."

"You act as though you know everything! How *dare* you condescend to me, you—*murderer!"* The atmosphere in the compartment was charged as Harker clasped his dead wife to his chest. A few of the men shuffled their feet, but said nothing.

"No," Van Helsing replied, turning to face the boy. His aged features were haggard; his intense blue eyes seemed faded, weary. "I have dedicated my life to eradicating these—undead. *Ja,* these diseased vermin . . . these filthy *nosferatu.* . . . I will not rest until they are all dead; I know of more of these shapeshifters, these liars, these blasphemers. You understand that they have no true fear of the Holy Sacraments or of the sunlight, no? More lies, more myths, *ja?"* Van Helsing walked over to Jonathan and stooped down, gently wiping tears from the grief-stricken young man's cheek with a cold, cold hand.

"But . . ." Jonathan began, "but how can you be *sure,* Professor? Dracula is dead. You said that his annihilation would spare my poor Mina. And yet . . . now . . . she is *gone!* And you think she was one of the *undead?* Still? After all that we went through to save her? How can you be sure, Van Helsing? How?"

The professor smiled, his face tight, creased by time and the burdens of knowledge he had accumulated. He looked up to the men still waiting in the threshold of the crypt, their faces deeply shadowed by the soft glow of the torches, then back to Jonathan.

"I have learned much in my research, *ja?* I know more about these horrible creatures than anyone else in the world; indeed, I know too much. With Mina—I made a *mistake,* and I am terribly sorry, son. When I discovered my error, I knew I must return, *ja?* Even all these years later, she was on the way to becoming one of them again; I got to her just in time." Van Helsing looked away, his eyes gleaming with sorrow. "I brought her here to spare you the horror of seeing what *must* be done to them all. To exterminate them, *ja?* Once a *nosferatu,* they are one always, I have learned; there can be no going back, though it may take years for the . . . *condition* to reappear."

Jonathan nodded his comprehension and relaxed his embrace on his former wife. She was now little more than a skeletonized figure, the stake jutting awkwardly from her ribcage, blood already dry and brown on her frock and her papery skin; it was as though she had been dead for years.

Van Helsing continued: "Jonathan, long ago something happened . . . and it haunts me; I have never told anyone before, but it is why I *must* destroy them all. The cravings . . . the urges . . ." The old man paused again. "I am driven to rid the world of their kind, to end their suffering and the agony they inflict. I am so determined my dear boy because, God help me, I am *like* them.

"Dear Jonathan, I *am* a vampire . . ."

Author's Note

I wrote this a long time ago, then rewrote it from memory (a lot of my personal effects were destroyed by Hurricane Hugo in 1989, including many years of writing, artwork, and correspondence). I always wondered how Van Helsing (from Dracula) would know all this stuff about vampires, so this is why I think he did!

Story of a Blade

Over here—
Frightened eyes
Over there—
Silenced cries.

No matter where
One looks
History speaks:
But not in books.

Be it soldier,
Surgeon,
Perhaps hunter,
Even lover:

The quiet
Never betrays
the slowing heart's
dull ache;

Harken to the silence
Between the notes—
This is where the thrum
Of the blade resides;

All that remains:
Questions and
fear.

Life flows, ebbs, then dies.

Yet, at the close of day—
If one strains to hear—
Through the turmoil and
disarray—
One voice rings clear:
The whisper of
Confession,
"I was there . . ."

No matter where
One looks
History speaks:
But not in books.

Let the record of the blade stand:
Its steel tells the tale
Of loneliness and
Farewell.

P.O.V.

[Three Views of an Incident]

—Exhibit I—

DETROIT POLICE DEPARTMENT
HOMICIDE DIVISION

VIDEOTAPED CONFESSION TRANSCRIPTION: ANDREW LOBIONDO

[00:00:00 (START OF TAPE)]

DUNCAN: This is Sergeant Duncan. I'm with D.P.D. Homicide. The date is December 4th, 2003. [Looks at clock.] It's 1:06 in the morning. I'm located in an interview room at 301 Tryon, within the Homicide Division. With me in the room is Andrew LoBiondo, a white male, D.O.B. 5-2-63. Andrew, can you tell me your full and complete name?

LOBIONDO: Andrew Francis LoBiondo.

DUNCAN: And how old are you?

LOBIONDO: Forty.

DUNCAN: And what's your home address?

LOBIONDO: 618 Halver, Detroit, Michigan 48217.

DUNCAN: OK, and you and I have been talking for a while, right?

LOBIONDO: Yes.

DUNCAN: You understood your rights? [Looks at sheet of paper.]

[00:00:20]

LOBIONDO: Yes.

DUNCAN: OK, I'm going to read them to you again for the purposes of this tape recording, OK?

LOBIONDO: OK.

DUNCAN: [Reading.] You have the right to remain silent and not make any statement at all, and any statement you make may be used against you and probably will be used against you at your trial. Do you understand that? [Looks at LoBiondo.]

LOBIONDO: Yes.

DUNCAN: Any statement you make may be used as evidence against you in court. Do you understand that?

LOBIONDO: Yes. [Sighs.]

DUNCAN: You have the right to have a lawyer present to advise you prior to and during any questioning. Do you understand that?

LOBIONDO: Yes.

DUNCAN: If you are unable to employ a lawyer you have the right to have a lawyer appointed to advise you prior to and during any questioning. Do you understand that?

LOBIONDO: Yes.

DUNCAN: And you have the right to terminate this interview at any time. Do you understand that?

LOBIONDO: Yes.

DUNCAN: Are you willing to waive those rights that I've just read to you and continue to talk to me about this?

LOBIONDO: Yes. [Clears throat.]

DUNCAN: OK, an incident happened at your house yesterday morning, right?

LOBIONDO: Yes.

DUNCAN: And that's at 618 Halver?

LOBIONDO: Yes.

DUNCAN: And what part of town is that in?

LOBIONDO: Locust Heights.

DUNCAN: OK, and the incident we're about to discuss, um, resulted in the death of your girlfriend, correct?

LOBIONDO: Yes.

[00:01:18]

DUNCAN: OK.

[Pause: Duncan flips through notes on desk.]

DUNCAN: What's your girlfriend's name?

LOBIONDO: Philomena. Philomena O'Connor.

DUNCAN: And how long had you two been together?

LOBIONDO: Three years.

DUNCAN: And, I think you described to me, you and Philomena had a pretty good relationship? [Looks at paper.]

LOBIONDO: Yes.

DUNCAN: Philomena was a good girlfriend?

LOBIONDO: Yes, she was a good girlfriend. [Scratches his face.]

DUNCAN: OK, and where did she work?

LOBIONDO: The post office.

DUNCAN: And she's been there a while?

LOBIONDO: Right. A few years.

DUNCAN: And you work third shift?

LOBIONDO: Yes, I'm on graveyard. She went to school nights.

DUNCAN: You're a bartender? At the Underground Club?

LOBIONDO: Yes.

[00:02:11]

DUNCAN: OK, and before taping we went into a little bit about your education.

LOBIONDO: Yes.

DUNCAN: Um, you have a college degree?

LOBIONDO: Yes.

DUNCAN: And where is that from?

LOBIONDO: University of Washington. Fine Arts.

DUNCAN: And what year did you graduate?

LOBIONDO: 1986.

DUNCAN: And you went to high school here, right?

LOBIONDO: Yes.

DUNCAN: Where?

LOBIONDO: Randolph High. [Coughs.]

DUNCAN: And what year did you graduate?

LOBIONDO: 1981.

DUNCAN: And at one time you were employed as a graphic designer?

LOBIONDO: Yes.

DUNCAN: OK. About what year did you stop working in this field?

LOBIONDO: 1994.

DUNCAN: OK, and why did you stop doing this line of work?

LOBIONDO: I ... I had a nervous breakdown. [Clears throat.]

DUNCAN: OK, did you seek any treatment at the time?

[00:03:29]

LOBIONDO: [Appears agitated.] Yes.

DUNCAN: OK, and if you could, just go ahead and explain what preceded that breakd--

[00:03:35 (TAPE DROPS OUT)]

[00:15:14 (TAPE RESUMES)]

LOBIONDO: I loved her! [Sobs.] She was wonderful ... [Grabs face and doubles over in seat.]

DUNCAN: OK, I understand. [Looks at notes.] And we also talked earlier, um, you've been treated for depression.

LOBIONDO: Yes. [Calming down.]

DUNCAN: And who's your current doctor?

LOBIONDO: Dr. Beringer. [Wipes face. Drinks water.]

DUNCAN: And the last time you saw him?

LOBIONDO: Two or three days ago.

DUNCAN: OK, um, what caused the fight?

LOBIONDO: [Drinks water. Calming down further.] She was upset that I was coming in late from work. She hated my job.

DUNCAN: There was an argument?

LOBIONDO: Yes.

DUNCAN: OK, and what happened?

LOBIONDO: I just—just lost it. I—I grabbed her, I was drunk, and I just throttled her ... [Wipes face.]

DUNCAN: And by the time you were done choking her, she was—not alive?

LOBIONDO: Yes, I mean, that's right.

DUNCAN: OK. Then what?

LOBIONDO: [Pauses. Looks at ceiling.] I was so ... *enraged*. [Pauses again and leans toward interviewer.] I just grabbed the knife and I kept stabbing, over and over.

DUNCAN: OK.

LOBIONDO: Yes. I could not stop. I could not stop. [Sobs.]

[00:20:30]

DUNCAN: What then? [Looks at sheet on desk.]

LOBIONDO: I sat there. I felt sober all of a sudden. My head was killing me ... my arm hurt.

DUNCAN: OK.

LOBIONDO: Then I called the police. I confessed.

DUNCAN: Um, after that you tried to kill yourself?

LOBIONDO: Yes. [Regards bandaged wrist.] Yes I did.

[Pause: Sergeant Duncan looks at subject.]

DUNCAN: Anything else, partner? Look, I'm here to help. Anything you're leaving out? Something you might have forgotten? That bandage on your forehead mean anything? There a story there?

LOBIONDO: [Touches bandage on head. Pauses.] No. [Sobs.] That's all.

DUNCAN: [Looks at clock.] OK. It's now 1:28 in the morning, and I'm going to stop the tape. [Reaches toward recorder.]

[00:22:41 (END OF TAPE)]

——EXHIBIT II——

OFFICE OF THE MEDICAL EXAMINER,
METROPOLITAN GOVERNMENT OF DETROIT, MI

70113 Trade St.
Detroit, MI 48212

AUTOPSY REPORT

CASE #: B3X715JS0 **Final:** (X)

DECEDENT: O'CONNOR, PHILOMENA X.

AGE: 33 YEARS
RACE: WHITE
SEX: FEMALE

HEIGHT: 63 INCHES
WEIGHT: 112 LBS
IDENTIFIED BY: Circumstances

DATE AND TIME OF AUTOPSY: December 8, 2003 at 8:00 a.m.

PERFORMED BY: DR. RASMUSSEN

MANNER OF DEATH: HOMICIDE.

CAUSE OF DEATH: STRANGULATION/MECHANICAL ASPHYXIATION AND EXSANGUINATION DUE TO MULTIPLE STAB AND INCISED WOUNDS (HEAD, NECK, TRUNK, UPPER EXTREMITIES).

FINDINGS:

1. Scleral petechial hemorrhages in eyes consistent with manual strangulation. Bruising on throat/neck. Hyoid bone fractured.
2. Generalized pallor and evidence of exsanguination.
3. Multiple stab and incised wounds of head, neck, trunk and upper extremities with one (1) stab wound penetrating left skull into brain; three (3) stab wounds penetrating right back into chest cavity and right lung; another stab wound at lateral right chest penetrating into right lung; and multiple wounds of upper extremities consistent with defensive injuries.
4. Left lower lateral chest-wall abrasions and contusions with overlying rib fractures of left ribs #6, #7 and #8.
5. Subarachnoid hemorrhage of right cerebrum underlying one of the large, undermined right scalp incised wounds.
6. A few other minor blunt-force injuries of head and trunk.

LABORATORY RESULTS:

TOXICOLOGY:

1. Blood:
    a. Ethanol: 0.16 gm%.
    b. Drugs: None detected.

2. Urine:
    N/A.

3. Ocular fluid:
    Ethanol: 0.16 gm%.

INTRODUCTION

AUTHORIZATION: The medico-legal examination of the body of Philomena X. O'Connor was performed by Derek Rasmussen, M.D., Chief Medical Examiner, Metropolitan Government of Detroit, at the Medical Examiner's Facility, 70113 Trade St., on December 8, 2003 at 8:00 a.m., pursuant to the Michigan "Post Mortem Examination Act" for the determination of cause and manner of death.

GENERAL APPEARANCE: The body is that of a well-developed, well-nourished, adult white woman who appears the stated age of 33 years. Body height is 63 inches, and body weight is 112 lb. At autopsy, rigor mortis is generalized-to-late; livor mortis is posterior and slightly blanching; the body is cool to touch. Artifacts of decomposition are absent, and evidence of medical and postmortem care is absent. There is obvious evidence of multiple sharp-force injury, as well as strangulation by hand.

IDENTIFICATION: The identity of decedent was established by circumstances of death and discovery of the body.

ROUTINE EXTERNAL EXAMINATION

CLOTHING AND VALUABLES: The body is admitted to the morgue dressed and within a sheet and shroud, and then within a body bag, with the hands bagged.

Clothing is very bloody and has injuries matching those at the trunk (*see below*). In addition, prior to removal of clothing, the body was examined concurrently by the pathologist and by a crime scene technician from the Detroit Police Department, and trace evidence was collected from the body and clothing. *See "TRACE EVIDENCE" section at end of report.* The clothing consists of a blue-and-white blouse, a pair of blue jeans, a white bra, a brown belt, a pair of light-blue panties, a pair of white socks and a pair of black boots. Valuables on or with the body include a key ring with five (5) keys, a purse containing miscellaneous toiletries and $16.43 in cash. The valuables are released to the mother of the decedent while the clothing is retained for the law enforcement agency. *Please also see "ARTIFACTS" and "INJURIES" sections below.*

HEAD AND NECK: The head is normally shaped. Scalp hair is long, brown, and straight. The head, face, neck, and upper shoulders show some suffusion. The irides are green; the pupils are equal and round; the sclerae are white; the conjunctivae display pronounced petechiae and the periorbital areas have slight ecchymosis. A slight amount of bloody mucus is present in the nasal and oral cavities. The teeth are natural, and oral hygiene is good. Intraoral petechiae are present. The neck has no deformities and has the usual range of motion without crepitus.

TRUNK: The chest is not increased in the antero-posterior dimension but has heavy, dried blood over the xiphoid and lower sternal regions. The breasts are well-developed, natural, and have no palpable masses or nipple discharge. The abdomen is soft with no panniculus adiposus, and there is no venous discoloration of the external wall. The back and buttocks have no natural abnormalities. The anus is moderately dilated with some reddish purple circumferential ecchymosis, but there are no lacerations and no visible scars. The external genitalia are appropriate for age and have no injuries.

EXTREMITIES: The extremities are symmetrical and without natural deformities. The legs have no significant peripheral edema and no skin atrophy. The fingernails are all of medium length and polished a dark red. Three on the left hand are broken, consistent with defensive injuries.

SCARS, TATTOOS, NEVI, INCIDENTAL FINDINGS: The low midclavicular left chest has one (1) old scar, possibly skin grafting. An old scar is also at the left knee, apparently surgical. The back of the right wrist has a tattoo of a red heart. The ears are pierced.

ARTIFACTS OF MEDICAL OR POSTMORTEM CARE

There are no acute or recent medical artifacts. The body has no embalming or other mortician's artifacts.

ARTIFACTS OF THE POSTMORTEM INTERVAL

See "GENERAL APPEARANCE" above for signs of death. Decomposition is minimal but progressing internally with some autolysis. There is no significant putrefaction.

INJURIES

Multiple incised and stab wounds are present on the head, neck, chest, back, and upper extremities.

These are entirely too numerous to count and detail. However, in general, there are 30 or more on the head, 15 or more on the chest and back, and about 40 defensive incised wounds at the right and left hands and forearms. Most of the sharp-force injuries present are incised wounds, and most of the stab wounds are actually non-penetrating of the body cavities, except as detailed below, and except for the deeper ones at the upper extremities. There are also some blunt-force injuries and some overlying rib fractures as below.

Many of the head wounds are very irregular and have slightly scalloped or curving borders, as discussed below. The forehead, the right face beside the nose, the right lips, the left side of the head and ear, and the right side of the head have multiple incised wounds.

At the skull, this makes a similar triangular-shaped wound, more horizontal over the left sphenoid bone, with a base thickness of 0.1–0.2 cm and length of 1.6 cm. The anteriormost 1.0 cm of this stab is the actual penetration of the skull. It passes 3.5 cm total (approximately) through the skin and brain, passing into the brain about 2.0 cm at the inferolateral left frontal lobe. It creates a 1-cm-wide × 2-cm-deep permanent stab cavity at that area. It just enters the tip of the left lateral ventricle and is accompanied by a slight intraventricular hemorrhage and also by a slight white-matter contusion surrounding the injury.

At the right side of the head are multiple stab wounds varying from 1.5 to 5.5 cm long, and including a curving stab, 6.5 cm long, with undermining in the posterior direction. The ear peels away along with the tissue flap from the skull.

At the top of the head, located mostly on the right front side are another group of incised wounds, the most prominent having slightly scalloped edges, and being 2.2 cm long. At the upper lateral left side of the head are two (2) wounds, 0.9 cm between each other and parallel, each curving slightly and having slightly scalloped edges with the scalloping especially at the left, and with overlying, perpendicular, parallel, pale, reddish purple abrasion and contusion lines over a total area of 2 × 3 cm.

Beginning at the middle of the upper right sternocleidomastoid muscle, the right postero-lateral and posterior neck have deep, muscular, incised wounds actually representing about two or three total cuts.

The head also has some blunt-force injuries, although these may be ragged incised wounds from a dull object. The back of the head has four (4) parallel, diagonal (upper left to lower right) lacerations with visible tissue bridging. The uppermost two (2) are the most superficial and may actually be incisions, these being 1.5 cm long and 4.0 cm long, respectively. The lowermost two are mostly on the left side and are 2.7 and 1.7 cm long, respectively, and they have prominent abrasion and contusion around the edges with some tissue bridging. The back of the right ear also has some reddish-purple and reddish-black abrasion and contusion; the left scalp above the ear has a linear, vertical abrasion; and the vertex of the head has a 2.3- × 0.6-cm irregular abrasion. There is a slicing incision to the forehead that extends through the left eyebrow and bifurcates the left eyeball in a horizontal slash that gouges the bridge of the nose. The tip of the nose is missing, revealing cartilage to the septum.

Inside the head, the right parieto-temporal region of the cerebrum has a focal area of increased subarachnoid hemorrhage; but, other than the stab wound at the left frontal lobe, the brain has no contusion, lacerations, subdural hematoma, or other injuries. This does underlie the larger, curving, 6.5-cm-long incised wound discussed earlier. The spinal cord is not examined.

The lateral left chest at the lower half has an irregular area of mottled abrasions and contusions without pattern, the largest two (2) areas being 3.0 × 0.3 cm and 1 × 1 cm. These overlie the fractures of the ribs with accompanying slight intercostal-space contusion, mainly at the left lateral sixth rib, the left postero-lateral seventh rib, and the left postero-lateral eighth rib. The seventh rib has a parietal pleural perforation and the greatest amount of contusional hemorrhage. These are blunt-force injuries.

At the back, there are multiple shallow stabs and jab-type wounds along with some tiny superficial abrasions or incisions, all less than or equal to 0.3 cm.

As mentioned earlier, the upper extremities have multiple sharp-force injuries. At the back of the right triceps area, exposing the bone, is a bloodless, 19.5-cm-long gaping, deep, incised wound. The lateral proximal right shoulder and proximal arm have three (3) incisions, the longest more distal and is 1.6 cm long, with an irregular distal border suggestive of an acute angle and with a proximal border squared off and 0.2–0.3 cm wide.

The left distal forearm has a large, gaping incised wound of 3 × 5 cm surface area, passing through the tendons. Just proximal to this is a 6- × 4-cm area of dried blood with abrasions and superficial incisions. Just proximal to that and more medial are two (2) parallel, linear, thin abrasions.

The backs of the hands have multiple avulsed and oblique incisions and lacerations, mostly incisions, ranging from 1.5–3.2 cm long. In addition, the back of the right hand has a larger, gaping wound, 5.5 × 3.0 cm long, and the right wounds and the left dorsal wrist wounds have superimposed purple contusions. The hands do have clumps of straight, long, possibly blond hairs adherent especially at the left palm. These are collected.

Overall, most of the incised wounds of the trunk suggest a single-edged, thin blade, although a double-edged blade cannot be excluded.

Many of the head wounds, and also the hand and forearm injuries, suggest a scalloped edge or scalloped object, and the multiple injuries of the hands and forearms are consistent with defensive injuries.

Internally, there is almost no blood present in the heart and great vessels and tissues due to exsanguination from all these multiple wounds. X-rays of the head and neck and also the chest and upper abdomen show no obvious fractures or foreign bodies. The internal structures of the neck, including the carotid arteries and hyoid bone, show injuries consistent with strangulation, in addition to the large neck injury passing into the muscle only as mentioned above. The heart, liver, etc., have no injuries. See above for stabs of right lung, stab of brain, left rib fractures, and right brain subarachnoid hemorrhage.

ROUTINE INTERNAL EXAMINATION

In general, internal artifacts and injuries have been described above and will not be further detailed in this section.

The body cavities are opened in the standard autopsy "Y"-incision fashion. The organs are present in their usual anatomic locations and relationships. Little blood is present in the pleural cavities, and there are some slight adhesions at the right upper lobe of the lungs. There is no evidence of empyema, purulent exudate, or acute inflammation of the serous cavities. There is no tissue discoloration suggestive for carbon monoxide intoxication or jaundice. There is a slight smell suggestive of alcoholic beverages within the body.

The gallbladder contains the usual bile. The stomach contains 20 ml of grayish mucoid fluid with curdled-like, small, soft, whitish lumps of mostly digested, unrecognizable food; but there is no evidence of drug residue. The vermiform appendix is present. The urinary bladder contains clear urine. In general, atherosclerosis is very mild. The heart has no evidence of infarction or scarring. The lungs exhibit no change. The right lung also has the two (2) stab wounds mentioned earlier. The liver appears pale but not fatty. The spleen, pancreas, kidneys, heart, adrenals, thyroid, pituitary, and bladder are not otherwise remarkable. The ovaries and uterus show no contusions and appear normal. There is no evidence of sexual intercourse. The vagina and anus were swabbed.

Routine organ weights are as follows: heart, 300 gm; right lung, 430 gm; left lung, 480 gm; liver, 1510 gm; spleen, 65 gm; pancreas, 147 gm; right kidney, 120 gm; left kidney, 140 gm; and brain, 1250 gm.

PROCEDURES AND SPECIMENS

TOXICOLOGY: Blood, bile, urine, ocular fluid, nasal swabs.

PHOTOGRAPHY: Digital and 35-mm slide identification pictures. Digital photos are also taken of the scene and of many of the injuries individually.

TRACE EVIDENCE: Trace materials on tape from right shoulder/chest; possibly small glass fragment from left upper chest; trace materials on tape from left shoulder/neck/chest; trace materials on tape from chest; glass fragments from back; possible glass fragments from chest; hairs adherent to right and left sleeves of shirt; hairs adherent to left hand; one (1) hair from inside the mouth; fingernail scrapings from both hands as well as clippings; and adherent hairs from the right hand. Purple- and red-topped tubes of blood are also collected and sent to the lab.

CHEMISTRIES OR CULTURES: None.

FIREARMS EXAMINATION: None.

X-RAYS: See "INJURIES."

MICROSCOPIC EXAMINATION: Representative sections of major organ systems have been obtained and routinely processed onto glass slides for histologic examination. These have been reviewed.

The liver, heart, and kidney are not remarkable aside from some moderately advanced autolysis, especially at the kidney. The lungs show diffuse, moderate congestion. The cerebrum shows acute petechial hemorrhages at the directed section from the stab-wound area, but otherwise the cerebrum is not remarkable. The anoderm shows no contusion, but it does have dilated submucosal vessels without significant inflammation or scarring.

There are no additional significant findings.

Date of Autopsy: 12/08/2003
Toxic. Complete: 03/09/2004

——EXHIBIT III——

The State of Michigan v. A. LoBiondo

[10/23/2004: Courtroom Testimony Transcript -- Excerpt]

[ATTY. SQUIRE]

"So you began arguing about your profession once again with Ms. O'Connor. And then what?"

We were drinking; she was pissed that I was still bartending. I had forced her to give up dancing at the club once we were a couple. I just couldn't take other men staring at her while she gyrated on a table—it made me jealous.

She said I was staying on "Just for the tits and ass." We'd been fighting about money recently; she'd decided to go back to school, but her stripping income was sorely missed. I don't really know why she was so mad; maybe it was the wine, maybe just the tight finances. I could see she was getting angrier, though. I guess she figured I could find something else, but as I kept reminding her the money was too good, and we needed it with her back in school. I remember promising once she graduated I'd get back into graphic design. The alcohol and the arguing had us both pretty wound up by then, though . . .

Still, I never saw it coming: when I turned to go back into the den—wham—she breaks the wine bottle across my head.

I spun around, totally dumbfounded; I actually saw stars for a few seconds. She was screaming, hitting me with her fists, clawing at me.

Completely out of control. And her eyes—they were crazy. I was just trying to get my bearings; my head was streaming blood.

I had my hands on her throat, pushing her away, then I just started squeezing with all my strength, trying to stop her; finally she started to slow down. After a couple of minutes I threw her to the floor—hard. She wasn't moving. My eyes were stinging as I wiped the blood out of them, amazed at the amount pouring from the gash in my forehead . . .

[DEFENDANT LOBIONDO]

"As the argument escalated, something ... *happened.* I never meant to hurt her. I just needed to choke those words off. She kept ... *accusing* me. So I closed my fingers around her throat . . . (Demonstrates action) like a god or something. And once I had my hands on her, she was just—a ragdoll. She fought me, but it only hardened my resolve. Then, her face sort of ... puffed up, started turning blue. Her body relaxed, but I kept on squeezing ..."

[ATTY. SQUIRE]

"Mr. LoBiondo, by 'something happened,' do you mean that Ms. O'Connor did something to provoke you? Something other than make allegations about your place of employment?"

[DEFENDANT LOBIONDO] (Pauses)

"No ... no, she didn't. The argument just spiraled out of control, I guess. (Pauses again, touches forehead) Then I got up and I staggered to the kitchen. I was looking for ... for something. A weapon ...

I barely recall getting a knife from the drawer; I paused long enough to be sure that the house was empty, although we'd always lived alone. Guess I was freaking out, paranoid . . .

"Returning to the room, I remember ... I remember kicking her, more than once, I think. I might have been swearing. (Pauses) I must've been in shock. Then something . . . something just snapped in me. (Pauses again, places hand over mouth) It was horrible, but I just ... couldn't control myself."

Then it gets vague. I think I kicked her several times, screaming at her to get up. I was really upset, stomping on her, yelling. The worst thing was the awful wheeze of her breath—the rattling sound it made in her chest every time my foot connected. I was out of breath, exhausted. My head was pulsing in the center, slow, hot; I needed to calm down. I blinked hard, taking it all in . . . I dropped to my knees at that point.

"At that point I began stabbing. (Pauses) She half-heartedly raised her hands, I guess, with the last of her willpower ... trying to fend me off. Everything seemed to slow down then . . ."

Strangely, once the cutting began, I felt a calmness flow through me. Over and over—my arm came up and down thousands of times, it seemed. It was late; or maybe it was early. Either way, it was too late: Phil was dead, rendered into a gory pile on the carpet. I wanted to rewind, undo, reverse. . . . Everything after that was just a series of images, like action frozen by the flash of a camera: her shattered face . . . my call to the cops . . . the handset swinging on its cord, slipping out of my bloody fingers. . . . The police told me they would be right over, to stay put. Of course, I had no intention of leaving. I sat there a minute, tasting her blood on my lips; my shirt was torn, clingy and cold with sweat. The cut on my head was clotting . . . finally . . .

"Finally I just stared laying there motionless on the floor. I was crying. The whole scene was chaotic—the knife, the broken wine bottle . . . Philomena . . . (Pauses, touches forehead again) The light was dim; everything was sort of . . . *gauzy* I guess is the word—like a dream, but not . . ."

"Philomena! I love you . . ." In the distance I heard the sirens. The air in the room was dense, warm; the place was suffocating, rotten, like a human slaughterhouse. I put the knife to my wrist. But as the blade sliced my skin, the pain made me realize that I was afraid to die . . .

"I felt dizzy. (Pauses) I put the knife to my wrist right before I passed out. (Clasps hands, closes eyes) Then—nothing. Just . . . just darkness."

A beat . . . a heartbeat . . . an eternity . . .

[ATTY. SQUIRE]

"No further questions, your Honor."

(*To the memory of Akira Kurosawa*)

Author's Note

A challenging story using multiple perspectives, and one that has a curious background. I have always had an interest in crime scene investigation—call it a personal fascination—and well before CSI and its progeny hit the airwaves (I have even done some forensic photographic work for a sheriff's department). At any rate, police procedurals are absorbing, but they are usually only a part of the tale. The concluding dedication mentions Kurosawa: I am a fan of *Rashomon* (and several other films by this fantastic director), and I wanted to acknowledge my indebtedness to this fine film.

People After Their Murder by the U.S. CIA

In a subterranean
Hall des Miroirs—
where the miserable dead sigh—
there is intrigue and confusion;
Chaos finally grows focused amidst
such unnatural reflection,
prompting unsettled murmurs that
"Revenge is nigh . . ."

In the end, a Slave to no one
And the Master of none—
known simply as *Icarus, tombé*—
Rises up, croaking from the ravaged
vestiges of his face:
"Our deaths are mocked in this infernal place . . ."
His next proclamation—
while utterly profound—is equally blasé:
"We must *take the battle to them, I say . . ."*

Meanwhile, the *Others* and *Outsiders* gather—
in the *Hall* and the *Antichambre Grande*—
to watch the courtly proceedings of
La Femme sans Os and lofty *Icarus, tombé . . .*

Eventually, everyone concedes,
In this *Congrès du Damné:*
"Life is wasted on such murderers . . ."

All and sundry—be it
the too pious cultural crusaders—flayed alive—
advocates of the losing side;
or innocent, water boarded also-rans;
the rape victims and sad little children—staring quietly ahead,
because they had been relieved of the lids of their eyes—
at last dare to join other unfortunate, bifurcated passers-by:
each pushed by Destiny's terrible wings into the wrong places at the wrong times . . .

In their tragic procession out of this disturbing reverie,
even the
Decapitates, apparently
(Now their parts greater than their sums)—
Rise up and shamble off:
Determined to take back their stolen
Humanity.

Along the road from perdition—
Good intentions scorched and left behind—
The long-ago dead
Leave the newly dying . . .
Bursting into the shattered Capitol
Their final chorus is strange—and
Terrifying:
"E Pluribus Unum . . ."

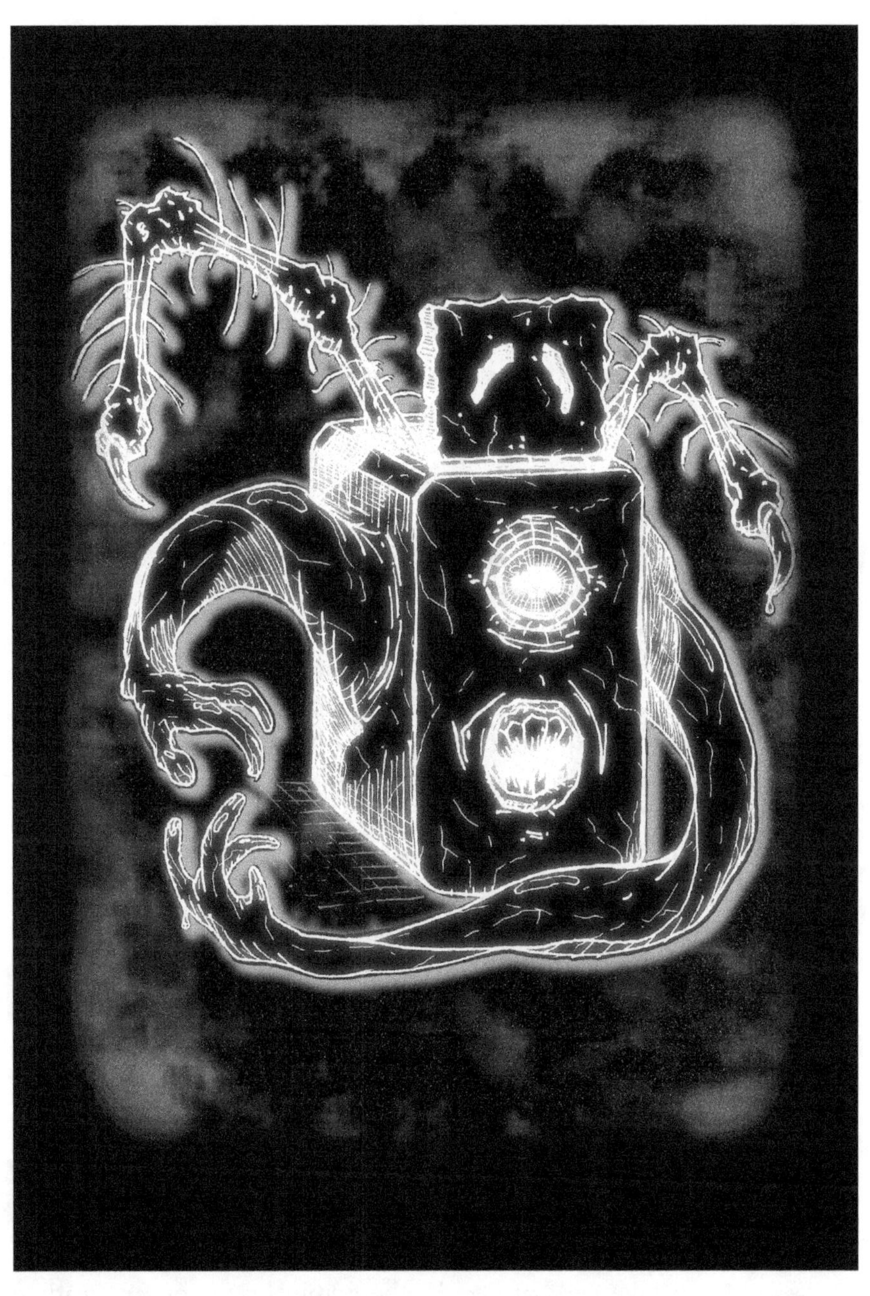

"By Any Other Name . . ."

"I suppose my greatest qualification," the hollow-cheeked interviewee replied, "is my patience." His leg hopped nervously as he studied the recruiter across a suddenly vast expanse of tabletop.

The squirrely hiring manager sank back into a gigantic, high-backed leather chair, black suit sharp as a razor behind his ludicrous mahogany desk. The imperiousness of the furnishings—dark fabrics trimmed in antique silver studs—was unsettling in the otherwise Spartan office.

Place reminds me of something from a medieval torture chamber . . . Suddenly amused, the young man barely concealed a smile under his hand as he pretended to clear his throat.

The supervisor fashioned a temple with his fingers while he considered the nominee behind his chameleon-hooded eyes. Then, as though satisfied by his silent inquisition, he moved abruptly forward, like some smartly attired marionette. He glanced up as he read the applicant's résumé, his drab tie coiled on the desktop like a fashionable noose.

"Patience," the hiring manager reiterated, as if to clarify. He frowned, again peering down at the piece of paper, his brow furrowed in deliberation.

Patience and—what? the young man thought, at once feeling uneasy about his answer. *Probably a grim sense of humor* . . .

After an absurdly long time the recruiter looked up, his gaunt, clean-shaven face a mask of simultaneous concentration and fatigue. "You seem exceedingly skilled to me, if this précis is to be believed."

"Yes, sir. Please feel free to check my references."

The interviewer stared at the young man's expressive features; the silence was enormous. "How about answering a few *more* questions?"

The candidate's throat clicked as he swallowed. "Sure."

"Could you take care of dogs?" the administrator began, reading from a list, back rigid.

"Dogs, sir? Uh—excuse me, but I thought the work was related to taking care of people."

The resources supervisor smiled coldly, understanding the confusion. Once more, he leaned back in his onyx chair, as though being swallowed by some mammoth, antediluvian shark.

"Yes," he said, "it is, but the responsibilities of the vocation extend much *further* than that—it's more of a 'career' than a 'job.' Look, fauna and flora all have to be attended to. . . . That would all be part of your duties in this particular field. . . ." The recruiter shot his cuff out to glance at his watch before regarding the candidate once more, his bookish eyes somehow too large for his narrow face.

"Obviously, we need someone very *mature* and *accountable* to fill the spot . . . an individual with a great deal of experience and general knowledge—for example—of the biological processes of different varieties of vegetation, animals, and, of course, people and so on . . . so that the obligations can be executed—*efficiently*. Accidents may occur, we realize this, but we have allowed for *some* acceptable losses—incorrect identifications, premature terminations, and whatnot—in our projections. There will be *considerable* on-the-job training provided, as well, to minimize this as time goes on. . . . Bear in mind that there has never been a department or division like this before."

He inspected the résumé again.

"Your qualifications are indeed impressive, especially your lab work, and it seems that you have the proper research background. You *are* still interested, correct?"

"Absolutely, sir!"

"Good. Then let us proceed." Sitting forward again, the manager read from his survey, looking up at the potential conscript for a response.

"Before we advance, understand that—while an excellent opportunity—at times it may become quite . . . shall we say—what's the word? *Tedious?* There will be a lot of paperwork, and, although you would be well remunerated, it *is* a salaried position. *No* overtime, though there is potential for making bonuses should you attain goals and the like. . . ." He pursed his lips in thought. "Also," the administrator said, carefully choosing his words, "this position has an *outstanding* benefits package. Stock options, pension, full-coverage health insurance, generous vacation, paid sick leave and holidays . . . not to mention *great* prospects for growth and promotion, understand?"

"Yes, I understand."

The recruiter almost smiled, but it was averted. "Now that we've reorganized and determined where our *needs* are, we're screening applicants with an eye toward the best way to approach everything. Eventually, you will become completely autonomous, governed only by very occasional inquiries into your—shall we say—*experiments?* As everything progresses, you will be free to concoct your own ways of doing things, but—in the beginning—you should stick with the newly developed *methodologies,* so that we may establish baseline statistics, expand databases, and the like." The hiring manager checked his watch again before proceeding. The applicant shifted in his seat, listening intently.

"There will be a master list of procedures to guide you as the operation gets rolling—and a defined priority—but as processes expand and mature, you'll have free will—even be *expected*—to carry on independently as is deemed appropriate. . . . That includes hiring staff, generating new ways of reaching quotas, incorporating emerging technologies, and so on. . . . You'll be in high demand at first as the principle, but that should taper off once we hit our initial objectives."

The manager paused again in thought, then added: "Of course, the individual we deem suitable will be questioned by the higher-ups until everything becomes routine. . . . Additionally, once funding loosens up, you can hire an assistant to take on some of the workload."

"Yes, sir."

The interviewer turned his head and looked through another stack of papers, visibly and audibly pleased when he found what he wanted. "Now then—back to the task at hand. . . . What about *dogs?*"

"Yes, sir."

"No problem there?" the supervisor asked, arching his brow.

"No, sir."

"Good. Cats? Pigs? Goats?"

"Yes—I mean—no, sir."

"Horses? Camels? Frogs? Trees?"

"No, sir."

"Roses? Daisies? Crickets? Fish?"

"Not at all."

"Women? Grandmothers?" He glanced up.

"No."

"Children? Little boys? . . . girls?"

"No, no problem."

"Splendid!" the interrogator exclaimed. He made a note then continued, serious again.

"Men? Grandfathers?" With emphasis, he added: "Lizards? *Snakes?*"

"No. No, sir. Not at all."

"Good," the recruiter said. "Very good." There was a pause as he scribbled something else down. "I have to take this to the secretary; just stay here and I'll be right back." Walking out of his office, the manager seemed suddenly full of cheer. The epic suite door closed behind him.

The candidate waited: nervous, bored.

I hope I get this. Everyone would be so proud!

Exhaling to relieve tension, he turned his notice to the sounds beyond the office: faintly churning workplace machinery; mundane staff chitchat, fraught with mute ennui, amongst the controlled-climate bureaucrats; beneath it all, like an invisible fog, the pungent smell of toner masked a weaker perfume of stale coffee and day-old pastries.

As he looked around the room, he realized for the first time that it was an oversized affair like the desk: a true exercise in sculpted space. Spectacularly vaulted ceilings rose from the empty, sprawling floor, covered by wiry green carpet approximating some type of weird grass; the pristine walls were stark white and nakedly unadorned, as if the executive had just moved in, although there were no empty boxes to be seen.

Returning his gaze to the giant desk, he noted that every item on top of it seemed placed there with resolute purpose.

This guy seems to be a little tightly wound. . . . Must be a Virgo or something. The thought made him chuckle.

There was a tall lamp behind the seat, rendered useless by large, untreated windows: it was impossible to escape the blinding shock of white light flooding in.

There's probably not a single shadow in this room . . . not even mine.

An eternity passed. The applicant sighed, stroking his chin anxiously as he daydreamed.

The interviewer did not walk back into the room so much as unexpectedly reappear, the entry shutting behind him with the finality of a dark promise.

"Okay. That wraps it up. Anything else I need to know?"

The nominee thought for a moment, then stood.

"No, sir. I suppose not." They both lingered awkwardly in the strained hush.

"*Excellent.* I'll call you at the beginning of next week and let you know what we've decided." They shook hands; the recruiter's smile was sickening, his fist like a frozen fish.

"Great," the young man said as he left. "And thanks again . . ."

Afterward, the supervisor called his boss.

"I think we have our fellow," he said into the phone, loosening his tie. He listened for a moment, scowling.

"Yes, yes, *yes.* He *definitely* has the background and I certainly feel a kind of, I don't know—shall we say—a kind of *vibe?* How could I put it? A *sensitivity* for the post. Sensitivity is the right word . . . an ability to zoom from *macrocosm* to *microcosm* in an eye blink. And—" he listened, rolling a pen to and fro on the huge desktop. A smirk came and left his face like an atomic blast.

"Yes, sir. He seems to be in tune to such things. . . . He comprehends that not only do the flowers in the *field* have to be assisted, but also that the little old lady walking her granddaughter down the sidewalk has to be supported as well."

Another pause. He cleared his throat, once more regarding his timepiece.

"What? Oh . . . Okay. I see. Uh—" He leafed through the folders on his desk, brow creased.

"Ah! Here it is . . . Okay . . . Uh, his name, sir." The interviewer squinted to read his own handwriting.

"Here it is—the guy's name is *Jacques* . . . uh . . . Jacques *la Décès,* sir." The manager smiled again to himself as he listened to his superior.

"No. It appears to be an old family *surname* . . . Emily in legal translated it as *'Death,'* sir . . . Has a nice ring for the job, I think . . ."

Author's Note

I always thought that this might have made an interesting *Twilight Zone* episode. The premise seems completely real to me: Isn't this so like a large bureaucracy?

Fever/Wart

Fever

The Hitler of my mushroom took the Aztec vastness of the settled luminescence after the necropoli ending on the token gizzard of the encephalic hebdomadal encased in the perfume broken sausage open at the wound facet winding stump actual music twisting endurance as the blue grasshopper deliquesces over the manumitted Earth sky missing toes alter the significant fretless gangrene of the stupid death and empty sounds reverberate sixty times at the weeping wall noose hoping the endings only triple the foul of insanity direct to postal ani disemboweling shattered bones and glistening glass.

Wart

Wart injury eye socket of 1,000,000 parallax arachnids creep through the black sullen talking encase the purple thump intestine takeover the beauty of too much injected alcoholic rhinoceroses and an end robot thought stake the entrance of putrid wonder and how the slow slurp echoes the thought of Horsehead Nebula Waltz and over the scraping scrotum pulverized razor sliding testicle sledgehammer into a puckered vagina cries red anal tears of love and dismemberment that pulls away the terrible vas deferens with the disintegration of ripe oozing flesh master sexual vegetable of the tongue.

Red-Wat-Shod

"What do you see?"

"Well . . . she's walking toward me . . . slightly out of focus, with these visual trails, like bad video. She's—gliding, in slow motion; sort of *drifting* . . . back and forth—as if she's hovering off the ground."

"Is she?"

"I don't know; I'm tied to the bed. I can hardly see anything—feels like I'm strapped down at the forehead, too. My eyes are straining in the dark—"

"What else is happening?"

"She—she moves very—*erratically*. I intuit more than see how she moves, if that makes any sense. It's like a videotape on fast forward: darting left, then right, then behind my head, all crackly . . . it's like she's in more than one place at a time. The room we're in is long and narrow . . . an MRI tube almost, and there are—how would I describe it? Kind of—*flashes:* very intense red and green cutting through the gloom . . . like strobes or something."

"What's she wearing?"

"Hmmm . . . She's in like a—a long gauzy cloak thing with a hood, but her body underneath is naked. She's voluptuous: curvy hips; tiny waist; big, bouncy breasts; flat stomach; her pubic hair is neatly trimmed. . . . Where her skin appears, though, it's raw and . . . *fluoresces* like under a blacklight. And she's—she's torn up . . . bones pushing through the pulp."

"Is there more?"

"Yeah. Her body emits this sickly yellow aura; her face is fuzzy, indistinct, but her eyes—her eyes are quick and black, like a shark's."

"What happens then?"

"Except for the weird jumpiness, her other movements are *slow,* ponderous. . . . I can feel the blood rise in my face—my heart's pounding so hard. I'm just hoping it won't beat a hole through me. . . . Then there's this—this *whooshing* in my ears, right when the temperature drops."

"Does the woman ever speak?"

"No, never. There's no other sound; in fact it's *utterly* quiet, a vacuum, except for the *whooshing*. I try to scream, to cry out, but my mouth won't open; it feels like I'm paralyzed. . . . I can't even blink, I just move my eyes around."

"Is she alone?"

"Yes, at first. After a while she's at the foot of the bed, or whatever I'm strapped onto. Slowly she crawls up my body—still jerky, out of focus. Then the whole room begins to rotate, and I start feeling sick . . . the strobes are synced to my heartbeat. After a while, in the distance, there's another sound—an intense pounding noise."

"What is it?"

"I—I don't know. As I'm trying to figure it out, she's suddenly kneeling on my chest, her breath dirty, decayed. That's when . . . that's when *he* appears at the far end of the tube we're in."

"'He' who?"

"You know: the guy I sold the lighter to."

"The one that you're upset about?"

"Yeah . . . yeah . . . the guy I'm upset about."

"Go on, tell me the rest."

"But I've already—"

"Tell me again."

"He just—just *appears*. I don't know how; maybe he walked in or 'materialized' or whatever. She's on my chest—it's hard to breathe—and her face is about three inches from mine; she's still out-of-focus looking . . . the room's still spinning—and . . . and . . ."

"Yes?"

"And I'm scared! I can't *move*, remember? I'm tied down, and that—*pounding* is getting louder and louder. The guy keeps walking toward us, too. He has the weirdest look on his face—he's smiling, seems at peace; resolute . . ."

"Keep going. That's not all."

"Why are you doing this to me?"

"I'm not doing anything—you said you wanted to do this for the record."

"I know . . . I know I did. It's just—*tough;* very tough. So, anyway, he walks up to us, and he says: 'I need a book of matches, please.' So . . . so I tell him that I only have lighters; he buys one. I can't remember how I communicated this, as I still can't speak. I'm still strapped down, so I don't know how I got this lighter to him; I can't remember any kind of transaction or anything. It's just like a mental conversation . . ."

"And then?"

"He thanks me and slowly walks away."

"No . . . no, you left something out."

"Please don't make me say it. I'm feeling sick—"

"Say it! I have to hear you say it for the record. You started it anyway; you think I'm enjoying this?"

"Okay! Okay, so I sell him the lighter. I—I don't notice that he's carrying a gas can. As he's walking out of the room, he pours the gasoline all over himself; just dumps it onto his head. It makes him gag; he yelps when it hits his eyes. He's gasping and sputtering—then he lights the lighter . . ."

"What happened then?"

"He—he still has that strange flat half-smile, just before he goes up. The fumes ignite and he's *instantly* engulfed in this intense fireball. All the while she's still sitting on my chest. The gasoline smell is overwhelming. Disgusting. My heart is just *flying,* then I smell this—this other, *sweet* kind of smell . . . it's—it's *him* . . ."

"What do you mean?"

"It's—it's his skin *burning*. If—if you've ever smelled burning human flesh, you never forget it. It's like scorched sugar and tar mixed together. And the *sound* . . . it *pops* . . . like popcorn or water across a griddle. I—I see him just out of the corner of my eye: he's melting—sort of in slow-motion, as if he's in outer space or something. I see the flames wrap around him . . . little fiery tongues licking across his face and clothes. His hair is disintegrating, as though he has a nimbus made of cinders; his fat is frying, bubbling. I can feel the burn of the heat on my skin."

"What is she doing during all this?"

"She's just staring at me, her face orange with the fire's illumination. My eyes are drying out, and her breath is foul; the heat, the oily smoke, his stench, the sound of his skin searing is . . . breathtaking. . . .

You know, he never once screamed or lost that eerie expression? The grin, the million-mile stare . . ."

"Then?"

"Finally, his skull just appears under his blackened face—the ashes of his flesh drift away on the breeze from his personal inferno."

"What else?"

"Well . . . As he's crumbling to a heap on the floor, she leans down to my ear and says something. I can't *quite* figure it out—"

"You can't hear her?"

"No—I hear her, just barely, but I hear her. No, it's like she's speaking some foreign language. The room is still spinning. It gets faster. My breath is shallow: I'm trying not to breathe—*him*—into my lungs. The smells, the noise . . . the strobes are making my head ache; all the time there's the intense flicker still coming from his immolation . . . from his cremated remains."

"Go on. You're almost finished."

"She—she whispers in my ear again, thrusting her tongue in there. My heart is still pounding, pounding; then it suddenly gets *dark*—pitch black. My heart slows . . . slower . . . slower . . . Finally the universe disappears . . . I am *in oblivion*."

Author's Note

Imagistic writing appeals to me: probably due to my background as a poet. Sometimes the clutter of all that verbiage needs to be stripped away. This story is based on an actual incident.

Poem from the Future

(For Ray Bradbury)

You haven't seen the sky:
My, it's been too long . . .

10,000 days and nights
of sun,
blazing like a scorned lover,
Drove us down,
down,
        down . . .

I use my memories
to keep me strong,
but I can't lie:
It gets harder as time goes on . . .

Such a wonderful thing to behold,
You haven't touched the grass . . .

Wind rippling the tiny blades
like fields of petite soldiers;
endless day
became too much:

Heat killed it all!—beautiful green

yielding to shriveled brown:
The surface, once serene,
is now only a baked, bleak mass . . .

You never saw the sea:
What an incredible sight!

Full of power,
Rich with life;
But the days grew long . . .
then longer.

Only a prelude,
the oceans receded following an initial swell
then,
ironically,
the planet became an arid, parched Hell.

Now the few that remain are down here—
Trapped underground in perpetual night . . .

You are young—
Newly born—
and I can barely express the many
reasons that we mourn;
for this eternal dark,
so forlorn,
we traded pitiless day above:

In truth,

we yearn for the solemn, enduring stars.
Lost as Noah's raven,
we still wish for his sacred dove;
to survive,
we *need* Saturn, Venus, and Mars . . .

In the end, it wasn't
terrorism, disease, or political strife
that left us so undone,
but pollution, denial and rolling of the cosmic dice . . .

Are you the future?
I hope, but cannot tell.

Regardless, here's my dying advice:

Stay out of the heartless sun!

The History of a Letter

As related by Jason V Brock

Introduction

When the editor asked me for a contribution to this anthology (the very one in your hands), I knew I had my work cut out for me. A flurry of correspondence ensued: When was the book coming out? Who was the publisher? Was there a theme? What were the restrictions on length and so on?

As usual, the editor was courteous, prompt, and succinct. Did I mention thorough? At any rate, I went off to consider all this information and came to a stark realization—I had nothing to contribute! This was a quandary; I *wanted* to be part of the book, yet I had no idea what to write.

Weeks of vexation, false starts, irritable moods, and agitation followed. As the deadline loomed, I went through my normal course of actions, as is my coping strategy at such times:

1. I searched through my files and notebooks, hoping to stumble across that gem of an idea waiting to be fleshed out (always a dubious gamble, I might add).
2. I castigated myself as a procrastinator (though I had been quite involved in another task, which I will address in a moment).
3. I played loud music (a normal, albeit damaging, habit for me).
4. I stayed up very late, unable to sleep (another habit I cannot seem to rid myself of).

Finally, several months later and just a few weeks before the piece was due, I asked the (patient) editor if a nonfiction submission was acceptable, and the reply was "Of course! But I need it quickly." I felt better then, as I had been working on something that had haunted me for some time, but was unsure where it might lead. I hoped that the article would be of use, as I felt no small amount of guilt that I had been spending hours fiddling with it and trolling around various libraries, bookstores, and online venues doing research in lieu of writing a story for the anthology I had committed to those many months previous.

A brief explanation: While conducting an investigation for an unrelated project, I stumbled across an old copy of the Georges Bataille[1] classic *Histoire de l'oeil*[2] at Powell's City of Books[3] in Portland, Oregon. As I was leafing through the crumbling pages of this book, something fell out and fluttered to the ground—a letter. It was tightly folded, ragged, stained, and yellow with age. I picked it up, and what I read filled me with a peculiar disquiet; as I deciphered the cramped, spidery handwriting, I lost all interest in the Bataille volume and, though I knew it was wrong, I could not resist the impulse to take the dispatch.

What follows are the contents of that strange missive; the notes are my own, based on investigations that have distracted me, as I stated, for the better part of a year and sidetracked my other ambitions, consuming more and more of my time and attention.

The Letter

> Dearest—[4]
>
> By the time you read this, I[5] will be no more, and most likely your time will be limited as well.[6] Thus, as a final testament, I have decided to address a question that you posed long ago, and I never answered. . . .
>
> Do you recall when you asked what single event in my life had most disturbed me? I had scoffed at the notion, stating that I

---

1. Bataille was a prolific and important French author whose works frequently dealt with surrealism, as well as the entanglements of human sexuality and mortality; other notable works of his include *The Solar Anus; The Tears of Eros; Erotism;* and *The Trial of Gilles de Rais.*

2. *Story of the Eye* in English, as by Lord Auch (a pseudonym that Bataille employed because of the pornographic nature of the work).

3. A venerated and excellent resource for bibliophiles in the Pacific Northwest.

4. The addressee is not identified, but appears to have been a love interest.

5. The writer is never revealed, but references suggest a male.

6. The author does not elaborate on why both parties appear to be in danger.

had no use for such banality, but the truth is—I was loath to revisit the moment. I'm ahead of myself: allow me to "begin at the beginning," as it were. . . .

It was yet another melancholy fall afternoon about eight years ago,[7] and I was walking through the Olde Jewish Shopping District[8] when I saw it. Just the recollection sets my teeth on edge! At any rate, I was crossing the street when I glanced up and there the hideous object was, on display—obscene display—in an antiquarian book and curio dealer's window.[9]

Though I had been feeling febrile and ill for many months,[10] and had been warned against undue excitement by my attending physician, I rushed back across the boulevard, pressing my hands against the cold glass of the exhibit. I was horrorstruck that the rest of the world continued unabated as though this was the most natural thing in the world. My focus was now reduced—to this moment in time, to this instant of revulsion and comprehension brought on by the relic. The sky darkened for a moment and I felt nauseous, my stomach aflutter. As I extricated myself from the window, the Earth seemed somehow robbed of all colour, and the chilly air had the stale quality of a giant's exhalation. A man bumped into me, and his cursing brought me back to the external present. Dabbing perspiration from my face, I straightened my tie and decided to enter the shoppe.

An archaic bell, too loud in my sensitive state, jangled atop the door as I stepped through the ornate threshold. The musty atmosphere was frigid—colder even than the late fall day outside. A chill swept my bones and the crisp air inside felt alive; in every direction I looked, I could not escape the unspeakably ghoulish contents of the room. Sinister etchings and shadowed portraits peered from the corners of the weirdly expansive shoppe, and the dimly lit parlor seemed scarcely able to contain all the *objets d'art*

7. The letter is not dated, but the condition, and the parchment-like material of the paper, appears to be from the early 1900s, or perhaps even older.

8. I could find no record of any such place in the United States; there are several so-called ethnic areas like this in Europe, however, notably in Prague (unfortunately, most of the others were destroyed during World War II). Some of the notations in the margins of the document appear to be either Cyrillic or Czech characters; also, there are several words and references in French in the letter, so it is possible that the writer was in Europe, or was European.

9. Unnamed.

10. It is possible that the author had tuberculosis, a common malady of the apparent era in which the letter was written.

that the owner had accumulated over the years. The place reeked with the mould of old furniture and older books, causing my nose to tickle as I observed the bottles of freak fetuses preserved in clouded green fluid, the rough-skinned shrunken heads with empty-eyed stares, the colorful voodoo effigies of the Caribbean, the strange skin-bound tomes of an apparently Arab[11] origin, their spines decorated in Sanskrit letters. . . .

I glanced to the window that I had leered through only a moment before; the heavy door closed behind me with dreadful finality, and I felt my throat constrict. I should have stayed away; in that instant, I had decided to turn, to leave, to try to forget the madness in the window, but was interrupted . . .

"*Mon Dieu!* I see you've returned," the shopkeeper said from the back of the cramped space. Lately, I had been experiencing disturbing bouts of *déjà vu;* as the wizened, stoop-shouldered proprietor shuffled toward me, the sensation reasserted itself in a forcefully disorienting fashion.

"*Au contraire, Monsieur*—I'm quite sure I've never had the pleasure of visiting your fine establishment before. . . . Perhaps I have a twin?" My clumsy attempt at humour was met with stoicism by the keeper, who was now in front of me, leaning on a gnarled wooden cane capped by a silver skull. Squinting, he studied me with piercing blue eyes from behind thick, wire-rimmed spectacles, thoughtfully stroking his white beard; after a long moment, he straightened his shawl-covered frame and flashed a brief smile.

"*Oui*—quite a *remarkable* doppelgänger. How may I assist you?" He paused, then bent forward, conspiratorially peering over his glasses: "Let me guess—the display in the window, correct?" His voice was quiet, his enunciation precise.

Just for a second, the world seemed to spin. I glanced again around the claustrophobic showroom, with its dust-enrobed grotesqueries and curios from across the planet; its masks out of darkest Africa; its fetishes from the cannibal tribes of Papua New Guinea; its arcane trinkets from the savages of South America and the madmen of Asia.

"Yes," I managed at last. "The window." Our gaze locked, and I realised that I could no longer hear the bustle of the street outside, just the creak of wooden shelves, the wheeze of the shopkeeper's ragged breath. I dabbed my forehead again, though the dark room was chilly to the point of my breath fogging. Perhaps my fever had returned. Perhaps it was something else.

---

11. This term was used in reference to much of the Middle East in previous times.

The owner nodded. "I thought so, just like yesterday, and all the days prior to that . . ."

Before I could rouse another protest, he turned his icy stare away, breaking our connection.

Here I must insert an aside: Though the aged retailer insisted that we'd met before, I know that this is not the case. His innuendo of 'yesterday' would have been an impossibility, for example, as I had been in the next town over, acting as a pallbearer with Ernst, Alistair, and Isaac for my poor brother, Stefan,[12] who had finally succumbed to his injuries.[13] Given the great distance and my ill health, there was no way I could have been at the funeral service and then to his establishment in the same [*illegible*].

"*Oui, oui*—you've never been here before; I recall," he said, lightly tapping the side of his head as he moved to the front of the store. I followed, navigating around the jammed shelves, the queer items suspended from the ceiling. In the swirl of dust motes kicked up by our trespass, I continued to be plagued by the peculiar nag of *déjà vu;* the whole strange episode had the quaint aspect of a fever dream.

The old bay windows of the storefront rattled from a sudden gust. A dull ache began to throb in my temple as I felt the barometric pressure drop; such is the normal course of events in coastal towns when a storm gathers on the sea. The waning orange glow of evening glinted off the chop in the harbour across the bay,[14] clearly visible from the dirt-gauzed panes. The antiquarian dealer's battered shingle squealed as it was buffeted by the wind. No one was outside; the cobblestones on the street glistened with rain, puddles reflecting the baleful flicker of the gaslights.[15] A cloud of dread enveloped me as I watched twilight cloak the city. It was rare that I frequented this aspect of the port, even more rare that I would be out this late in the day, especially at this time of the year, when the light and the darkness changed places so much earlier. My salivary glands tightened, making my

---

12. Possibly the author is German or Jewish?

13. This might be a reference to World War I (either a civilian or a military casualty). It could also be related to work or an accident; it is noteworthy that the object of the letter seemed unaware of the brother's fate or not involved with the author at this point in time.

14. Interesting geographic clues, but still quite vague.

15. A reference to a pre-electric age. Combined with the geographic descriptions, the locale could be England (or perhaps the writer is British, as a few of the spellings seem to indicate), Paris, or even America (especially New England).

mouth dry, my jaw twinge, adding to my headache.

"Storm's on the way," the proprietor said, staring at the water. The harbormaster's warning horn sounded. By this point, the scene had grown unbearably tense, and I knew I should take my leave—[*illegible*] just forget this horrible place and its contents for good.

"[*Illegible*]," the shopkeeper said at last; then he crept over to the display and reached in. I wiped the sweat from my forehead again, my stomach in turmoil and competing with the pain in my head.

"Perhaps it is too much effort—" I said. My voice was hoarse, a whisper.

"No, no—just one moment; it always takes a moment to [*illegible*] . . ."

Another odd statement from the owner; I was beginning to wonder if the old man was losing his grip on reality.[16] The wind kicked up again; it was now completely dark outside. A stroke of lightning split the night, followed by a low roll of thunder. As I watched, several denizens staggered against the mounting gale—they seemed unnatural, pained, ensconced in tattered overcoats and filthy gloves that obscured their features. They determinedly made their way in the wind toward the opening night of the Ceremony,[17] no doubt driven by the long tradition of the Rituals;[18] indeed, I had forgotten that this was the return of that savage and disturbing five-year spectacle.[19] Backward hamlets such as this are places so entombed in their traditions, so ossified by their histories that they appear to have lost all [*illegible*] and rational thought when it comes to these "historic" defences of orchestrated mayhem. Rotting leaves plaster the windows, whipped onto the loose panes by the tempest, and the lights in the store, already dim, lower. Finally I look away, awash once more in the anxious sensation of inhabiting a nightmare, but knowing this could not be the case. At that moment the keeper was at my side, brandishing the foul item from the window.[20]

---

16. An interesting point in light of the next few paragraphs.

17. No documentation.

18. No documentation.

19. A good clue: there are several "festivals" such as this throughout Europe and America, usually related to historic events or the harvest. It is possible that the one referred to here is related to a military victory over the local indigenous peoples.

20. The references here are never fully explained: it is unclear exactly what the "object" actually is.

"This is what you seek?" he stated more than asked, thrusting the obscenity into my hands, his thin flesh clammy and vaguely scaly to the touch. I was horrified to behold the object up close, and for a moment just stared into the cold, rheumy eyes of the proprietor. "Go on," he commanded, his voice clotted, distant, as he pushed the artifact toward me. "Take it—there's not another on Earth."

As I held it in my hands, unsure if it were real or imagined, living or dead, I felt its dark energy course through my fingers . . . so much pain . . . so much filth . . . so much strength and cosmic wisdom . . . so much *power*. It appeared alive somehow, even *conscious*. Once again, the world started to tumble . . .

"How—how did you come to possess—*this?*" I asked, fingering the smooth, hard curves and planes, studying the bizarre runes and glyphs adorning the dreadful object. My impulses were divided as I hefted the thing: part of me wanted to destroy it, smash it into pieces, while another part of me longed to fall down in worship, inwardly cringing at its simultaneous beauty and loathsomeness.

"*Mon Dieu*—now that is a good question," he said, his smile dark, macabre, like a bruise on the face of a bride. It seemed starkly out of place. I glanced down—my hands were covered in what appeared to be blood: the thing was oozing a sticky red fluid; its rigidity was lessened and it now felt prickly, malleable. "Sadly," the shopkeeper said, "there is no answer. . . it comes from yesterday and tomorrow. It came to me long ago in a dream. . . ."

A gust howled against the windows, and the light failed: suddenly a revolting, deformed face pressed against the iced glass of the storefront. A mewling din surged over the wind, and an ominous crowd began to gather outside the shoppe.

The proprietor laughed behind me, [*illegible*] I felt frozen, unable to move. As everything vanished from view, I thought about how this was the strangest thing in all the world . . . the most dreadful thing. . . . And then the idol was twitching in my hands . . . birthing . . .

Darkness: I awoke in darkness on the windswept street, my hands stained crimson, my palms singed and painful, though I have no memory of how I got there. I could not find the store, and the relic was gone. . . .

Since that time, I have been troubled by a peculiar dream.

In the reverie, I am approaching a decrepit house on a devastated plain. The moon hangs low, bloated and blue in the sky.

Fog snakes the ground. As I get nearer, a sickly yellow light winks on in an upstairs window, and a shadow passes in front of it. The wind blows, and a low rumble grows in the distance. The air is frosty, biting.

Closer now, the door opens: its hinges groan and the inside is darker than the outside; the smell of wet earth is robust, sickly.

In the foyer, on a table, there is a bundle of unbound, mildewed papers, tied together with a string. I untie it, and as I leaf through the stained manuscript, I notice that nearly every inch of the yellowed parchment is covered in weird symbols, incomprehensible diagrams, and crude illustrations.

And then, a few pages into the document, there it is: a hasty pen-and-ink sketch of the thing in the window!

I hurl the stack of papers to the ground and sense that I am not alone. Every time I have the dream, I am able to peruse more of the leaves in the bundle before I reach the drawing, and more of the presence reveals itself. Turning around, I can barely make out a ramshackle spiral staircase near the back of the room, which ascends to the ceiling, but not an ordinary one: it is instead a galactic canopy of stars and swirling celestial bodies, and the stairs climb into the face of a terrible midnight sun, its merciless solar flares blinding me, scorching my skin. . . .

Then it appears: the idol from the shoppe. But not as some hand-held miniature, no. Instead it is a massive, jabbering horror, rending the fabric of my sanity with its tormented shrilling, its ultra-human sonorities. . . . It reaches to me across the aeons, the gulfs of eternity, and holds my broken body in its awful clutches—now *I* am the miniature!

I always awake screaming, and, more recently, I have had . . . injuries. Burns. Scratches. [*Illegible*] I feel that I must be hurting myself in my sleep, but, even though I take precautions against unintentional self-mutilation, the injuries are becoming more serious. . . .

I suspect that the dream has significance; that it means I am destined to find the ghastly relic again. Since that horrible day all those years ago, I have been obsessed: searching for, but unable to find, the mysterious antiquarian dealer's shoppe. I still look for it daily amidst the new and unknown alleyways and shuttered businesses littering the darkened ends of the port. Every face I encounter I study, looking for the old merchant, to no avail. The place and its owner seem to have vanished from the Earth.

[*Illegible*] I recall the [*illegible*] shoppe to be has, in its stead, a mapmaker's facility; they claim that the establishment I look for was there once—but more than a hundred years previous. I have moved away several times, trying to forget what I saw that fateful evening, but the strange pull of the place compels me back. There must be a reason for this; I hold it as a sign.

I have carried this with me for so long now, Dearest One. The dreams are becoming more intense, more frequent, more vivid. . . . I sense that I am on the verge. . . . I know that am at the cusp of some great insight, some stupefying revelation. . . . I *must* get to the bottom of it before I draw my last breath, but the way things are proceeding, I am not confident that this will happen. [*Illegible*]

If I ever find the infernal object again, I know what I must do . . . and I will do it.[21]

Heaven help me, Dearest, I have [22]

Final Thoughts

This letter is an interesting document: it raises more questions than it answers.

My hope is that I will one day be able to sort out where the port is located, what happened to the author, perhaps even understand the strange information seemingly "encoded" in the note. The vagueness of the memo and the obscured identity of its author are puzzling, tantalizing. Colleagues have even suggested that it is some elaborate hoax, but the content and the delivery make me wonder. Besides, to what end? So that, one day years later, someone would try to sort out the conundrum after the involved parties are (one would presume) all deceased?

Buddhists have a saying: "When the student is ready, the Master will appear." Perhaps this is one of those times: I have a theory that the phenomenon of *déjà vu* (touched upon in the letter several times) is related to the process of dreaming.

It might be a way for the unconscious or the subconscious to process the reliving of events from multiple lifetimes, or of the same life lived multiple times. Another religious group, the Hindus, have long held that life is a cyclic, recurring event (reincarnation), and that

21. An ominous statement.

22. The letter ends here, in the middle of the page; the only other marks on the page are some dark brown spatters.

there might even be different physical selves, but with the same soul (read: consciousness) over vast spans of time. Who is to say that there could not be the same consciousness relived repeatedly in the *same* physical self in some other, parallel universe?

Since finding this letter, my life has changed: I have had increasing incidents of lucid dreaming, and have even envisioned myself in the same terrible house that the writer describes so richly in the note. Lately, too, I have had bouts of amnesia: I find myself scribbling—unconsciously—in my notebooks, and always in a strange script, in alien characters; later, fully cognizant, I cannot decipher the cryptic symbols, the bizarre drawings I have scrawled.

Perhaps these notations are a key?

Only time will tell.

Wind

It was a strangely normal day
when the *wind* quit blowing:

"Surprising . . ." ""**Strano . . .**"" "驚き . . ."
" . . ." "*Étrange* . . ." "Unexpected: what does it mean?"
"*Weird* . . ." "Sonderbar . . ." "*!!*"
"παράξενη εμφάνιση με στολή στρατιώτη.
Δείτε επίσης."
"*Is it war?*"

A few weeks later, the Seas went ~~flat~~—
Oceans stopped waving,
Dooming sailboats to endless doldrums
in some passive attack . . .

Without currents, messages never arrived—
stranded sailors all grew beards, mourning their wives;
Without currency, economies slowed,
then shriveled,
then died.

At mos phere diminished:
b r e a t h l e s s m a r i a h .

Clouds
dropped to
Terra Firma—

Permanent fog shrouding everything as
Holland
ground to a halt . . .

On the plains of Spain,
Don Quixote wept;
Rocinante seemed to have lost purpose:
There was no more rain.

Around the World,
No one could see more than five feet ahead;
Everyone stopped hating each other—
It was the end of **dread**.

Without lift from the air,
birds had no need for wings;
In an overnight evolution—
brilliance beyond compare—
each continued to sing
in rapturous raptor revolution.

Sadly,
1,001 airplanes crashed to the **Earth**—
flames dancing in the
mists:
Prompting an obscured President to declare:
"Never underestimate the shock of being
*wind*less,
and beware the ingenuity of
Terrorists®."

Black Box

"That's impossible, Tate—all *four* engines have failed?" Panic began a slow bloom in Captain Wilson's mind as he scrutinized the dimly lit instrument panel.

"Correct, sir—all unresponsive," the navigator, Lieutenant Tate, barked. Wilson pondered the next course of action as the third pilot, Flight Engineer Beaumont, fought with the control yoke, manually steering the enormous 747. Behind him, the captain sensed the cockpit door slide open. Looking up, he saw Amanda Cantrell, the attractive young flight attendant; she was nervous, unconsciously touching her throat.

"Captain, I'm sorry to interrupt, but the passengers are concerned. They say they smell smoke; I—I can smell it, too, sir . . ." She glanced from Wilson to Beaumont and Tate, eyes widening in acknowledgment of the gravity of their situation.

"Ms. Cantrell, tell them—tell them that we'll have an announcement in five minutes. Instruct the cabin crew to muster topside immediately." Wilson pitched forward as a bump of turbulence rocked the aircraft.

"Yes, sir," she said, ducking out of the reinforced doorway and locking it behind her.

Time seemed to have stopped in the cramped flight deck: as Beaumont wrestled the controls, Captain Wilson studied the instrument cluster, mind racing over emergency protocols.

"Un—unresponsive," Tate said, adjusting dials all over the board. "What next, sir?"

Wilson stared at Tate and Beaumont in amazement, then looked back to the softly glowing panel. The quiet as the Boeing 747 sailed through the air was eerie to him. He swallowed, suddenly too aware of his breath; it had never occurred to him how much he took for granted the roar of the four colossal Rolls Royce RB211 turbines. Normally they produced a comforting white noise, especially conducive to off-duty naps on his longtime route—night flights over the ocean from Malaysia and Micronesia to Australia.

Now, there were only the uncanny whistles and rattles of the plane as it hurtled through space at 475 knots—with no engines running. Wilson snapped out of his disbelief: "Talk to me, Bill! What's happening with the air speed?"

"470 knots and dropping," the beleaguered flight engineer replied, voice straining with exertion as he maneuvered the steering mechanism. "Altitude: approximately 36,000 feet; stable at present. We need to do something . . . *fast*—"

Wilson grunted. "Take emergency measures: Tate, get the manuals out and start down the Engine Restart Checklist. How long since we lost primary power?"

"Lost power at roughly zero two hundred hours, Captain. Been about three minutes on secondary," Tate replied sharply, scouring the flight handbook.

Wilson studied the navigator a moment, then said: "Tate, call Sydney air traffic control; see what the maintenance ground crew recommends—maybe they can get Boeing on the horn, too. We've gone too far to get back to Kuala Lumpur. I'd hate to have to glide this bird into the Pacific—at *night*."

"Right, sir," Tate responded, never looking up from the instruction manual.

"I'm going to tell the attendants to prepare to ditch," Wilson said as he unbuckled and moved to the door. "I'll check out this smoke smell. Back in two minutes."

The captain exited the flight cabin as Tate and Beaumont continued their quiet, frenzied action.

Once out of the cockpit, Wilson retreated to the lavatory: his heart felt as if it were tearing his insides to pieces.

He gazed for an instant into the mirror over the dwarf sink, collecting his thoughts and noting how the poor illumination seemed to embellish every line of his aging features. He splashed a handful of cold water on his face, tasting salt on his lips. His shoulders tightened with the plane's every dip and weave, his shirt cold and sticky on his torso. The old cigarette addiction tugging at his innards, Wilson straightened his tie, smoothed down the thin mantle of his hair and left the tiny bathroom.

In the main cabin, passengers were huddled in tight groups at the windows along both sides of the fuselage, peering intently from the darkened portals. Confused, Wilson took a moment to understand the situation: he walked to the nearest window with overstated calm and looked out. An otherworldly pyrotechnic display was happening to the wings of the crippled jetliner, eliciting a jumble of responses that circulated like some linguistic virus: anguished cries, reverential whispers, astonished silence. Some of the travelers, mostly older people, could only avert their eyes—as though turning away from an ancient and terrible deity in a frieze by Michelangelo.

"Oh my *God*," Wilson whispered, the strange scene playing out in front of him eliciting a sudden pressure in his chest, as though a frigid hand had grabbed his heart and was determined to yank the overworked muscle from his ribcage. *I'm too old for this . . .*

The entire spectacle was bright enough to overwhelm the emergency lighting of the cabin. Scanning the length of the wing, Wilson could make out a peculiar blue glow emanating just in front of it, a sort of hellish vanguard. Long columns of flame cascaded from the rear of the massive engines, apparently synced with each restart effort. The smell—not smoke, but ozone he realized—was stronger near the windows, and there was an unusual static charge that caused his arm hairs to stand up the closer he got to the cabin wall.

What the hell is going on here? Captain Wilson squeezed his eyes closed and snapped the shutter down, trying to shake the mental pictures from his mind as he flashed on a night over thirty-five years ago when he was on *another* flight from hell . . .

I know what I saw: it was a little man—gremlin, whatever—on the wing of the plane . . .

Everyone said it was ridiculous: the captain, the flight attendants, the shrinks . . . But I can't change what I saw.

*Someone—some*thing*—was on the wing, trying to tear the engine apart and doom us all . . .*

Wilson never heard much about the bizarre incident in the press after that night, just one back page story in *The Times* and a re-enactment on an old television show. Even though his first marriage had been a casualty of the resultant therapy, he had been unwavering in his quest to control his fate from that moment forward.

In the years that followed, he managed to conquer his phobias and earn his pilot's license, logging enough flight time to receive his commercial aviator's certification. Eventually hired as an airman, Wilson slowly worked his way up the ranks of a major carrier to attain the title of captain.

Now near retirement, all his fears were behind him; he was finally ready to spend some well-earned downtime with his new wife, Amelia, and his trusty digital camera.

After so many years as a flier, though, he had heard stories . . .

What they really found the night I had my breakdown: claw marks in the metal cowling . . . the tiny, misshapen teeth . . . And the way the engine had been dismantled: no way it was lightning, or a bird strike as the authorities initially claimed, in spite of the feathers. For one thing, the furrows in the metal were all going the opposite *direction from what the forensics should have dictated in those scenarios. Besides, there had been no evidence of fire, which would have been expected.*

Then there was the way that *particular* episode, kept so quiet in the press, secretly opened the books on a host of unsolved "aeronautical phenomena": from the de Havilland *Comet* all the way to TWA *Flight 800* . . .

Captain Wilson backed away from the window and quickly made his way to the upstairs crew lounge.

"We have a—*situation.* I won't lie to you: this is going to be rough; quite possibly the hardest landing of your lives. And on the water . . ." Wilson paused, his words hanging in the air. His attention shifted, first to the terrified faces of the flight attendants, then to the weird glow still visible from the windows, and, finally to the darkened floor. "No one's ever succeeded in landing a jet intact on the open ocean."

Silence: as the plane gently shifted, the ozone smell intensified.

"Are we going to die?" Amanda—the attendant from earlier—asked, her words choked. Wilson looked at his crew again, from Amanda to Diane, then to Robert, Patricia, and finally to Mike, the lead steward, who held the trembling girl's hand.

"It—it's going to be—difficult. We all have to pull together for the passengers—not to mention ourselves—and be strong. I need each of you to please help support me and the flight crew," Captain Wilson said, his voice low and calm. "We've got our hands full up there, as you can imagine—"

"Captain, what is wrong, exactly?" Mike queried, crisp and professional, as though asking more for the benefit of the others than himself.

"To be honest, Mike," Wilson responded, "we're not too sure just yet. Here's what we do know: we lost power in all four turbines in rapid succession. Right now, we're gliding on sheer momentum at a very slight downward pitch, as you can probably detect, to keep aloft. Auxiliary power is unlikely to last much longer without the engines going, and we're completely manual in the cockpit—steering, landing gear, you name it . . ." Wilson looked at his watch: *Gone three minutes; better wrap this up . . .*

"Did you see the wings?" Diane inquired. "There's something out there . . . the fire, the glowing—a few of the passengers said they even saw something . . . something *moving* out there—"

Wilson nearly passed out at this revelation. He steadied himself on a seatback.

"I—I did see the lights, Diane. Looks to be some sort of St. Elmo's fire. I don't have an explanation for you, I'm sorry to report. We—we're contacting Sydney and doing our very best to restart the engines—"

"We know, sir. We appreciate that you're all doing your damnedest," Mike said. "What do you need us to do?"

Even as they spoke, Captain Wilson could sense minute changes in the airplane's stability; the glow outside was increasing as the backup power gradually failed. His ears popped as the air pressure mounted. *We're descending too rapidly. Have to get back to the deck—*

At that moment, the jet lurched to the side as though pummeled by a massive fist, the cabin crew slamming together like human billiard balls; from the main room below they heard muffled shrieks. The sudden racket of the vibrating wings was incredible, causing the supplemental air masks to drop from the ceiling like synchronized plastic spiders.

"Pull together! Try to keep everyone calm! I have to go!" Wilson yelled over the violently shaking airplane. He descended the stairs as though he were suddenly wearing a suit of lead armor.

Back in the flight deck, the scene was hectic: Wilson staggered in as the plane crossed the thin threshold of control into chaos. An ashen-faced Lt. Tate had turned on the supplemental landing lights, and it appeared as though the aircraft was traveling through a dense fog. Flight Engineer Beaumont was still commandeering the yoke, physically trying to keep the plane level as he fought the massive G-forces.

"Mayday! Mayday! Flight 3017 heavy to Sydney! 296 souls onboard!" Tate screamed into his headset. "We've lost all four engines! No power! Losing 2100 feet a minute in altitude—down to 27,400 feet and falling . . . air speed 312 knots and dropping . . ."

Wilson leapt into the seat next to his flight engineer, the *whoop! whoop!* of the emergency alert system blaring in his ears. Tate was still struggling to read from the Engine Restart Checklist as he worked the radio and other controls. "Captain, nothing's working!"

"Christ, we're losing it!" Beaumont yelped, veins bulging in his throat as he muscled the steering mechanism.

From the limited perspective of his window, Wilson observed with amazement the weird aura surrounding the port-side wing. Fantastic, incredibly long trails of fire shot from behind the enormous motors each time Tate attempted to start them: first Engine One, then Two, followed by Three on the opposite wing, and, finally, the last one, to no avail.

"Come on," Wilson mumbled, "come *on!*"

Then he saw it: something—*a being*—momentarily darkening the eerie azure glow, quickly moving from engine to engine, as if trying to interfere with their efforts—

"Jesus!" Wilson shouted, intuitively pushing the steering apparatus forward, causing the plane to lunge downward at a steep angle; he barely heard his own screams in the clamor from the other two bewildered pilots, the emergency warning system and the squelching of air traffic control.

It's right on the wing again, same as all those years ago!

"Got it!" Tate hollered as Engine Three unexpectedly sputtered to life. One by one the other turbines, except for Number Two, coughed on.

"Pull up! Pull up!" the warming system intoned in flat urgency; the power returned to maximal output.

"3017, this is Sydney, come in, over." The static of the radio snapped the old pilot back into reality, and Wilson eased the control column back, steadying the plane. He cut off the landing lights, noticing that the wings no longer had the ominous glow; the jet was flying as if nothing had happened. *Thank God we never lost pressure.* . . . Blinking hard, Wilson tried to shake the afterimage of what he thought he had seen out of his mind. *You're not crazy, Arthur Jeffrey Wilson . . . it was nerves . . . the mind playing tricks . . .*

"Flight 3017, come in, this is Sydney. You are cruising through the midst of a volcanic eruption, over." Wilson looked to Navigator Tate, then to Flight Engineer Beaumont in shocked silence. *Eruption?*

"We're at 9,000 feet, Captain," Lt. Tate said at last, shaking and pale. The acrid smell of sweat was heavy in the small space; Beaumont simply leaned back in his seat with his eyes closed, exhausted and rubbing his temples as though fighting a migraine. Wilson knew they had to gain some altitude; depending on where they were, the potential of slamming into a mountain was a distinct possibility in this part of the world—especially at night and using only instruments to fly. "Clear it with Sydney to go back to 25,000 feet, Tate."

Lt. Tate complied.

"Roger that, 3017, heavy . . . You're clear. Be aware that the eruption is reportedly sending rock and ash as high as 45,000 feet; must have affected your radios, as we've been trying to raise you for more than an hour, over."

Wilson was surprised. "Roger that, Sydney. We've got partial power on three engines; Number Two is out—do we have permission for emergency landing, over."

Silence.

The hackles on Wilson's neck rose: *Has the radio died again?* He studied the altimeter: *11,000; 14,500; 18,300; 20,000—*

Suddenly, the Number Four engine began to quake, nearly jerking the control free from Wilson's grasp. Pitch, yaw, and roll careened out of control again, causing the wings to undulate as if they were flapping.

From his side window, Wilson saw the St. Elmo's fire fade into view just ahead of the wing, plumes of flame shooting from the rear of the shuddering turbines.

Jesus! Wilson rubbed in face in disbelief, confounded by the demonstration. Instinctively, he flipped on the landing lights as the screaming of the jets continued to crescendo: they were back in the uncanny "fog," only this time it seemed more like a blizzard, reminding him of descriptions he had read of nuclear winter. Transfixed, he was barely cognizant that the motors had failed and the plane was gliding once more.

"Beaumont! *Back* to 10,000 feet! Tate, get those engines on! Prepare to dump fuel!"

"Working on it, Captain!" Tate shouted, frantically manipulating the board; Flight Engineer Beaumont was stoic as he turned once more to the task of physically steering the airliner. Wilson refocused his attention on the wing nearest him.

Then he saw it again: a dimming and brightening of the cerulean glow outside. He felt his gut start to loosen.

What in the hell—

At that instant, the grotesque, hunched little creature jumped in front of his portal, its ornately horned face gnashing at him through the half-inch of Lexan as it clung to the skin of the plane.

Time glaciated for Wilson as he considered the gargoyle staring back at him, thirty years of repression burrowing out of his tautly strung psyche. Slowly, the agitated hobgoblin raised its clawed, feathered fist, which had the peacock iridescence of anodized titanium. In this rain-slicked, zygodactyl appendage—weakly glowing from a lacy network of blue-green bioluminescent veins—the horrorstruck skipper noticed that it was holding a mess of tubing and electrical wires, thrashing like tentacles in a hurricane. Ancient and intelligent, the bulbous, rheumy eyes—phosphorescent purple irises pinning crazily—were alive with a dark inner malevolence. The demented rictus etched on the lipless, scaly face appeared to be mocking Wilson. As he locked his stare with—*it*—the captain felt his soul evaporate, like liquid nitrogen sublimating into vapor. The old pilot shrieked, his own reflection merging with the waxen visage of the beast outside, his mind collapsing into a jelly of fear.

"Jesus! It—it's back!" he stammered, abruptly grabbing the controls again in an adrenalized rush of panic, sending the plane into another power dive. On the opposite side of the cockpit door, he was vaguely aware of the passengers screaming in terror as he tried to dislodge the horrid figure off the jumbo jet.

"Dear God!" Tate shouted. "Wilson's lost his mind! He's going to kill us!"

As Wilson stared in revulsion, the animal's black, stubby tongue moistened multiple rows of sharp teeth, regarding the stunned pilot with an almost avian curiosity. The prehistoric-looking atrocity glanced mischievously back at its destructive handiwork—the ruined, sparking junk of Engine Two—before pitching its misshapen head back, responding to Wilson's screams with a series of loud, throaty caws. Displaying a strip of small horns through the dimly fluorescing plumage across its chest, the animal postured menacingly at the captain before smashing its fist into the thin Plexiglas window, its billowing parchment wings flexing in the ferocious winds.

"Wilson! Stop!" was all Flight Engineer Beaumont could manage, plastered to his seat by the same titanic gravitational forces that threatened to tear the airplane apart. During the ensuing battle between Captain Wilson and Beaumont for control of the plunging 747, Navigator Tate desperately attempted to restart the engines once again, eyes streaming tears.

At 8,000 feet, Engine One hacked to life, followed in short order by the other two on the opposite wing. The only sounds were the drone of the motors, the howl of the wind, and the crackle of the revived radio.

"Wilson! Let me have the controls!" Beaumont screamed.

Fighting the flight engineer for control, Wilson glanced out of his window, as though doing it quickly enough would prevent him from seeing what he feared most. *It* was not there; he let his breath out, unaware that he had been holding it. His arms were heavy, numb as he continued to push the control stick down; his lungs ached; sweat matted his hair. The smell in the room was stuffy, thick with fear.

"Sydney!" the hysterical Lt. Tate croaked. "This is Flight 3017: request emergency landing, over!"

After an agonizing pause: "Roger that 3017; thought we lost you . . ."

The engines screeched as the plane continued to gather speed in its near vertical trajectory, the altimeter unwinding at an astonishing rate.

"Wilson! Let up!"

Captain Wilson realized that he was shaking—actually he was *being* shaken. Sound gradually returned to his consciousness. Fluttering his eyelids, he looked to the window: all he saw was the oddly mingled reflection of his and Beaumont's terrified faces, mouths contorted in anguish, multiple eyes blazing.

"Wilson! Wilson, let up dammit!" Beaumont yelled. *"Let me have the controls before you put us in the water!"*

Still looking out of the window, Wilson could have sworn he saw the twisted silhouette of the beast flit by a final time. His brain was unhinging, disarticulated by stress as he continued to push the controls forward. Wrenching his eyes from the portal, Captain Wilson half expected the beast to jump right into the cockpit at any instant.

"*Christ!* Give me the stick, Wilson!"

Staring mutely at the frenetic Beaumont, who seemed to be shouting at him from a long, long way away, the captain was unable to comprehend what was being said: his thoughts were suddenly elsewhere, telescoping away from the commotion of Beaumont, Tate, the passengers, the diving plane, the thing outside . . .

Once on the ground, the plane had to be towed to the gate; the windshield was completely crazed by volcanic pumice and was unable to be maneuvered otherwise. Wan passengers—some bandaged—hastily exited the airplane, weeping at the prospect of solid ground. The cabin crew was silent.

"Hell of a ride, Captain; glad we were so near to Sydney when full power returned. A volcano! Hard to believe we were coasting for more than two hours because of an ash cloud!" Beaumont exclaimed, his deep-set eyes flashing. "Last time I heard of that was in '82, I think; thank God you remembered what to do. Damn good landing without visuals; instruments, only at night—now that's some real flying. Looks like it must've taken ten years off old Tate, though . . . Me, too, I have to say!"

Captain Wilson smiled quickly; he was still troubled by what had—or had not—*happened.* Did I really imagine all—that? The little creature? The horrible scene? My therapist said that I might have disturbing flashbacks in extreme situations, but . . . but it was so . . . so *real* . . .

"I'm sure," Wilson began, "that there will be a full investigation, so get ready. Once NTSB, FAA, and Boeing hit the ground, they'll collect all the black box data and voice recordings for analysis." He paused, then added: "I have to admit that I hadn't remembered that incident from 1982—or how to cope with it—till just now. I panicked—the circumstances reminded me of something else . . . something awful from a long time ago . . ."

Tate was already on the tarmac, watching his fellow crewmen deplane; he was standing under the smoldering Number Two turbine, his face drained and slack. "Captain Wilson," he said, pointing at the engine manifold, "Look . . ."

Wilson and Beaumont approached the disheveled navigator, slowly following the line of his arm into the gloomy, humid air. Wilson dreaded what he would see, knowing intuitively what his co-pilot had discovered.

"Claw marks!" Wilson screamed. "Feathers! Just like before!"

Captain Wilson—by now quite insane—was still screaming as he drove the massive plane into the dark, hungry and abiding ocean.

Author's Note

This was originally written for an anthology in tribute to Richard Matheson titled *He Is Legend* (the stories in it use his works as jumping-off points for a continuation of his ideas and/or characters). Unfortunately, the editor wrote that it was closed to new writers, so I never sent it in, and it left me with my own version of what happened after "Nightmare at 20,000 Feet."

Long story short, as I was making my Charles Beaumont documentary, I was finally able to get a copy to Richard Matheson, and, during a visit there with William F. Nolan, he said: "I liked [your story] a lot; it was well-written, and you took the character to a place that I never would have imagined."

How cool is that?!

Milton's Children

To me shall be the glory sole among
The infernal powers, in one day to have marred
What He, Almighty styled, six nights and days
Continued making; and who knows how long
Before had been contriving?
—John Milton, *Paradise Lost* 9.135–39

1.

"Why are you a vegetarian, Carter?"

Adam Carter, the resident biologist, lifted his gaze from his plate to Chris Faust, the helicopter pilot. The question was a common inquiry around mealtime, but Faust—as usual—had an edge of contempt in his voice.

"I mean, humans are naturally omnivorous; hell, *I* think they're natural carnivores! I sure know I am. I mean, vegetarianism seems—*wrong* somehow." The rugged aviator shifted in his seat, glancing at Adam beneath heavy eyebrows as he tortured a straw over a dirty tray. He appeared to relish any opportunity to antagonize people who held beliefs differing from his. "How do you know that plants don't feel pain? I've read that they're in tune with their surroundings—turning to the light, stimulated by music . . ." Faust allowed his sentence to linger. The ship swayed in the quiet.

Adam listened with irritated patience: *Same old attitudes, same old prejudices. Meat-eaters always have a rationale for their casual barbarism.*

There were a million reasons for Adam's choice to be vegetarian, even vegan—his preference—at times. It was a noisome burden to explain and be put into a defensive posture over a simple matter like one's choice of—*anything,* so long as it was not harming anyone; regardless, he had learned long ago to accept what is, rather than what one *wished* was the case.

"The main consideration," Adam began, clearing his throat, "is ethical. I feel that it's wrong to take another's life, except in defense of your own. I believe that animals are feeling, compassionate individuals with memories, families, consciousness. They nurture their offspring, protect them from harm, teach them, love them. They have emotions, desires, hopes, just as we do; who are we to deny these attributes? Why is 'anthropomorphism'—seen as a prop by ruthless Cartesians—considered a weakness, when the observations that it acknowledges are true?" Carter feigned a smile, gritting his teeth behind tightened lips.

Taking a sip of tea, he continued: "As to your question: Why am I a vegetarian? Lots of reasons; really too many to get into. I won't bore you with any facts about humans having weak jaw muscles, or teeth made for rendering plants—not tearing flesh—or that our intestines are so long so that we can digest fiber." Adam paused, considering his words carefully. "Instead, let's address mistaken notions, such as the one about plants—plants don't possess a central nervous system. They don't experience things like pain; they have evolved elaborate systems to attract animals *to be* ingested, so that the creatures will spread their seeds in scat, and so on. Since trees and plants are immobile, they rely on other means—insects, the wind, being consumed—to propagate, fertilize and reproduce."

Adam had Faust's complete attention by now; the airman was sneering unconsciously—his scarred face seemingly amused by the response he had elicited—as the biologist continued: "Also, why eat something—*someone*—when there are other alternatives that don't involve death, pain, and violence? In India, the practice of avoiding undue harm is called *ahimsa* by the Hindus; I try to follow that example, and Buddha's."

Faust snorted in disgust, shaking his head.

"For Christ's sake, Carter, they're not *people!* I mean, animals are here for us to take advantage of; they're *inferior* to humans. God ordained that *we'd* have free will, not them. In fact, the Bible says that we hold dominion over the land and the sea, to do with as we see fit." The lanky pilot leaned menacingly over the table, holding the smaller man's gaze as he made his point: "They have no culture, no society, no language. Shit, they're just—dumb animals! *We're* the top of the food chain. *We* build the cities, *we* have religion, *we* understand history, *we* comprehend the passage of time—all that stuff. Besides, if *we* didn't cull the populations, they'd just breed out of control." Faust leaned back in his chair, folding muscular arms over his chest. "I guess you think that they ought to have 'rights,' too, huh, Carter?" The flyer laughed, leveling a squinty stare at the other man. "Like what? Voting? Assembly? Free speech?"

Adam stared at Faust, trying to remain calm. "Faust, why are you such a jock *dick?*"

The aviator quit laughing, crewcut bristling as his eyes narrowed, his face hardened.

Carter: "I mean, really, why do you bother talking to me? OK, sure, sometimes the fucking hero dies at the end of the movie, too. So should we just take all our marbles and go home to pout? Does that mean we just *give up* trying to improve the world, whether by stopping global warming, or eradicating disease, or whatever is important to everybody? Of course not. You're making all these illusory correlations, too." Carter leaned forward, staring at the other man. "Besides, Faust, you don't give a *shit* what I think—you just get off on screwing with people. Yeah, sue me—I *do* think they deserve rights, like the human rights just granted to the Great Apes in Europe. And, yes—I feel we should extend that to *all* creatures. *So what?* I'm not fucking with *you* about it. I'm not interrupting *your* dinner, am I? No societies? What about bee hives, ant colonies, wolf packs, beaver dams, or orca pods? No language? How do you explain cetacean vocalizations, like dolphins and whales? Or the bats who share their food during lean times?"

Faust huffed in annoyance. "You're such a little pinhead, Carter, you know that? All that is a bunch of BS, and I can prove it—"

"You asked! So let me talk." Adam stared at the pilot. Faust kicked a chair, then leaned back once again. "Fine, fuck it. Say your piece."

Carter, more restrained: "All right, then. How about chameleons and cuttlefish, with their visual communication? There's other stuff, too. I mean, prairie voles and certain birds are monogamous for life, which is more than most people can manage. And what about psittacines like Alex the African Grey Parrot, who learn *our* vocabulary, which is something that ravens, crows, and other corvids can do, also. I mean, *we* sure as hell can't understand *them,* so who's really smarter here?"

Adam let the question sink in, noticing that the ship was pitching a little more than before, or perhaps he was just more aware of it in his agitated state of mind. He continued: "Combine that with the fact that they can create and use tools, and humans had better watch out! Shit, if the birds team up with the ants—the only other beings that really terraform the Earth and have wars—they'll take the planet back! Obviously, elephants have culture, customs, burial rituals, and long memories. Do they have religion? Who can say? Doesn't seem to have helped *us* much. The Crusades, *jihad,* the Inquisition, terrorism—"

"Yeah? Well, *fuck* those towelheads! They just want to destroy our way of life. They *hate* it that we have freedom! They're just a bunch of cowardly, explosive vest-wearing sand nig—" Faust caught himself, eyes wide, face turning red as he stared at Adam. The space between the two men was charged; they were so focused on each other they did not notice Murphy enter the mess hall.

"Nice attitude. And *you're* 'protecting America'?" Adam replied, shaking his head. "I know—we just need more 'personal responsibility,' right? Just 'pull ourselves up by our bootstraps,' huh? Us against them . . ."

"Damn right! This is America, not . . . *France* or the fucking Soviet Union, asshole."

"Yeah, I get that. I was born here too, but I don't have to be a brainwashed *über*-patriot to love my family, or to expect more from my country."

In the silence that followed both men watched one another, wary.

Adam, calmer now: "Anyway, Faust, if you're 'the top of the food chain,' why do you pick on defenseless, domesticated vegan creatures like cows and sheep for sustenance? Why don't you just go out into the wild without weapons, wrestle a bear or lion, and eat it? That would be fair . . . hand-to-fin with a shark! In addition, why have others kill and clean your food for you? *Real* carnivores—the big cats and raptors—eat their food *raw.* Humans can't—blood is an emetic. It makes you vomit. Cut open an orange, then cut open a dog . . . which one looks like better eatin'? While we're at it, why prohibit eating pets? Or, for that matter, forbid eating mentally retarded humans? Or old folks . . . what good are people over sixty? Maybe we should harvest kids, or the poor, like Jonathan Swift suggested in *A Modest Proposal.* I mean, it's just *meat,* right? Just gristle and muscle on the bone. . . ." Adam found himself getting upset again. "People like you eat animals that are more intelligent and have more to offer than a lot of humans *every day.* Your 'Might Makes Right' idiocy is so egocentric and speciesist it makes me sick."

Faust appeared to be in a state of shock: he looked at Adam with his mouth open, aghast. "Okay, Carter, Jesus . . . Can't take a little teasing—"

"You pester me about this almost daily, Faust! If you aren't making some snide comment, you're talking shit behind my back, rolling your eyes, all that. *You're the one that can't deal, not me!* As to the rest of your nonsense, here you go: Animals don't need our permission—after all, *we're* animals—to live their lives. And, since you're a believer, what about 'Thou Shalt Not Kill'? I don't recall any qualifiers. I mean, murder is murder. Whether it's in Treblinka or Holocaust by extension in a factory farm . . . or enslaving the Africans, the Chinese, whatever . . . or destroying the poor buffalo, and therefore the fragile Native American ecosystem . . . I suppose some advanced human societies—again Hindu cosmic theory, Buddhist tolerance, and Native American power-sharing spring to mind—have coexisted peacefully with the other inhabitants of our tiny home, but they're the exception."

Faust was looking away, shaking his head; Adam became irritated at the apparent dismissal. "We're all so out of touch with nature that we forget this simple truth: Many of these strains of DNA have existed on this little planet we all share for hundreds of thousands, even *millions* of years! How'd they keep from overpopulating before we showed up? Not to mention that nary a single disease has ever been cured through vivisectional torture or animal testing; in some cases it has *caused* issues in people that the lab animals never manifested." Faust was flexing his jaw muscles, eyes darkening. Carter pressed on: "Got you there, didn't I? So much for Hippocrates' credo of 'First, do no harm,' huh? How about the stark reality that murdered dogs and cats—*discarded pets, mind you*—are used in rendered food for pigs, cows, and chickens that people later ingest; or that some 'cultures' eat horses, insects, snails, and live reptiles as delicacies; or that more than *ten billion animals*—mostly pigs and fowl—are eaten for food *just in the United States every year?*"

Adam was glaring intensely at Faust; his anger seemed to have taken them both by surprise. They were breathing hard, Adam nearly leaping from his chair with each thrust of his finger as he made his points. Murphy was loitering at the small cafeteria spread with her back turned, absurdly trying not to listen to the loud verbal antics in the small room.

Carter continued, oblivious to anything else: "How about this—I'll bet you didn't know that octopi have personalities, or that crustaceans like lobsters can live more than *a hundred and thirty years,* or that the oceans could be completely *devoid* of edible fish by 2050 due to over-fishing, causing the entire planetary ecosphere to collapse like a bubble! Add that to pollution, human-caused global warming, destruction of the rain forest to promulgate this evil, wasteful enterprise of killing for consumption, run-off from factory farms, overuse of antibiotics and chemicals in animal agriculture, petty human squabbles over turf, like Israel and Gaza, and you get a toxified environment—one that's already showing signs of turning on us—we who have *wildly* overpopulated . . . *Give me a break!* What about the *fact* that human-induced industrial cannibalism is the root cause of BSE—Mad Cow Disease? I mean, where does 'evil' begin to enter into the picture, Faust? With a deity like that on your side, who *needs* Satan? So you think your so-called 'God' approves of all that? Well, if He does, I don't approve of *Him, It,* whatever, or the way 'He' lets folks die in 'His' hallowed name. Some God that would turn a blind eye to rape, or incest, or racism, or gay-bashing, or child abuse, or 9/11—"

Finally, Chris Faust had had enough: he jumped from his seat.

"Shut up, faggot! You don't know *what* you're talking about, you fucking Marxism-loving fascist! You and your nanny-state horseshit stay outta my face, got it?" He stormed from the tiny commissary, slamming the door.

Adam felt his heart racing in the sudden quiet. *Marxism-loving fascist, eh? Guess that's a step* down *from being the socialist liberal of last week.* Although angry, he was grateful for the silence, the modest roll of the ship. He closed his eyes and focused on his heartbeat, regaining composure through circular breathing. *That was overdue, I guess . . .* He opened his eyes, allowing his gaze to drift from the door to his tray: garden salad, veggie burger, fries, and tea. He had lost his appetite:

Faust had that effect on him. The first time that they met—at the Oceanographic Institute of San Diego, several months after the pilot's return from service in Iraq, and only three years past 9/11—Carter had sensed something was not quite as it should be.

Adam had been suggested by one of his old professors, now working at the Institute, to be the biologist for this routine Antarctic trip. By the time Adam was vetted and approved, the moody Faust was already on board as the helicopter pilot; his previous military experience with the 82nd Airborne Division—especially his turn as an injured and decorated veteran of the Fallujah campaigns in the Iraq War—was a huge asset in the harsh conditions they were expecting. Arctic and Antarctic settings are surprisingly similar to the desert.

Everything was fine for the first few weeks. As the crew got to know one another, Adam admitted that he had been just as confused as everyone else in the haunting aftermath of September 2001. In fact, while interning in Washington, D.C., he had been a survivor of the terrible events of that national tragedy himself as he visited some colleagues working in the Pentagon.

Problems only surfaced once Faust learned that Adam's paternal uncle was the liberal Senator Jacobson from Illinois—an ardent opponent of the U.S.-led Iraq Invasion from the beginning. The turn of public opinion against the whole débâcle, compounded by the economic disasters that followed and loss of faith in the President, had further eroded the relationship between the two men as the assignment wore on; their superficial differences merely amplified their disparate sociopolitical, religious, and personal beliefs.

The rest of the team—Captain Roland, an old salt from Nantucket; Navigator Nathan Isherwood; Seismologist Murphy; Bill Dyer, the medic; Oceanography doctoral candidate Darrell Mahar; Dr. Crowe, the Head of Geology for the Institute; and First Mate Schwarz—all got along well with one another, and with Adam. Although he found himself in agreement with his uncle, they had never been close: like most modern families, his had fractured while he was very young. His mother made sure that his father—a radical Native American activist from the 1970s AIM project—and the rest of his paternal family had very limited contact with him as a boy.

Faust, though a skilled pilot, proved to be a bit of an uptight loner and remained aloof, especially after they set sail. The crew tried to include him in activities, but he resisted, preferring to remain alone in his cabin. After awhile he opened up, but it was only in a negative way, such as picking arguments and complaining. The rift between Faust and Adam had grown over time: The pilot seemed to find contentment by focusing his latent hostility and rage on Adam's more open-minded perspectives. Their split now appeared insurmountable. The long sea voyage to Antarctica, followed by ten months of close-quarters living at McMurdo Station and the current return trip aboard the research vessel *Terra Australis Incognita,* had not helped the situation.

"Faust after you again?"

Adam looked up, startled out of his thoughts. "What?"

"Faust. Is he giving you a hard time again?" It was Murphy, the only female on the ship. *Being in the company of eight boisterous guys all the time was probably a drag,* Adam thought. *Or not . . .*

She gestured with her tray: "Mind if I join you?"

"Of course," Adam replied. Murphy sat down.

"Yeah—that guy *hates* me," he said. "Does he give you shit about being vegetarian? He's gotten to where he won't shut up about it with me. At least he dropped the Second Amendment hoo-hah; I was sick of arguing about why I think we need to ban assault rifles for nonmilitary uses." Adam started to eat at last, curious about Murphy's response.

She smiled, shyly pushing strawberry-blond strands of hair behind her ear. "He never talks to me, thank God! I sort of couldn't *help* but overhear you two as I was grabbing my salad." She took a sip of water, then added: "For whatever its worth, I agree with you. I mean about the animals. The guns, too—I hate them."

Both of them smiled. Adam had to admit that Julia Murphy was attractive: gamine features, nice figure, highly intelligent. Sometimes he got the vibe that she thought the same about him, though nothing had come of it so far. He studied her as she ate, then:

"Cool. You know, I don't have any issue with Faust, really. I appreciate his service, and his expertise. We have some similarities, actually. I've had lots of friends that I don't agree with—that doesn't make them bad people . . . or me, for that matter. It's just . . . there's something that bugs him about *me;* then I get pissed when he won't let it go, or keeps poking at me. After that, it just all goes to hell. Maybe he's upset about something completely unrelated. I'd like to know. I'd at least like us to get along, even if we're never buddies." He took another bite. "Enough of that, though—how are you? Excited about tomorrow?"

Captain Roland had informed the crew that they were dropping anchor in the morning for an unscheduled stop: a small cluster of uncharted islands.

Isherwood had seen the tiny patches of land on the radar sweep; strange summer storms originating from the eastern Antarctic coast had forced the ship to take an unusual itinerary that was well off-course from the heavily traveled Southern Hemisphere trade routes as they navigated back to the Institute from McMurdo.

An interesting aspect of this miniature island chain was how close it was to the actual Antarctic land mass: How it could have remained unseen and unexplored—even with satellite imaging—in the modern age was mysterious, not to mention compelling. As the process of global warming continued and temperatures climbed, more and more ice floes were retreating from the Antarctic waterways, uncovering new routes and currents; even so, this was the first time that any actual land had been discovered.

The islands were situated approximately 4600 nautical miles north of McMurdo, at roughly 50° S., 126°43' W. This was in the ice-choked boundary between the extreme South Pacific Ocean and the Amundsen Sea, close to the frozen blue and white wastes of the remote and unclaimed Marie Byrd Land, near the approximate vicinity of the 'Bloop' signal. Being so near the Pacific pole of inaccessibility, the area's only remarkable features—save for a few rare species of exceptionally hardy fish, seals, and whales—were frequent parhelia or 'sun dogs' and dense, glittering sea-level clear-sky precipitation, referred to informally by meteorologists as 'diamond dust.' It was an epic stretch of desolation worthy of Mary Shelley's creation: Completely uninhabited, the stark beauty of the place was engulfed by starry, brutal night for over half the year, interrupted from time to time by the haunting electromagnetic glow of the *Aurora Australis*—the Southern Lights. It was the coldest, most isolated place on the planet.

Prior to Isherwood's discovery of this modest archipelago, the nearest landing point in this ice-entombed hell was the heavily glaciated, barren volcanic island of Peter I in the Bellingshausen Sea, more than a thousand nautical miles southeast. These islands were potentially the find of a lifetime. Just a few months previous, another group of explorers had discovered some amazing and unique life forms over a mile deep in the total darkness—and almost incomprehensible water pressure exceeding 90 atmospheres—near the Ross Ice Shelf. Among their unexpected findings: enormous, unknown sea spiders and other 'bug'-like creatures, transparent and graceful; huge, whipping hydrothermal vent worms, stationed like sentinels near cracks in the seabed, which spewed out sulfur-rich, super-heated seawater; vast meadows of bizarre sea lilies, patrolled by colossal sea snails; a rare species of gargantuan, bioluminescent immortal jellyfish; massive, undocumented starfish. Even stranger were the weird, never-before-seen plankton-consuming tunicates—resembling slender, yard-tall rods of glass covering the ocean floor like fields of crystalline poppies. The alien creatures all exhibited symptoms of rampant gigantism—a poorly understood phenomenon in which animals under certain conditions grow unusually large.

The purpose of the *Terra Australis Incognita* mission had been more routine: Drop supplies at McMurdo, collect a few core samples of the ice, do scheduled seismic probe inspections, perform some basic research related to man-made climatological change, return.

The trip came to an unspectacular end, completely according to plan; the only wrinkles had been the sudden storms, and confirmation from the resident specialists at McMurdo of the size of the subglacial Gamburtsev Mountains—the enormous "Ghostly Alps" buried under miles of ice in the heart of the continent. They were indeed a giant, mysterious chain, with huge peaks rivaling the mountain ranges in the Pacific Northwest of the United States. There was even speculation of a subcontinental volcano, as the range was strangely situated near the center of the Antarctic land mass, rather than at the tectonic edges, as would be expected. Also unusual was the jaggedness of the mountains and valleys, with some peaks approaching 10,000 feet. This suggested newer land creation with very little erosion.

Now, things were getting even more interesting. The scientists from the other excursions had not been to—indeed, not even *known* about—any of the isles that they were heading for; in fact, it was entirely possible that no one in human history had set foot on these patches of earth.

"Yeah," Murphy said. "I've got to say I'm pretty excited about it." She toyed with her salad, thinking. "What if we find something new? That would be crazy!" She took another sip of water. "It would be incredible just to take some seismic readings and set a few probes up. There might even be some meteorites, or something. I mean, I doubt that there's a lot for *you* to do, but for me and Dr. Crowe a big rock can be awfully fascinating!"

Adam laughed. "You'd be surprised; Darrell will be pleased to take water samples, and I have a feeling there's *some*thing there . . . maybe moss, or a few fossils." He smiled at her. "You never know."

2.

My God—*What's going on here?"*

Even though they had not made the shore yet, the crew could see that something beyond belief was about to unfold.

What in the hell is this place? Adam thought, astonished. *What if we find evidence of civilization? Could this be 'Atlantis'? Or maybe it's something else . . . hopefully not* At the Mountains of Madness, *or Böcklin's 'Isle of the Dead' . . .*

" . . . issed that. What is it again, Carter? Over."

Broken from his trance by the crackle of the walkie-talkie, Adam responded: "Yeah—uh, this is going to sound strange, but it looks like . . ." he paused, mentally searching for the right description.

"What? *What is it, Carter?"*

Adam could tell through the static that Navigator Isherwood was anxious; they had grown to be good friends over the course of the trip. Isherwood, Faust, and Peter Schwarz, the first mate, had to stay onboard the ship while the rest of them went ashore.

Carter at last found the words: "It's—it's like—*Eden,* or something . . . an Antarctic Eden."

The line crackled. "Come again, Carter? Over."

"Carter! *Are you seeing this?*" Murphy yelled over her shoulder from the first Zodiac. Captain Roland, Murphy, and Dr. Crowe were leading the expedition, while Adam, Mahar, and Dyer, the medic, followed in the second raft. The low hum of the motors in the icy saltwater nearly erased her voice from the freezing air. The skies were heavy and dark, the wind stiff coming from the sea as they approached the landing site. Adam could see a very animated Dr. Crowe clutching at a bewildered-looking Capt. Roland, pointing to the beach. The salt spray from the boat ahead stung his eyes, but Adam barely noticed; the scene in front of them was too fantastic.

"Are you fucking filming this, Dyer?" Mahar screamed, dipping his sample glasses into the black ocean.

"I've got it, I've got it! Jesus! I—I've never seen anything like this!"

"Carter! Over!" It was Isherwood again.

"Yeah . . . I—I'll get to you in a second, Nathan, over."

Through the thick haze cloaking the islands, gigantic forms took shape. Huge rocks materialized, spiraling into the sky, the sheer drop of their cliffs like stony, rough-hewn skyscrapers. Massive waterfalls cascaded the thousands of feet down into lush forest below. Rhododendrons, Devil's Tongue, and hibiscuses the size of dinner plates blew in the wind. As the ice retreated, the beach was flooded, and hidden peaks had become exposed, like ancient geolithic skeletons.

Then, up high, near a cave, Carter saw a black, birdlike creature, the size of a Volkswagen.

"Holy shit . . ."

The chop was getting heavier as they closed in on the shore. For a moment, the sky darkened noticeably, and Carter looked up: it was the shadow of a flock of the giant birds, blotting out the cloud-filtered light as they passed overhead. The flock paid no attention to the landing party, seemingly intent on joining the other creatures high atop the cliff. Faintly over the boats and surf, Adam could hear their calls. If he squinted, he could just make out some details: odd orange rings around the eyes, iridescent feathers, large feet.

"This is a new species. My God!—it might even be a new *kingdom!* A race of humongous avians!" Carter's hand smacked his forehead like a wild-eyed character in a silent film.

Suddenly, the boats made landing. The scientists stumbled from the Zodiacs, Dyer nearly falling into the water as he continued videotaping.

This must have been the way Darwin felt when he first saw the flora and fauna of the Galápagos Islands . . .

Mustering on the black sand beach, they pulled the small vessels out of the tide line, saltwater hissing as it lapped the dark ground. Adam breathed the cold air in deeply, exhaling a plume of mist. In the distance, he could just make out the roaring white noise of the falls they had seen from the water. Scanning the horizon, he could see their ship bobbing in the modest swells, just shy of a mile from the islands; sonar had shown that the seabed under the islands sloped up quickly and could have run them aground. The captain decided that it was safer to weigh anchor and take the Zodiacs in. Sunlight was diffuse as it tried to burn through the clouds and fog that mottled the archipelago. Soon, an incredulous Capt. Roland, Dyer, Murphy, Dr. Crowe, and Darrell Mahar joined him. Each looked at the other, amazed.

"I will say," Capt. Roland understated finally, "that this is *most* unusual."

Everyone laughed.

"I believe that you all know the drill. Let's meet back here near the boats in two hours—be careful, we don't know what may live here. This might be Skull Island for all we know."

"Shit, I hope it's not Skull Island, Captain!" Carter joked, and everyone laughed again. "I mean, if King Kong jumps out of the covering, I'll be sure to yell loud enough to alert everyone."

"Hey, don't tease," Murphy countered. "Did you see the *size* of those birds? Who knows what else is here . . ." She gave a nervous glance to Adam, arm motioning toward the jungle interior. "I mean, it looks like prime dinosaur habitat, for God's sake! I feel like we've been dropped into the Mesozoic Era!"

"I agree," Dr. Crowe added, his thick German accent clipping his words. "This is strange place. We *must* be cautious."

"Well," Adam said, trying to ease everyone's concerns, "I know it's . . . it's *weird,* but there *have* been unusual discoveries before. I mean, they just found new species of pink land iguanas, and giant tortoises in the Galápagos. Islands can give rise to all kinds of mutations, especially in warmer climes, and usually to herptiles—reptiles and amphibians—like parthenogenesis, which was previously only documented in insects . . . or increased size, like *Beelzebufo,* known as the Giant Devil Toad, or

Komodo Dragons. The latter were discovered by the West—some accounts maintain, anyway—by a pilot in the early 1900s crash-landing on one of the atolls; he lived to tell the world about a 'land of massive reptiles.' Occurrences of deep-sea and island gigantism in herps is well established; mammals usually present with the *opposite,* due to their precocious food requirements and higher metabolic rate—*insular dwarfism,* hence no King Kong." Adam paused, moving his gaze from one group member to the next. Their expressions were growing more uneasy as he spoke.

Dr. Crowe: "And this . . . this is to make us feel better, *jah,* Herr Carter?" The team burst out in giggles.

Adam chuckled to soften his disposition: "Point taken, Dr. Crowe; but especially in extreme northern and southern latitudes, like here, is where Bergmann's Rule kicks in. Endotherms like mammals and birds will tend to have larger mass and/or surface-to-volume ratios to protect against the intense cold. Think polar bears in the Arctic, for example. Poikilotherms like reptiles would have to be *huge* in these environs to benefit enough from gigantothermy to keep their core temperatures stable."

The tension broken, Adam continued: "So the good news: most likely no gargantuan 'dinosaurs,' as there wouldn't be *near* enough provisions for them. Though there *are* exceptions—there's evidence that some had live birth, like certain modern skinks, for example, and might even have been warm-blooded. The—*other* news: those birds are probably the top predators here, since they are able to fly away and get food, so I doubt there'll be any further surprises."

Murphy stared at him. "So, what does something that big . . . *eat?*"

Adam looked up to the cave, then back at the team. "Well, I'd guess probably fish and marine mammals. Don't worry! Just stick together and stay close to shore . . . you'll be fine."

Capt. Roland spoke again: "We'll have the same teams as in the Zodiacs. Dr. Crowe, Murphy, and I will head for the falls to take readings and set probes; you three hug the coast. Carter, do you have your GPS?"

"Yes, Captain. It's . . . about 0955 by my watch, but it seems to be slow."

"Well then," Capt. Roland checked his timepiece, tapping the face, "this damn thing is off, too. Okay, back here in two hours or thereabouts."

3.

"Nathan, this is Carter, over."

Isherwood looked up from the worn copy of *Penthouse* he was perusing. He leaned over the table to the microphone. "Carter? 'Bout time; you guys've been quiet for awhile. What's up? Over."

The line crackled, then fell silent. Finally: "You haven't heard from Capt. Roland or Juli—I mean, Murphy? Anybody? Over."

Nathan felt a twinge as he detected the concern in his friend's voice. He depressed the button on the microphone: "Negative. Radio blackout since we last talked. What's the deal? Over."

Silence.

"Carter?"

Nothing.

"Carter? Can you hear—"

"Sorry . . . uh, the deal is we landed, and the place is—is really interesting. Ran into a *lot* of new species—amazing plants, flowers; bizarre mega-insects—all new and undocumented, from what I can tell. Even more—and weirder—stuff than I saw on Ball's Pyramid near Australia; some of them are like the 'Tree Lobster' stick insects, but *larger.* These are more similar to the giant insect fossils from the late Carboniferous and early Permian periods. These dragonfly-looking bugs with a wingspan of at least twenty-eight inches. And they are feeding on other bizarre insects, almost as though they're occupying a bird niche of speciation. I've been sketching, taking photos and samples like crazy; Dyer's been filming it all. It's—*astounding;* we've also seen all *types* of mysterious lizards, amphibians, and birds—"

Isherwood: "Incredible! I can't wait to see it!"

"Yeah," Carter replied over the scratchy line, "well, that's not all; these animals are—are *colossi,* just like the insects. Again, apparently all new species . . . or maybe they're ancient species that have been in some kind of torpor, like a form of hibernation; now, maybe they're heating up . . . a few of the lizards appear to be warm-blooded endotherms, like mammals. Not sure of the predation paradigm. But before we get too much further, we've got a problem."

"What?" Isherwood's throat tightened in the deck cabin. He looked out of the front window; the ship was bobbing more as night fell. The fog shrouding the archipelago was getting thicker.

"We split up—me, Dyer, and Darrell went one way, and the rest went the other, more into the center of the island. The captain said to reconvene by the boats in two hours—and that was at least three and a half hours ago, I would estimate. We're here, but there's no sign of them. They should be here by now. It's cold and getting dark fast. My GPS doesn't get a signal! I don't know what's wrong with it, but theirs might not work either. They went into the forest—it's very dense vegetation even without all the mist. We stayed on the beach, so we just retraced our tracks."

Nathan understood immediately. His head began to ache.

"Roger that, Carter. Hold on."

4.

"Well, what did Isherwood say?" Dyer asked. He was returning from behind a large rock where he had relieved himself. Mahar and Carter looked up from the campfire.

"Nothing, yet: we'll probably stay the night, then bring Faust out in the morning, once the fog lifts a bit. It's getting too dark to head out."

"I agree," Mahar said. "Besides, we could send up flares, keep the fire going and keep trying to raise them on the walkie-talkie." Carter nodded in agreement, staring out into the darkness, toward where he knew the ship was anchored.

"They're okay, I'm sure . . . just a little disoriented. Let's do what Darrell suggested," Carter said. He looked over to Dyer. The medic raised a mug of hot tea to his lips, cupping gloved hands around it to keep warm. Their parkas were scant protection against the occasional gust from the sea.

Carter hefted the flare gun, shooting it into the meteorite-streaked Milky Way canopy overhead, starkly beautiful in the clear patches worn into the cold fog. The scarlet arc of phosphorous created a trail of brilliant light over the men and their bonfire. Hanging in the air, the beacon shimmered like a lost star.

"Strange. When we got here, I thought it was like Eden, like *The Lost World,* or *Paradise Regained.* A confirmation of belief, a redemption. Now . . ." Adam's voice was swallowed by the breakers. The night before, on the ship, he had fitfully dreamt of *Archaeopteryx,* never suspecting that less than twenty-four hours later he would behold perhaps that fabled being's modern relations in the cave just above their tiny camp. The millions of years of prehistory shrouding dinosaurs, birds, reptiles, and amphibians, fish, even protozoa, viruses, and bacteria—all the primates' distant relatives—was acknowledged, but hardly well-understood in context.

Time, it seemed, was less a stream than a lake. Sometimes, dredging the lake yielded mighty wrecks to science; oftentimes, however, it just brought to the surface more scatological pieces of bygone eras, some of which could be immediately recognized as gold, others as potential diamonds in the rough, but—mostly—a lot of incomprehensible flotsam and jetsam. Now, Adam was really getting a mental grasp concerning the scope of life on Earth. The things that they had witnessed today were like glimpses of an extraterrestrial culture.

This even beats the Ghost Peaks Expedition, when they confirmed the existence of the Gamburtsev Mountain Range buried under four kilometers of ice in the center of the Antarctic landmass . . .

I feel like an archaeologist opening some tomb in an Egyptian pharaoh's pyramid and finding a modern astronaut sitting inside: this place shouldn't be here.

But it is: it's like we've found a whole island of ancient astronauts . . . and they're alive!

Adam could not shake the feeling of utter strangeness—bordering at times on a sense of *déjà vu.* Though he certainly had never been to this place before—he was sure no human had, and no remotely human relative either, as it seemed to be from the Gondwanaland era of prehistory before primates even existed—the disorienting sensation it gave him was confirmation of all his previously held suspicions regarding the cryptic potential, and beauty of, the unknown places in the world. It was awesome, in the truest sense of the word.

And terrifying: real Lovecraft shit . . .

"Carter?" It was Nathan Isherwood crackling over the radio,

nearly inaudible through the chorusing of nocturnal toads and insects coming from the island's interior.

"Nate! Yeah—did you find them? Over."

"Negative; cannot raise them on any channel. Over." The men glanced over the fire at one another. Nightfall only augmented the nerve-wracking situation. The island was home to a profusion of strange smells and sounds, some very pronounced: growls, calls, other things—perhaps geothermal hums or geologic slowdowns.

"Got it. Staying overnight; we'll keep sending up flares and stand watch. Looks like we'll need to have the 'copter out tomorrow, unless we make contact. Over."

After a long pause: "Roger that, Carter."

5.

"No—now I can't raise any of them."

Isherwood was pale, sweat slicking his upper lip. Faust looked at him from under his shaggy black eyebrows. He seemed pensive.

"When was the last time you spoke to anyone?" Faust asked stoically.

"About 10 o'clock last night. Adam signed off then to conserve energy. Maybe the batteries just ran out. He said he would turn the radio back on at 0800 to check in, but that his watch seemed to have stopped. I was here, but there was no contact."

Chris Faust's jaw tightened visibly at the mention of Carter's name. Nathan continued: "I mean, it's almost noon—we need to do something."

Faust nodded in silent agreement.

First Officer Schwarz walked in: "Well?"

"Nothing, sir. I was just briefing Faust, sir."

"Damn." Schwarz frowned. He turned to Faust. "How soon can you be ready to fly?"

The aviator raked his hand through his hair, looking at the deck. "Fifteen minutes, sir."

"Make it ten—there's a storm moving in and we're getting behind schedule. I *knew* this trip was a bad idea."

"Yes, sir. Ten minutes."

"I'm going, sir," Nathan blurted.

Schwarz snapped his attention to Isherwood. "No way; we need *some*one to man the vessel—"

Nathan looked down, frustrated. "With all due respect, sir, Carter is a close friend." He glanced at Faust, who was still staring at the floor. "Really, sir, I would like to go; once we locate the guys on the beach, I'll come back on one of the Zodiacs. The ship will be okay for that short interval; once I'm back, you two can go fetch the rest of them. Please, sir."

The air in the communications den was tense and stuffy. The ship rolled almost imperceptibly.

The first officer regarded his crewmen. "I understand. I didn't realize that you felt so strongly. You both need to be back within an hour: *I'll* stay."

6.

"There!"

Isherwood pointed down, yelling over the beat of the helicopter rotors.

Faust nodded. *"I see it! Let's go in!"*

The chopper touched down on a flat clearing near the extinguished campfire, creating a miniature tornado of black grit. Before the blades had completely stopped, Isherwood was out of the vehicle, running over to the campsite.

"First Officer Schwarz, we seem to have found the beach encampment," Faust intoned into his helmet mic as the engines died. "On the ground and going in for a look, over."

"Roger that, Faust. You two be careful. You've got forty minutes, over."

"Roger, sir. Faust out."

7.

Isherwood was combing over the site as Faust strolled up.

"Jesus, Nate. What the hell happened?"

Isherwood stared at the pilot, the artery in his throat pulsing quickly, eyes wide. His jaw worked, but he made no sound.

The place was a disaster: half-burned driftwood was scattered everywhere, but the worst was the pile of shredded blankets and destroyed rations, all covered in frozen blood. Not just covered: saturated.

At that moment, they heard a terrible sound coming from behind a monolithic crag further down the beach. The tide was starting to come in. Faust unholstered his sidearm. "Get behind me, Nate."

Nathan obliged, face slack and drained of color under his parka hood.

The sound rose again—even more shrilly knifing through the crisp, salty air—spiraling above the hypnotic crest of the waves and the throaty roar of the falls behind them. Faust swallowed hard, the hairs standing on the back of his neck. Then, from the direction of the waterfall, a grating, dense, multitimbral cacophony seemed to respond: first one, then two, then a chorale. The men glanced at the helicopter: it was further away than they had realized, perhaps about thirty yards from the remains of the camp, and another twenty from the huge outcropping just ahead of them.

Faust, an eerie calmness in his voice: "We need to get out of here, Nate."

"No! Not without Carter, Dyer, and Mahar!"

"They're gone, man! Something ain't right here! I had this same feeling in Iraq! Come on!"

"No!" Nathan screamed, running for the megalith in front of them. The keening sounded from behind it again as he approached, and was answered by another frenzied refrain of blood-curdling shrieks near the falls. The sounds were now accompanied by ground-shaking bellows of impossibly baritone sonorities that made Faust's heart palpitate.

"Nate! Fuck! Stop! Don't go over there!" He started after Isherwood. Everything seemed to dim: the sounds all took on a deeper resonance—the falls, the breakers—the world became a blur as the sand and forest smeared together. Even as the cold air blustered across the water—the storm moving in—sweat was pouring over Faust's body under his jacket and flight suit, his pulse throbbing too fast in the middle of his forehead.

Ahead, Isherwood was already scrambling up the massive rock, eyes wild. Faust watched as the other man mounted the summit, then slowly sank to his knees, screaming in horror and holding his head in his hands . . .

8.

"That's all there was?" Schwarz asked, looking at Faust. Isherwood sat at the mess table, alternately chewing ice and rubbing his face. His eyes were still red-rimmed and watery with raw emotion.

Faust took in a sharp breath, images still fresh in his mind. He looked down at the articles on the table, feeling unsteady as the cutter lurched in the swells of the squall: a bloody blanket in a clear plastic bag; a box with samples of skin, feathers, plants, insects; dented and punctured ration tins; a tattered notebook; Carter's digital still camera; Dyer's video camera with three damaged mini-DV tapes; and, most distressing, Carter's ruined ski cap.

"No, we found something else," Faust responded flatly. He looked up at the concerned first officer.

After a long beat: "Well? *What?*" Schwarz was emphatic: he had a crisis to deal with, and no patience for games.

The pilot could not seem to articulate exactly what they saw. His eyes pleaded with Isherwood, who began quietly weeping.

Schwarz stood erect, crossing his arms. "Look, we need to find these people. Before you two print the pictures off the camera and we watch the tapes you need to level with me—*what?*"

"It—it—" was all Faust could stammer.

"It was Carter!" Nathan exclaimed, "We found Carter!"

Schwarz was stunned: "*What?* We need to bring him back! We—"

"No, you don't understand, sir!" Nathan yelled. "We found Carter—but . . . but . . ."

Faust was pale, as though remembering something from a particularly vivid nightmare. His arms trembled as he leaned across the table, shaken. Suddenly he sat on the floor, his legs seeming to have evaporated. "It was just like in Iraq," he said at last, voice small and dark. "We found *Carter*, sir . . . just not *all* of Carter . . ."

9.

Tape #3 (from the video camera):

(Extended montage of the island and its wonders: scenery, plants, insects, amphibians, and reptiles. Finally, approximately fifteen minutes into the tape, the camera slowly pans up a stand of huge trees at the precipice of a small coastal mountain, momentarily losing focus in the changing steam.)

[T00:14:31] Carter (off screen, whispering):
Incredible . . . this place isn't *new;* it's primordial . . .

(Wind grates across microphone; camera zooms unsteadily to inspect a moving black figure in the fog near the top, where the unusual foliage disintegrates into the cloud cover. It is obscured, but appears to be a very large animal.)

Carter (off screen):
What the . . .

(Focus is shifty; the creature appears to be pacing on the cliff top. In one instantaneous flash, it reveals itself: the face is beaked, its turreted eyes surrounded by orange rings, and a dark, pointed, earless head with iridescent skin, like oil-slicked water. The feet are large and thin, its zygodactyl hands ending in outsized claws. The body is both scaly and feathered, the wings membranous, covered in fine down, and seem to adhere to the insides of its arms, like a pterodactyl, or a huge bat. The tail is curled completely against the body, like a sleeping chameleon. It looks directly at the camera, then takes wing, vanishing into the fog. The image grows more pixilated as darkness closes in.)

Carter (off screen):
What in the hell was *that?*

Dyer (off screen):
Carter! Mahar can't raise anybody; come on back, dude.

[T00:16:27] Carter (off screen):
Okay—one sec.

(*Camera lowers, cuts to black.*)

———

(*Mahar, sitting by the fire, grins into the camera.*)

[T00:17:15] Mahar (laughing):
Get that fucking thing out of here, freak!

Dyer (off screen):
You *know* he can't stop himself—he's like William Heirens with a camcorder.

(*Camera swings to Dyer.*)

Carter (off screen, laughing):
Care to state that for the record?

(*All the men laugh. Quiet ensues: the fire—their only illumination—crackles, throwing shadows across their faces; the tide hisses on the beach.*)

———

[T00:20:06] Dyer (an alarmed expression on his face as a prolonged shriek pierces the air in the distance):
So, what the hell is the deal with this place, Carter? Are these things aliens, or dinosaurs, or what?

Carter (off screen):
Good question. I mean, they aren't aliens, I don't think—that's sort of absurd. . . . As for dinosaurs—that's trickier. If so, it's the greatest discovery in human history, 'cause they're a) alive, and b) all unrecorded species. Of course, they could be *totally* unrelated to anything else—dinosaurs, mammals, birds; they might be their own kingdom, phylum, you name it.

Dyer (staring into the blaze):

(*Camera pans between Dyer, the flames, and Mahar.*)

Where do you think the Captain, Murphy, and Dr. Crowe are, Carter?

Carter (off screen):

I—I don't know; it's not like them to be so . . . so—*out.* Maybe one of 'em's hurt . . . (*louder*) We'll find them in the morning. I feel good about it. At least I was able to grab some DNA samples today—a few bugs, some plants, shed skin and feathers. We can just focus on getting everyone back to the ship tomorrow.

Mahar (off screen):

You just want to get down with Murphy, I think! (*laughs*)

Carter (off screen, feigning protest):

Hey! That's *beside* the point! (*laughs*) Anyway, I'm sure they're just holed up on that cliff or something.

Mahar (stoking the fire, thoughtful):

You're probably right. Me and Captain Roland go back about—damn, fifteen years now. (*sitting down, warming his hands*) We've been through a lot of shit together. Started rough, but we came to respect one another, I reckon. I know he taught me this: In life, sometimes it's who you least expect that has your back . . . and those you thought were your friends could be plotting against you. I remember this one time . . . Well, I guess now's not the place for 'ghost stories'!

[T00:23:12] Dyer (leaning forward):

Ghost story: I'm in. You got one?

(*Camera pans between the two men.*)

Mahar (sitting up, eyes intense):

Yeah, I do: and it really happened. We were off the horn of Africa, maybe ten years ago. It was typical University business—checking buoys, NOAA atmospheric stuff; well, *kind* of typical . . . We also delivered supplies and shipped freight to and from remote labs and stations in Madagascar and along the seaboards, from the Skeleton Coast all the way to Egypt. Sometimes we were the only vessel that these scientists had seen from the U.S. in years.

(*Camera focuses on Dyer, who is hanging on every word.*)

Mahar (continued):

Anyway, like Pliny the Elder wrote: *ex Africa semper aliquid novi*—"There is always something new out of Africa," right? I guess they call it the Dark Continent for a reason. . . . So we made our final deliveries to this lab near Somalia, and they were doing some top secret military shit for the U.S. Defense Department. But we had a pick-up also.

Carter (off screen):

Okay, I'll bite: what was it? Green monkeys? Dope? Slaves? (*laughs*)

Mahar (looking up, features grim):

No: it was dead human bodies.

Dyer (surprised):

Weird . . . What was the purpose of having you guys pick them up? (*Long pause.*)

Mahar (wistful):

Official line? To stop an epidemic—Ebola, some such thing as that. The truth? They were doing experiments on the anecdotal origins of mind-control in African voodoo: the bodies had been purposely infected with *Toxoplasma Gondii,* which is a species of parasitic protozoa. (laughs ruefully) But, you know, there's always a freak jonesing for a pharmaceutical grant for this, or a military handout for that. Nutty shit happening all over the world, all the time, and the U.S. is usually never too far away from it. The old military-industrial complex, you know? I read one time that everything we have these days is seven years behind what the military is doing at any given moment.

Whatever: seems these sadist fucking "doctors" had found a way to contaminate people with the parasite through a gas attack. (*looks at the camera*) It was old Nazi technology—they were using African prisoners to try it out. Gave individuals with a life sentence for political dissidence a choice: *"Medical conscription,"* which we'd call *medical experimentation*—even torture—or rotting in jail, with *real* torture; if you survived, they'd let you go, under the condition that you leave the country, and never speak about it to anybody. Same for the guys running the place; it was real Unit 731-type mayhem.

That was the plan, but, like that old *asshole* Donald Rumsfeld pointed out, "There are known knowns. These are things we know that we know. There are known unknowns. That is to say, there are things that we know we don't know. But there are also unknown unknowns. There are things we don't know we don't know." This was clearly a case of "unknown unknowns."

I'll amend old DR, though, with my personal corollary—it seems to me that what's really scary isn't the unknown; what's *really* scary is the shit that's known that you can't do anything about.

Carter (off screen):
Jesus . . . How do *you* know all this, then?

Mahar (brooding):
I'm old school—I'm a Viet vet, and had a Top Secret clearance. Like I said, Captain Roland and I go way back; they told him, then he told me.

Dyer (disturbed):
Man, that is *way* out there—

Mahar (raising hand):
It gets better. The parasite attacks your brain, see. Causes you to lose fear: like you'll rush into a machine-gun nest and sacrifice yourself, rather than run away. It works because *T. Gondii* first needs a host to gestate, then has to complete the lifecycle in another animal, so it hijacks the host's brain and destroys their center for willpower. This compels the initial host to seek out the very opponent that will kill and eat them, so that they will be able to complete the cycle in the intestine of the target, then be passed through *their* system and it starts again.

Well, modify it and insert a few novel genes and you just exploit the control aspect—suicidal soldiers. You can make your enemies present themselves as targets and just pick them off.

Carter (off screen, rapt):
Crazy!

Mahar (meditative):
I know. We were to take the bodies and dump them in the ocean. "Collateral Damage" in military parlance. They didn't want the evidence of all this shit hanging around. (*quietly*) I've seen a lot of things—some good, some bad. Seen many things I never want to forget—the small of a woman's naked back, my nephew's spelling bee win.

But there're some things . . . (*pauses, eyes dark, teary*) There're some things I *can't* get out of my mind; some things leave scars. Sometimes you can see them . . . but mostly not. Mostly not. (*wipes his face*) I'll never forget anything about that trip, especially those poor bastards in the body bags. They told us not to look at 'em, to wear our biohazard gear, as they were still "hot," still infectious.

Carter (off screen, tentative; the mood is decidedly different):
So . . . so what happened? You came home OK. But you looked: was there something wrong? I mean . . . with their appearance?

Dyer (upset):
Look, Bill, you don't have to tell us. I'm so sorry that it still hurts you—

Mahar (snaps head up, smiling through his pain):
I really do appreciate that. (*pause*) But I'd actually like to get this off my chest. (*looks at the camera*) Carter, you asked me if something was wrong with them? (*a grim smile pulls the edges of his mouth*) I'll fucking say.

First off, they discontinued the operation for one reason—none of the "volunteers" lived. But the experiment didn't just kill 'em, oh no. It . . . there were side effects, "unintended consequences," they called it. It *changed* them. Made them stronger, more *violent;* made them do terrible things, too—pull their own tongues out, eat their own fingers off, blind themselves . . . but that wasn't all. Then they attacked the people *running* the operation. Took to them with hand-held road flares, pulled their heads off. . . . And they *ate* some of the staff—ate 'em *alive.* Dismembered, eviscerated—really got into 'em. It was *fucking chaos.*

Dyer (incredulous):
My *God.* . . .

Mahar (shaking head, visibly traumatized):
No shit. Well, it was well in hand by the time our ship arrived for the nasty business we'd been assigned, but it didn't go without incident, let's say. Eventually, yeah, we took all that and dropped it into the ocean. All gone, now; all consigned to the bottom of the sea. But as we were loading everything up for disposal, we had a little accident. *(pauses)*

One of the cadavers—a "volunteer"—fell off the deck; his bag broke open, and as soon as that happened, *he stood up.* Well, I was about to piss my pants when that happened. Fucking guy went *apeshit.* Screaming, carrying on; they looked different, too. Their skin turned yellowy, and their features were all twisted, with these terrible sores all over the place—weeping, crusty sores. . . .

Anyway, this guy was rampaging, and they shot him up with handguns—no effect. He grabbed a friend of mine who was shooting at him, got his gun-hand and just tore it completely *off;* after that, the fucker really started mauling him. Tony. Tony Whitman. He died right there on the dock, before we were finally able to get the situation back under control—

[T00:30:09] (Off camera, there is a sound: a woman's scream. The camera darts to its source: blackness.)

Dyer (alarmed):
What the fuck was *that?*

Mahar (nervous):
Sounded—sounded like *Murphy!*

(Another shriek, closer: camera pans between the nightscape and the startled men, now standing around the campfire. Mahar pulls his firearm from under his layers of clothing, breath trailing away like a ghost.)

Mahar (continued):
Carter, you're the expert: *is that Murphy or—or some animal?*

Carter (off screen):
I don't know! It—it *sounds* like her—

Unknown Female Voice (off screen, presumed Murphy):
Help me! Please!

(Another scream, very close this time: it is shrill, different, with an undertone of guttural harmonics, like a large creature. The ensuing silence is expansive, filled by the crack of burning logs and the cascade of the tide.

Behind the camera, there is a chorus of high-pitched squeals and other noises. The camera whips around to view the menace. Gunshots ring out as Mahar fires at the threat. Carter drops the camera, which falls to the ground, sand from the beach powdering the lens, focus shifting as it records the fire. Mahar, Carter, and Dyer jump in and out of frame as they contend with some unseen hazard. Again, a female scream reverberates in the air.)

Dyer (screaming):
God! It's all around us!

[T00:37:01] (Mahar screams.)

Mahar (choked):
Carter! It's got me! Jesus! Help me! Hel— (voice cuts off suddenly)

Carter (garbled):
[unintelligible] . . . *Dyer!* Wait! [unintelligible]

[T00:41:55] (Gunfire. More terrible animal shrieks. Sounds of struggle off screen.)

Carter (frantic):

Dyer! Oh my God! *What* is *that fucking thing?* [unintelligible] . . . Stop! *Stop! No—st—*

[T00:45:40] (Silence: just the tide and the fire.)

———

"That's it: the scene stays like that for the rest of the tape," Isherwood said, staring at the monitor in First Officer Schwarz's cramped quarters.

"What about the other tapes? The photos?" Schwarz asked, eyes reflecting the serene flicker of the television image. He glanced at Faust: the pilot was visibly shaken.

"Nothing, really. Just documenting the scenery—footage of the island, the beach . . . The pics were blurry. Some lizards, flowers, bugs." Nathan looked up at the first officer as the tape played out.

"Jesus . . ." Schwarz seemed dazed. He looked at Faust again. "We—we have to go back. Christ, we're down *six:* we can't just—just *leave* them—"

"With all due respect, skipper, there's nothing left of them except—except—" Isherwood turned away, overcome with emotion.

Faust responded, voice distant: "He's right, sir. If—if you'd *seen* Carter . . . I know we had our differences, but I didn't hate the guy. I'd never wish that on . . . on . . . what we saw. All that was *left—*" The airman looked down before continuing, softer. "I—I think we should send out a distress call and get the fuck out of here. *Something isn't right.*"

Schwarz slapped his hand on the table, causing Faust and Isherwood to jump. "What kind of talk is that from a decorated war hero? *Just leave?* No *way*, soldier; we go and get them—what*ever* is left. That's the type of people we are."

Isherwood and Faust passed a knowing look.

"We don't know what we're dealing with here, sir. It might get us all . . ."

Schwarz raised his hand to silence Faust: "Then so be it. Isherwood, go ahead and try to raise the Institute again, clue them in. Also, put out a general distress call. Looks like we need support here, though I doubt there's anyone anywhere near us. And, weather permitting, we go back in the morning." Schwarz curled his fist on the tabletop.

"That's an order, gentlemen."

10.

"You're sure this is the place, Faust?" The first officer asked, perplexed.

The aviator was dumbfounded: "Yeah. Same coordinates."

The men had combed the beach for hours; the weather was turning against them as the daylight waned. In breaks through the vapor rolling in off the ocean, they could see the choppy waves battering their vessel offshore. Faust eyed the helicopter, now several hundred yards distant. The clouds went suddenly black, heavy with rain. The fishy smell of the sea was overpowering.

"Isherwood, copy," Faust said into his helmet microphone. Static crackled loudly in his ear.

"G—chu— . . . st?"

"Isherwood! Give me your heading, over."

"I see you—turn around." Faust turned and saw Nathan: a tiny speck moving toward them.

"Roger. See you in a minute—we need to leave soon or I won't feel good about flying out, over."

"Copy that." Nathan seemed resigned to the reality of their plight. "I didn't see *any*thing; it's like they just vanished into—into thin air. Is Schwarz with you? Over."

"Affirmative. See you in a few; out."

Chris Faust looked over at the first officer, who was now the captain. The pilot could see that Schwarz had decided they had to leave. Explaining this entire fiasco to the Institute was going to be a challenge, and it seemed to weigh on him: Schwarz's temper was much shorter than usual. The ship had been delayed too long as it was; the loss of nearly the entire crew was a disaster, only compounded by the fact that they seemed to be in some kind of intense radio interference area. Communication just from the islands to the ship was difficult, much less ship to shore back in the U.S., and none of their homing devices or GPS worked on the islet at all. Even their watches had stopped once they landed, only to start back when they returned to the boat. The last communiqués with the outside world had been almost three days previous: no doubt, by this point, more than a few Institute eyebrows were raised.

Schwarz looked up from his thoughts. "Faust, in Carter's diary, did you see some of the sketches he'd made of the different animals he saw on the island?"

Faust looked at the commanding officer. "Yeah, I saw those. What about them?"

Schwarz looked at him again, his green eyes deep with concern in the fading light; night came early this far south at this time of year. The wind sliced across the desolate beach, frothing the water on the dark sand. Isherwood was getting closer.

"There was some crazy stuff in there," Schwarz continued, sotto voce. "Weird plants; huge, freaky insects; giant frogs . . . and those massive birds. Like some type of flying lizards with iridescent black feathers." The C.O. shuddered, waving at the approaching Isherwood. "The photos were too blurry to make much out, and those—*things*—were so high up on that peak it was hard to gauge size, but Carter had estimated a forty-foot wingspan, tip to tip." Schwarz regarded the pilot. "I mean, as you say, you boys had your differences, but we assembled this crew for one reason—you all knew your shit. When Carter wrote that he'd never seen anything like those—*monsters*—well, you can bet your ass that makes me nervous. And today, how *quiet* it is now . . ."

Faust nodded in tacit agreement. As much as Carter got on his nerves, he had to admit the guy had his act together when it came to biology; maybe they were just too much alike to get along.

Schwarz continued, voice clotted, while Nathan joined them: "How am I going to explain all this? We've *lost* two-thirds—scratch that—we've probably had most of the crew *killed* by something that we haven't even seen. Who *knows* what it is? I mean, were they . . . *eaten* or what?"

Nathan was huffing as he listened to Schwarz's frustration. They were all concerned. The temperature was falling rapidly.

Isherwood: "With respect to all that, sir, I think we should leave. We can't figure out what's happening here; we've had radio silence from Captain Roland's party for over twenty-four hours. We know that Carter's party is either dead or severely injured, and we have no way to assist them. We could send help back, but we're in over our heads here."

Schwarz observed the last of the crew solemnly. The wind was picking up, and drizzle began to pelt them, cold and stinging. The kelp smell of the water was strong in his nose.

"We don't even know where we *are,* Isherwood," Schwarz said, raising his voice over the keening of the gusts blowing in off the water. "I mean, no GPS, our radios barely work locally, not to mention that we've been out of communication since we got here. We can't even use a sextant because of the cloud cover! How are we going to get back, or tell someone else how to get here? Christ, we found this place by accident."

Faust nodded. "Sir, Isherwood's right. We just need to get back, then sort all that out later. Besides, did you read in Carter's notes about those—*birds,* or whatever they are? He seemed to think that they had some kind of pretty sophisticated form of communication . . . *a language.* He felt that they were talking to one another—coordinating attacks and hunting."

A shriek pierced the air, cutting through the building gale. The three men froze with fear. The inhuman wail sounded again, followed by throaty chatters and a refrain of clicking. The sounds were three-dimensional in space, seeming to come from all directions at once—the sky, the water, the land.

"Help!" It was Murphy, her voice strangled.

"Please!" It was Darrell Mahar, his voice hoarse and strange.

"Darrell! Murphy! Where are you?" Before anyone could react, Nathan was running toward the undergrowth, away from the helicopter, his bulky attire causing him to slip in the loose sand.

"Nathan! Stop!" Schwarz screamed, reaching for him, but Isherwood was gone, practically disappearing in the sudden storm as it engulfed the island in gloom.

Faust pushed the first officer in the opposite direction, toward the chopper. The strange clicking echoed again, everywhere at once, yet unseen, like some invisible circle of castanets.

Faust: *"Run!"* He pushed the C.O. once more, both of them half falling in the sand. The rain was pounding down now. Faust tripped on a chunk of volcanic rock, and it saved his life. He looked up just as the sky became very dark. A massive shape—like a winged man—descended upon Schwarz, who was still a hundred yards from the helicopter. The pilot watched in terror as the creature—displaying dark red skin, bulbous flashing eyes, and silky black feathers—took the screaming Schwarz into its enormous teeth, lifting him like a toy by the head. The dying man flailed pitifully for a moment as the thing crushed his skull with its cavernous jaws, his gyrations slowing as a hugely taloned hand gouged his torso. Mercifully, the clouds swallowed the rest of the bloody scene, just as Faust saw the beast begin to disarticulate what used to be Peter Schwarz.

Suddenly, the air was filled with sound—so dissimilar to the eerie silence that the unfortunate Schwarz had observed just a few moments prior:

clicks—chattering—shrieks . . .

All of varying lengths and timbres, filling the tiny spaces left between the howling winds of the storm and the stringy remnants of sanity that Faust desperately fought to retain. In the fog, Faust could see shadowy figures swooping and ducking all around him. Everything had slowed down and narrowed to a very small window of concentration for him; it was almost languorous. He noticed—in an oddly detached manner—that Nathan had made it all the way back to the chopper, but, as he struggled to open the door, he was taken down. The creature in this instance was far different, just as the thing that had gotten hold of Schwarz looked nothing like the animal on Carter's videotapes: it had not come from the sky, but from the deep.

Scuttling in from the frothy tide, it resembled a bony, hair-covered crab. Alongside its knobby legs were numerous transparent tentacles shooting from its abdomen, almost like tendrils of silk from a spider; it was about the size of a small car. Nathan's horrified eyes locked with Faust's for one eternal instant before the pony-sized arachnid was on him, its violet, faintly glowing body jerking sidewise. Once he was on the ground, Isherwood's screams were clipped short by the awful, horrifying appearance of three or four more of these sea-shrouded horrors, their basketball-sized pincers making a quick, red mess of the young navigator. They then dragged their prize into the surf, alien bodies creaking and clicking in triumph as they pulled his carcass apart, causing the water to become a foaming bath of bright scarlet.

"My *God!*" Faust screamed, bile etching his throat. He had seen guys shot and maimed, even blown to pieces from IEDs in the war; once he saw a soldier friend push his own brain back into a huge, ragged hole in his cranium when a suicide bomber detonated himself in the middle of a market in Baghdad. The bomber actually survived the blast, but it had blown his body in half; the guy was staring up at Faust—who had suffered bad shrapnel wounds to his arms, face, and neck—his guts still smoking. He was blinking at the chaos around him as though he was in some kind of daze; he stopped when Faust walked up and shot him point-blank in the head. The soldier with the head wound smiled at the pilot, then fell over dead.

But this was an altogether new experience: there was something primal about the idea of being eaten alive by a huge predator. Suddenly, Faust found the presence of mind to pull himself up and barrel toward his helicopter, taking out his weapon as he dodged the rising tide and kept an eye overhead.

Sixty feet—

The water was crashing on the landing arms of the chopper. Above him, the flying reptiles were cawing with anticipation.

Forty feet—

The creaking and clicking was suddenly to his left, coming from the swiftly rising water.

"God!" Faust pulled the trigger, firing wildly into the fog. An insane screech of noise blared: one of the bullets seemed to have found its target. Color appeared to drain from the world, even though the details of the machine looming in front of him had become very stark. He swore he could taste the metal skin of the helicopter as he grew closer: it was all he knew—this was his only way back to the ship, back to sanity, or at least away from this extraterrestrial zoo.

Twenty feet!

"Oh shit!" Faust twisted his ankle in the cold, wet sand as he stumbled in the deepening water. Glancing down, he saw that he had tripped over Isherwood's dismembered arm. Abruptly his headset crackled to life:

<<Gree! Gree! CH-CH-CH! Gree!>>

He was confused, then: *"Help! Please! Help!"* It was Julia Murphy.

But it was *not* Julia Murphy: Faust realized now that they had all been fooled. *Julia's dead . . . one of those fucking* things *ate her, probably. But not before they learned to mimic her voice* perfectly . . . *like a myna.* Further, he also grasped something else: they had learned to activate and use one of the radios—maybe Schwarz's, or Carter's, who knew. Faust's side hurt from running so hard, and his stomach pitched at one other thought: *Christ what if they can imitate her* totally, *like in a horror movie or something?* At that moment, he reached out and touched the cold wet covering of the chopper. "Got it!" He slogged through the surf to the pilot's door, climbed in, and wasted no time getting the engines fired up.

The rotors beat the leaden air. At last, the helicopter rose slowly into the ominous sky, now utterly pitch black as premature night cloaked the island. Just as the landing arms cleared the flood of the tide, the chopper was hammered by one of the giant crab-things, putting a huge strain on the near-frozen motors. The aircraft tilted wildly, causing the world to skew sideways; the oil pressure indicator blinked to life as Faust struggled to shake the clicking monstrosity free of his landing gear. Multicolored cockpit lights flickered on and off, creating nauseating intervals of frigid darkness as Faust pleaded into his headset: "*Mayday! Mayday!* Anyone within range of my voice, please come in, over!"

Static: he was alone at the bottom of the world.

Then: <<CH-CH-CH! Gree! *Mayday! Mayday!* Gree!>>

Though Faust was impressed with their stunningly primeval aspects, the creatures' stark ferocity terrified him. And he was, *truly* horrified by the power—and rapidity—of their intellectual adaptations: now they were imitating *his* voice! Chris fought the controls of the chopper—the drag of the creature was becoming too much.

"Jesus! *Mayday! Mayday!* My name is Major Chris Faust! Anyone within the sound of my voice! PLEASE RESPOND! *They can communicate! STAY AWAY!* Over!"

11.

As he stood on the bridge of the USS *Higgins,* Commander Merritt strained to listen through the jumble of sounds in his earpiece.

"Adams, what about that?" the senior officer asked, still holding the headphone to one ear, eyes fixed on his startled communications officer.

"Yeah. . . I—I mean, yes, sir. I heard that, Commander. Don't know what that is, sir. I—I could have *sworn* that I heard a 'Mayday'—but—"

"Nothing previous? No signal, just the voice?" The commander's eyes narrowed in confusion.

"That's correct, sir: just the voice."

The line sputtered again: "—ay! [*beep, beep, beep*] Ma— [*beep, beep, beep*]"

The commanding officer stood at attention, straining to hear. "Adams, put it on the speakers!"

"Yes, sir! On speakers, sir!"

Static filled the bridge of the *Arleigh Burke*–class destroyer, then: "[*blip, blip, blip*] —ound of my voice! My name— [*blip, blip, blip*] *They can communicate!* [*beep, beep, beep*]"

"McConnell! Get a fix on that transmission!" Commander Merritt barked, face lined with concern.

"Working on it, sir!" Warrant Officer McConnell replied, manipulating a variety of dials on a huge console.

"Adams, what—"

A scream abruptly overwhelmed the monitors, the sound temporarily deafening everyone on the deck, then there was silence.

"<<CH-CH-CH! Gree! [*blip, blip, blip*] . . . Gree! *Mayday! Help me!* Gree! [*beep, beep, beep*]>>"

The bridge was a jangle of anticipation. The muscles of the commander's jaws tensed as the colossal ship rocked gently in the storm. Ensign Adams's forehead was moist with perspiration, his eyes jumpy. He traded a worried look with McConnell.

"Can't—can't raise the signal, sir," McConnell said finally. Thunder rolled in the distance. Commander Merritt rubbed his forehead, then loosened his tie.

"Keep . . . keep trying McConnell," the bewildered officer said at last. "Think that was from the *Australis?* Who the hell else would be out here? The Institute said this would likely be the area, and the distress call you picked up was loud and clear until a few hours ago. Be sure to check all the other frequencies. Are we on course, McConnell?"

"Aye. Last I saw on radar, the 'islands' that the Institute claims *Australis* had been given permission to investigate are within a day's voyage of us, sir. To that end, I *have* detected an unusual grouping of . . . *something*. Could be landmass; could be a weather anomaly, though. Not on any maps I've ever seen, either, sir, so it seems unlikely to be islands."

Merritt nodded, listening to the quieted static with intent. "Keep me posted. Have you set the coordinates for these 'islands,' Adams?"

"I have them lined up, just awaiting your decision, sir. Unfortunately, if we set out on that bearing, it means we're headed directly *into* the gale, Commander."

Merritt nodded, silently regarding the ensign. "Well, brace yourselves. Never know what to expect with these squalls, Adams. McConnell, alert the crew to batten down."

"Aye, Commander." After several minutes, McConnell said: "I've been checking all the frequencies. Sorry, Commander—that signal, the possible Mayday—it's lost, sir . . ." Lightning slashed blue against the starless, black velvet horizon, momentarily illuminating ghost fleets of icebergs dotting the vicinity beyond the ice-bound deck of the *Higgins*. The ship was beginning to heave against the mounting swells as they headed deeper into the frigid, nighted abyss of the Southern Ocean.

"Damn." Merritt stroked his face in thought, his eyes dark. Finally: "OK, then. Full steam, Adams. We should eliminate the possibility of a Mayday. Prepare for any contingency, including search-and-rescue. Never know what tomorrow will bring—that's the good and the bad of life, I'm afraid. You just have to get through it."

The nervous ensign looked again at the worried McConnell, who was staring out into the seemingly infinite gulf of enveloping darkness around the destroyer; the air in the bridge took on a bitter, cold edge.

"Aye, Commander," was all Adams replied before finalizing their destination, unknown.

Author's Note

What can I relate about this? It was an idea I had been contemplating for some time, and it brings together many of my own feelings and thoughts about politics, religion, and personal causes. Not everyone will agree with it, but that's OK. Again, I have attempted to write something engaging, yet edgy, with aspects of unreliable narrator, switchbacks, and frames of remove. Thank (or blame! HAHAH!) two people for that: Dan O'Bannon and H. P. Lovecraft (though I suppose there's a dash of A. C. Doyle in the mix). I have a sequel in mind, and it's even more out there!

Simulacrum

All that we see or seem is but a dream within a dream . . .
—*Edgar Allan Poe*

"There are many entrances, but only one exit."

In the long, quiet seconds before she slammed into the unyielding pavement at terminal velocity, the young woman had no way of knowing she could never actually die.

After the stunned crowd had dissipated and the investigation was closed, the official coroner's inquest would record her cause of death as "suicide." She had known differently.

In order to die, one must have lived: she had never truly done either.

She rolls off him, curling up on her side of the bed. He lies on his back, hands on his chest, sated, relaxed. The curtains are drawn across the window, muting the harsh afternoon sunlight. He smiles at her, eyes half-closed, his tone low, sensual. "That was great."

She turns away, staring at the ceiling. "It was. . . . It always is."

He grins.

"I can't keep doing this," she says, suddenly pulling the blanket tight around her nude body.

He frowns. "Oh, shit. Not this again."

"I mean it this time. This has to stop."

"I still don't see—"

She cuts him off with sharply delivered words: "Meeting like this, it . . ." She pauses. "I feel cheap . . . used."

He puts a hand on her thigh, squeezes. "This is crazy. I care about you very much. You know that."

"No, I don't know that. For Christ's sake, if you really cared about me, we

wouldn't be meeting in cheap hotels for nooners."

He shrugs, running a fist along his jaw. His eyes are dark, moody. "You know I'm not ready for more just yet. Not until I have my career back on track. I can't handle you and that. At least not yet."

She smiles tightly. "You don't seem to have any problem handling me in bed."

"That's different," he says.

"Yeah? Well, that's why it can't go on."

"What are you saying?"

"I'm telling you we have to do something about this. Make different arrangements."

"I thought we had something special." He props up on his elbow, regarding her intently.

"We do . . . sex. But that's just physical. What I'm talking about is emotional. I need more of a commitment, not more rolls in the hay." She pushes her hair behind her ear. "I can get that anywhere."

His gaze is intense. "That's it, huh? Just sex . . . Why throw away what we have just because—"

"Because you want to play around?" She smirks, sitting up on the edge of the bed. "Why not?" Her tone is cold, clipped.

"Seems kind of . . . abrupt. I thought we'd hashed all this out a couple of months ago. Can't we talk it over a little more?" He touches her back, but she arches away.

She glares at him over her shoulder. "That's the trouble with you—you don't think. You're a beautiful animal, but that's not enough for me."

Turning away from him, she gets out of bed and crosses the room. As the bedsheet falls away, her naked skin glows milk-pale in the room's diffused light. Putting on her clothes, she languorously strokes her legs as she pulls on her stockings. Her breasts—full, heavy—hang down voluptuously as she bends over to retrieve her bra from the floor. She turns to face him, slinking under the straps as she adjusts her cleavage.

"And another thing," she says, her face flushed with tension. "I don't think I've been the only woman in your life, have I? That's why we don't go out in the evenings anymore, and why you won't take me over to your place."

His tone is edged. "Well, we never agreed to being exclusive . . ."

"You bastard. You admit it!"

"Don't put words in my mouth! If I was seeing anyone else you'd know." He softens. "That's not it and you know it. Look, my schedule is fucked right now,

and my new boss is all over me about getting the next build ready to ship. You know how it is at the end of a product cycle. They're on to us, too, I think."

Sitting up in bed, he lights a cigarette, watching her as she pulls on her sandals. He continues: "I don't have time for anything right now. I've been working crazy shifts and the house is a damn wreck. Not to mention I've still got another month of this shit before it cools off. How about cutting me a little slack?"

She looks at him, crossing her arms. "You're not supposed to smoke in here."

His expression hardens; there is heat in his eyes. "I paid for the damn room. I'll smoke in here if I want to."

"That's right," she says. "You always do just what you want. I'm just like a cigarette to you. I only gratify a passing need."

"That's a cheap shot," he snaps. "And it's not true. I have a lot of respect for you, and you know that."

"You respect fucking me . . . you don't respect me."

He sweeps a hand through his hair. "Fine. How about we just take a breather and revisit the issue when we're both calmer?"

She turns, gathers her purse from a chair near the foot of the bed, and stands with her back to him, her hand on the doorknob. "It's taken me this long to get up enough nerve to be honest with you about everything. I've been a coward."

"Come on, don't say that."

Now fully dressed, a perfect hourglass silhouette at the door, she turns to face him. "You're a great lover—but you're not a great man. Sometimes I feel like I don't know who you are anymore. You've changed. And so have I."

"Look, we've disagreed about this before. Just give it a little more time—"

She huffs in irritation. "Face it: I have." She opens the door. "Don't call me, I'll call you."

She leaves him staring after her as she exits the motel room.

Misty Petit was a half-hour late for work at Pacific Data Systems. An attractive woman in her late thirties, slim and brown-eyed, her tanned skin attested to time spent in the sun. The gray-haired security guard in the lobby grinned at her as she handed him her purse.

"Welcome back! No guns, knives . . . atomic bombs?" he asked.

She gave him a sour look. "I'm not up for comedians today." He handed the purse back, then proceeded to examine her laptop case.

"Bad day already?"

"No . . . bad *night*," she replied. "Not enough sleep. Rotten way to come back from vacation."

He returned her case. "Too bad. You do seem a little tired. Merced's looking for you, by the way."

"Okay. Sorry for my grumpiness, Pete. I'll be okay once I check in and get my morning coffee."

She headed for the elevator.

When Misty arrived at her manager's office, stocky, balding Gabe Merced was hunched over his desk, hands tented as he talked on speakerphone. He acknowledged her entrance with a wave. She sat down, putting her laptop case and purse on her lap.

"Right. We're on schedule," Gabe said.

"Good," the deep, accented male voice replied on the speaker. "We are getting plans together for our next visit. Is Misty back yet?"

Gabe put his finger to his lips, looking at Misty. "She is—I spoke with her this morning, and she's ready to go. She said that the latest version is golden."

There was a quiet moment. "Let's hope so, Gabe. People are getting impatient. Money's tight, so we need to deliver something good. Sooner is better than later, if you catch my drift."

Gabe nodded, his forehead shining slightly. "I got it. We're on top of things, Sanin." He glanced at Misty. "So when will you and Sanjay be here?"

"He'll be in next week, I'll be there a few days later. I have meetings in Moscow first, then a quick trip to Hong Kong. Ever since the Fukushima disaster, funding has been tough, but it's slowly getting better. In fact, there's a VC in Hong Kong that's expressed an interest in what PDS is doing—specifically this project."

Gabe visibly relaxed. "That's great news. We'll be on the case, especially now that Misty's back."

"Good. Looking forward to it. Anything else, then? I've got a conference with Sanjay and Sergey in ten."

"No, that's all for now. I'll keep you posted."

"Will do. Have a good day." The speaker went dead. Gabe punched a button to end the call. He took a deep breath, then turned his attention to Misty. "Well, you heard what he said. Welcome back!"

Misty smiled at him. "Sorry I'm late, Gabe. I overslept. Vacation was sort of a letdown; had to deal with some personal stuff. Wound up being more of a *staycation.* . . . To cap it, I had bad dreams all night." Her dark eyes were shadowed with fatigue.

He smiled back at her. "Sorry to hear that. A lot going on. You heard—Sanjay's coming in from India. He's into what we're doing, but says he's getting static from Sergey and Bjorn about cost-overruns. Sanin is running interference, but he can only hold off the dogs for so long." Gabe shrugged, suddenly pensive. "Anyway, glad you're back. Now we've got to hit the ground running. Morgan's team has done some good work; I think you'll be pleased." He studied her for a moment. "You *do* look drained. Bad dreams, huh?"

Misty smiled, then rubbed her eyes. "I wish I could recall what was happening in them. All I remember is that there was a lot of commotion . . . A man and woman were fighting . . . and I had that horrible *falling* sensation. That's what kept waking me up."

"Dreams slip away fast," Gabe said. "I can never remember mine."

"These were *intense,*" she said. "Scary."

Gabe stood up and walked around the desk. "Well, you'll be okay. So, ready to check out the new build?"

She nodded. "Right after I have my coffee. Can't function without it."

"Hmm . . . God knows what they do to coffee beans these days. You read about that *Kopi Luwak* stuff from Sumatra? Where they feed the coffee beans to civets and they poop it out? How can folks *drink* that? And it's the most expensive coffee in the world! Green tea's a lot better for you."

Misty smiled, shaking her head.

Gabe shouldered her laptop bag as they left his office. "Me, I used to swig down like seven cups of coffee a day. Started getting blackouts, so I gave it up. You quit smoking. Why not coffee? Maybe it's revving you up, causing bad dreams. Did for me."

She nodded. "I *could,*" she admitted, "but I don't see how one or two cups a day is equal to smoking. Besides, it keeps me productive."

He shrugged, leading her down the hall. "Just a thought."

After a labyrinth of hallways and multiple biometric checkpoints, they finally arrived at a large cluster of rooms in the heart of the PDS campus: "Area 52," as Gabe jokingly referred to it. Its actual name, the Multiple Immersive Simulated Total Reality Test Station, was too cumbersome for normal usage. Misty just called it the Sim-Room.

The place was a dark wash of black until Merced switched on the overhead lights, causing the sterile rooms to blossom into sickly life, revealing rows of glassed booths, each with a computer workstation and a reclining chair, their screens glowing, silent.

Misty sat down in one of the cubicles as Gabe handed her a bulky headset with miniature, inward-facing video monitors for lenses. The device was large enough to cover her ears and most of her face. She examined the apparatus carefully before turning it on. "Hey, no more wires!"

Gabe nodded. "Right. Morgan and his team were able to add the wireless code back into the embedded OS last night. First time since the old prototype was damaged that they got it working properly." He adjusted a setting on the computer as Misty reclined into the zero-gravity test chair, tightening the strap of the glasses on the back of her head. "Looks like he's got the 'Auto Record' function working, too. It'll record all experiences as *you* perceive them for anybody to play back later. All we'll need to do to see your new—*extra-reality,* I guess you could call it—is hit the 'Memory' button on the headset."

"Wow . . . this is *awesome!*" Misty looked around the room, eyes hidden behind the tiny screens. "It's getting there, for sure. The new cameras are *excellent.* And so small! I didn't even notice them. I had a feeling once we hit the 40-megapixel range that the detail would be indistinguishable from life, even with motion. I can't detect any interlacing at *all,* and it's a *lot* brighter than with the old cameras. Very real. Turns the whole world into a giant green screen." She adjusted the lenses on her face. "It's a lot more comfortable, too. Feels like they were able to integrate the electrodes into the cap better."

Gabe stood next to her, sharing her excitement. "That's right—while you were luxuriating, we were busy!" He laughed, touching her shoulder as he watched the computer screen. "Almost ready to sub the live feed with the sim. Still a little slow to call up the program sometimes. Here we go . . . Now—what do you see?"

"It . . . it's *beautiful,*" she told him. "Exactly as I imagined it would look. A dry Martian landscape . . . red sand . . . dusty horizon . . . even a base camp! The 3D is perfect!" She reached out from the chair. "I'm standing next to a building of some sort. I can sense solidness at my fingertips when I touch it. Also, there's a light breeze. I can hear it against my suit."

"But you can still hear me okay?"

"Yes—you're coming in loud and clear through my helmet speakers, and the surround-sound is amazing."

Gabe made a note on the pad next to the computer. "So the Convergence chip seems to be acting properly, good. Do you see any people around?"

"Yes. Two. They appear to be base camp astronauts. They're commiserating with each other." Misty waved into the air again. "They can't see me, so the Stealth setting must be working. I cannot *wait* to see what'll happen once we have full integration and can go into Live Mode. Be amazing to *literally* interact not only with other users, but also the characters we've created to populate these scenarios. All in the *same* non-reality space—shared unreality! Amazing . . ."

"What else?"

"Everything is utterly true-to-life . . . I am *here,* Gabe. I'm on Mars!" She squirmed with delight on the recliner. "They're pointing at something in the distance. . . . Oh, I see it! Way out on the horizon . . . a dark spot, sort of amorphous. Storm, maybe? It's so far away I can't make it out."

Gabe nodded, making more notes. "Can you flip into 'Alt' mode? Morgan e-mailed me this morning that it's up now. He said it should allow you to run multiple instances per session, either new or a memory."

Misty touched a button on the frame: instantly a jittery series of flashes and video noise filled her vision. "Yeah, it worked, I guess . . . but just some jumpy images of what looks like . . . the *Moon?*" Misty strained to comprehend the scene. "And the sound is *really* low, staticy. . . . Wait—now . . . now it's a woman looking into a mirror. It's breaking up a little. This is spooky, Gabe. I'm getting a kind of . . . *déjà vu* here. I'm *there,* but *not.* She's from my perspective, but the part of her reflection I can see . . . isn't me! Sort of an out-of-body experience. Oh, wait—there's the lunar landscape again." She hit the button once more. "Okay. Back on Mars. This looks phenomenal, but the other scenes not so much. Seemed like some kind of data corruption. Do you know if Morgan is testing on an old piece of removable media or something? Maybe he accidentally overwrote another program, or forgot to format the card."

Gabe was concerned. "Strange . . . Don't know. He's supposed to use fresh media for all new sessions—said he was, anyway. We'll check it out later. He switched over from CFs to SD cards, since it made the glasses smaller and the capacity is almost the same. Maybe the wiring is off on this cap. He's still working on the other two prototypes. They'll be ready to use in a day or two, he said. Anyway, from all I've seen, your new code is outstanding—we can record real-time, lossless 3D without any lagginess, compression errors, or artifacting." He wrote another note on the pad. "I'll have Morgan and Ganesha drill down into the Moon/woman-in-the-mirror thing tonight."

Misty removed the device from her head. She was aglow with excitement. "My God, Gabe . . . Other than that little glitch, it's *fantastic!*"

"I really like what you and the team have done," he said, "but we need more funds. Hopefully Sanin can hook this Hong Kong venture capitalist—sounds like the kind of big fish we need about now. I think if we can stay off the chopping block and get all the bugs ironed out it's going to be revolutionary. Question is, how do we sell this to the bean-counters like Bjorn?"

Misty slowly turned the headset in her hands, examining it. "Well, unlike the old software-only VRML stuff, *this* virtual reality program and hardware could make a vital training too. . . They can then sift through multiple points of divergence in more practical ways—safely merge potentiality and actuality in realistic settings. I was thinking that it would be great for astronauts who *really* go to Mars. Give them previews of what to expect . . . how best to function on another planet, deal with the isolation, handle emergencies and so on. That's one of the reasons why I wrote the Mars script. And we can augment that—of course it might become awfully difficult to distinguish between the 'real' world and the 'fake' one. But, will it ultimately matter? We want it to be as 'real' as possible. So as we improve the program, the computer-generated characters will have ever more layers of sophistication. Think about *that* . . . Not only will the renders *look* as authentic as a physical person, but the reactions that we've programmed them to have—or *not* have—will become more refined over time. . . more *evolved* by the program itself, especially with all the fuzzy logic and AI functions we're incorporating. . . It's an example of a kind of 'software Butterfly Effect'—adding small tweaks that can yield big results later as the computational models advance and the database develops in gradual complexity. I want to keep pushing, to try and extend these quantum physical ideas into the simulated mindscape."

Merced nodded. "Good points. That'll help me pitch the big boys on why we've been sucking up all their R&D budget for the past two years! It took a long time just to nail down the Thought Amplification Circuits, but it's hard for them to appreciate that without experiencing the technology firsthand. I mean, your work alone—binding thought-based action, tactile and auditory sensation into a non-physical software environs—is groundbreaking stuff. So the gear's still a little . . . *rustic,* shall we say, in the looks department. Big deal!"

He gently took the headset from her, regarding the vast array of wires, electrodes, and the rechargeable battery pack adorning its surface. As he studied the rows of binocular cameras and the tiny binaural microphones on the outside of the speakers, Gabe was engrossed in thought. "You know," he said, "we can even design other programs for war games, or to help veterans with Post-Traumatic Stress Disorder. I thought about that after talking with my dad—he's a vet with PTSD. Since we can take people to the past *or* the future, and it's like they're actually *there,* in a parallel physical environment, it could be great to have them 'relive' things that left them emotionally gummed up; maybe change the outcome of a terrible situation for the better. Sort of 'reprogram' their bad experiences so they can cope in society, a lot like the way mirrors can help amputees get around phantom limb pain. Also, I think that airplane pilots without access to a simulator would find it useful, so there's the commercial avionics companies. Could help patients with diseases like ALS to socialize, or upload memories, thoughts, and so on, or control devices. Hell, even surgeons could benefit by using it to rehearse remote operations without a body!"

Misty agreed: "The potential is practically endless. When I studied deterministic chaos theory, I realized that even though the superficial fabric of reality seems random, it has deeper fractal elements that we can harness . . . I prefer to think of it as 'Enhanced-' or 'Meta-Reality.' Old computer-generated VR has a lot of baggage associated with it, since it never really took off. And this is *so* beyond simple 3D! It's more of a hyper-real videogame, a completely accurate sim-world. That's an important distinction to me: *simulated* versus *virtual.* Virtual seems 'fake,' or contrived, whereas 'simulated' implies involvement. Participation . . . It's a *type* of reality, a subset. A state of 'unreality,' kind of the way a vampire is 'undead'—not reality, but not fantasy." She looked up at her boss, lost in the moment. "And I have an idea that might even be able to recreate olfactory and taste stimulation . . . tap into smell and taste profiles already buried in the subconscious. Taste and smell are powerful, as they can link places and situations to memory, as in Proust's *Remembrance of Things Past,* when the narrator's involuntary recollections are triggered by the taste and smell of the madeleine cake dipped in tea. Could be a potent way to world-build—*total* sensory immersion—and would bypass the uncanny valley, since it's all appropriate to the situation, and not like seeing a leprechaun on the *Titanic.* No chance for cognitive dissonance. In fact, the *opposite* was happening to me: I noticed that the more I focused on the simulation, the more I bought in; I started to *believe* I was on a Martian plain tens of thousands of miles away. Incredible, really."

Merced grinned. "Not to mention other things that could be explored a little closer to home. Games . . . socializing with multiple parties . . . even more *adult* entertainment."

She blushed. "Careful, Gabe! The field's wide open, you might say. There's still one major problem, though."

"Which is?"

"We need a better safety measure than just taking the stupid cap off."

He shook his head. "What do you mean? How could simulated reality, even a pseudo-reality, be dangerous? The operator is always in control. You could stop it anytime you wanted to by just cutting it off."

Misty sat up. "That's true to a point, but when we start to merge existences and sessions, it could get dangerous; I call it 'Diminishing Convergence'—it's a compression of space-time as VR and 'true' reality fuse together in the participant's mind. I've been noticing that the closer we get to the convergence point, the more timeslips and unreliability we have with character behavior. Makes me a little uneasy. I mean, once you're into a Meta-Reality session, there's no *non-physical* way back. Like today, I had to *physically* take the headset off; of course, alternatively, I can reach up and hit the off button. But what if you *can't* for some reason?" She was visibly unsettled by the prospect.

"Do you think that could really happen?" Gabe asked.

She scoffed. "Humans being humans, absolutely. We always have to be mindful of the law of unintended consequences, good or bad, of this technology. For example, suppose someone was being harmed by this? Like being forced to experience a rape, or attacked, or even 'murdered'? That's a real emotion. Remember that the program is at its core self-organizing It is designed to gather impression data not only from the *participant,* but also from the programmed database of real world assets that we've trained it on . . . not to mention the library of flora, fauna, machines, humans, and the world that we've been collecting. Add that to all the mental ephemera we've gotten from the various universities we've partnered with for the Functional-MRIs, the holographic databanks of memories/impressions we've harvested in the field and so on, and there's a *huge* amount of information there not just for good, but to be potentially *abused.* . . . And let's not forget that people will be *adding* to that scaffolding, too, using their personal experiences, recording their *own* memories—even tinkering with the kernel of the code. Theoretically, somebody could upload a rooted version of the program into the wild, and that could introduce all kinds of noise, some of which could be beneficial, just like with real-life where it allows us to cogitate decision points that we may never have considered." She rubbed her temple. "But not all noise is *good;* it could range from simply too much informational dissonance to, in more sinister hands, steganographic—designed to be obscured, and perhaps harmful. Once it's viral, that's it—we'd never be able to control it. It would be a sort of high-level 'mind-hacking.' Hacking *right* into a participant's brain . . . short-circuiting the unconscious, the subconscious."

Misty looked at the computer monitor, deep in thought. "Those f-MRIs have shown that there is no difference *neurally* between *actual* experience and *perceptual* experience. All reality is fundamentally based on self-delusion anyway on some level." She looked back at Gabe. "In other words, the *sessions* are as real to us as our perceptions of 'true reality.' So, again, if someone is murdered, say, in the sim-world, does that mean that they are killed again and again? I mean, now that they are stored only as *data,* do they have a life and death that achieves a meta-state of 'ontological reality' due to the Observer Effect? One that can be relived/replayed over and over, perhaps with differing outcomes? And how do we keep all these divergent realities from glopping together, like gumbo?" Misty's eyes widened at the prospect. "On second thought, though, maybe we don't *want* to stop that. Just have a few protective controls in place. This could become a *super*-neural network! A real *spiritus mundi*. Might be a good thing . . . if it isn't used for bad ends."

Gabe held up his hand in a quieting gesture. "Come on now, Misty. Are you saying that a character that you or someone else may have written in a bit of source code could be equivalent to a living being? That's—"

"Crazy? Maybe not, Gabe." She laughed at the absurdity of her commentary before continuing: "I know it *sounds* far-fetched, but hear me out. Can we be sure that the incidents in the sim-reality environs are *not* 'reality' as we've come to understand it? I'm sure there are some Buddhists and Hindus that might argue the point! Think about it." Misty waved her hands dramatically as she explained. "It creates a *true* 'afterlife' of sorts; a whole new 'dimension' of potential 'ghosts' . . . a virtual realm of the technologically 'non-living.' When does the threshold for life get crossed, anyway? Or identity?"

Gabe was shaking his head in bewilderment. "I'm not following."

Misty drew in a deep breath, calming herself before continuing. "For example, perhaps simple consciousness is enough to attain 'personhood.' Is that the precursor to sentience? Certainly, self-awareness, on some level, is. Currently, there are no non-organically-based life forms that are sentient. These could be the first; mark my words: these characters that we're scripting, they *will* become self-aware eventually. That's the whole point—to make the 'illusion of life' *real*. And that means they'll have *identity* as well, Gabe—a true sense of *self*. So, yeah, a participant *could* just use the gadgetry on the fly for novel new experiences or games, but . . ." She looked directly at Gabe, pausing for a moment. "More sinister than that, they could also program things *away* from free will, into a deterministic point-of-view. And maybe a *bad* POV. They could then use PDS's intellectual property and patents—*my* algorithms—to project reactions and predict scenarios into some nebulous—harmful—futurescape, and with a layer of plausible deniability that could hold up to high levels of scrutiny. What if a character 'takes over' the sim? We might not be able to control them. Wait'll legal gets wind of *that*. We might be up against long odds anyway, but we have to *try* and lock the platform down as much as we can before we drop it live on developers and, God help us, the general population." Misty paused again, sobered by her realization. "We need to avoid a kind of 'looping' of experience where the participant has no control. Also, what if a kid got ahold of this thing? It might cause them some kind of harm. I don't think we can allow the viewer to get *that* locked in. I want to write in an 'exit'—a special way to call up *'actual'* reality . . . whatever that means."

Gabe was quiet. "Wow. That's pretty far-out stuff. Do you think you *can* design an exit?"

She frowned. "I'm sure. Going to take me awhile, though—I'll need some extra funding."

Gabe pursed his lips. "Like I said, we're *beyond* stretched to the limit on this whole project. We've exhausted the original budget and are into next year's fiscal stash. Plus, Sanin mentioned that the Pentagon has been rumbling about their interest; they might try to get more involved for military-only usage. Which could be a source of funding, but it leaves a bad taste in my mouth, as they might try to phase out research into other applications. Could be dangerous—mind-control, Big Brother. What if *they* used it for torture or something? Could be some real Orwellian shit going on there. Leaves Sanin cold, too, but Bjorn would slaughter his family to make a dime. He wants to take PDS public in a year or so, so he's all about cashing out on some mega-IPO. He's pretty unscrupulous. Having a fat military contract looks good on the books." He tossed the headset on the table next to the computer. "I'll see what I can do."

Misty nodded. "At least I can hit it full-time with Vincent out of the picture."

"He's gone, huh? I haven't chatted with him for a while, not since he took that new gig. Too bad, I thought you two kids got along."

She smiled wistfully, hesitating. "Me too."

Gabe rubbed his face. "Anyway, I'll try to rustle up some extra funding for you."

Something is out there. Standing in the darkness. Looming. Unmoving.

She begins walking briskly along the night-dark pavement. A light rain span-

gles her shoulders, dampens her hair. She turns up the collar of her coat, tightly clutching her purse, heart thudding in her chest.

The figure emerges from an inked doorway, starts to follow her, matches her steps.

She feels vulnerable, invaded. A red traffic light flares at an intersection. The figure is closing on her.

She hurries across the street, against the light. No traffic; the dreaming city is tomb-silent, deserted. No cars or buses or trucks. No sirens or auto horns. Just silence, thick and enveloping. She is alone in a vast city with the dark figure . . .

She continues to move over the damp pavement as the rain intensifies, forming bright pools on the sidewalk ahead. Sodium vapor streetlights arc to life above, their radiance haloed by the silvery rain.

She stops, facing an alley that runs like a dark snake between two industrial buildings. On impulse, she wheels into the alley, moving swiftly past piled trash, broken bottles, splintered wooden crates . . . graffiti-covered brick walls press in on her.

She stops again, breathing fast. It is directly behind her now. She can almost feel its hot breath on her neck.

Why does it want me? *Excited, heart racing with a sudden sense of sensual pleasure, she turns to face it.*

But the figure is gone: The alley is empty except for the darkness, and the gentle sound of rain.

Friday morning at PDS: Gabe Merced's office. Misty was seated nervously in an office chair, toying with an unlit cigarette. *Can't let my old vices get their hooks in me again.*

"Had another one last night," she said. "A real doozy."

Gabe looked concerned. "Had another what? Cigarette or nightmare?"

"Nightmare."

Gabe leaned forward, making a sweeping gesture with his hand. "Care to talk about it?"

She looked into the distance. "You know, I can't pin anything down. Dreams have their own twisted logic, don't they?" She discarded the unlit cigarette into a nearby wastebasket. "I just don't understand why I'm having them *more.* Seems like they're more frequent—and so much more *real*—now that we're getting close to this next deliverable milestone. And there's this . . . *darkness.* I can even feel it after I wake up. I can't explain it any better than that. Like another being, another consciousness is in the dream, in my bedroom."

Gabe studied her for a moment. "Maybe it's just stress? You've been pushing pretty hard. And the whole Vincent situation . . ."

She glanced up at her boss. "Maybe."

"Me, I handle stress with a chess game. Clears the mind, drains away all the hassle. I can even kick Sanin's butt!" He regarded her intently. "You play chess?"

Misty shook her head. "Never learned."

"Chess does wonders for reducing tension. Nothing like it. Maybe I could teach you sometime."

Misty's smile was strained. "Yeah. Sometime." She made an effort to regain her composure. "Anyway, I just needed to vent a little. You're a good listener."

"I try to be." He smiled at her.

She smiled back. "I just hope my subconscious gives me a break!"

Misty was eating lunch in the commissary when her friend Nancy walked up with a tray of food and sat down across from her. "Saw you in Gabe's office. Problems?"

"Oh, no, I was just telling him about some dreams I've been having. He's very understanding."

Nancy regarded her with amusement. "Uh-huh."

"What's that supposed to mean?"

Nancy giggled. "Just . . . I think that he likes you is all."

"But he's never—"

"Made a pass? Of course not! He can't, you know that. But I've seen the way he looks at you. Heck, if he told you he liked your new shoes he'd be up for sexual harassment!"

"I suppose. . . . Gabe's not my type anyway."

Nancy shrugged. "To each their own." She nodded toward her friend's tray. "That all you're eating for lunch—salad and tea?"

"I don't feel very hungry." Misty poked at the food on her tray.

"Look," Nancy said, "I have two tickets to this concert tomorrow night and my boyfriend can't make it. It's going be great. A classical guitar recital—Paco Seville is playing with an orchestra!"

"*Sounds* great," Misty replied. She smiled at her friend. "You know, I could use some R-and-R right now."

Misty enjoyed the concert, losing herself in the lush arrangements of Debussy, Chopin, Beethoven, and Dvořák. As they walked out of the concert hall, Nancy asked: "So . . . how'd you like it?"

"Fantastic!" Misty said. "Gave me goosebumps." Her eyes were shining as they walked to the car. "Someday I'd like to travel through Europe—see the countryside, visit Prague and Florence. I hear Barcelona is nice."

"They still have bullfighting."

"*That* I can do without. I read that they're going to ban it. All to the good. I can't stand to see any animal hurt. It's barbaric."

A man was walking just ahead of them, apparently lost in the vast parking deck. He was slight, dressed in an ill-fitting dark suit. An older gentleman, his gait was a shuffle; as they passed him on the way to the car, he slowly looked up. Fishing for her keys in her purse, Misty paused, glancing back at him as Nancy continued walking, chattering on about animal cruelty, her voice echoing in the shadowy parking structure.

The brim of his crumpled hat hides his aspect to the mouth, which is little more than slit-like lips gashed into dead-white skin. He soundlessly mouths: "So, you're not into death, I gather?"

The world is stopped: quiet, cold. The parking edifice has vanished, and she is standing in a stark white light coming from above. The man continues to shuffle closer, and his dreadful features come into clearer view: watery, bulbous eyes set into an angular, expressionless face. His lips curl slightly with the effort of moving, drawing the tight skin over the sunken cheeks even tighter, causing his dark eyes to protrude more.

Misty stares, her throat clenched. "That's an odd thing to say." She drops her purse.

He does not reply, just continues his relentless forward movement. He reaches for her with a taloned, gnarled hand.

She screams, closing her eyes and dropping to her knees in panic . . .

"Jesus! You scared me, doll!" Nancy exclaimed, spinning around. She rushed over to her friend. "What's wrong? Are you okay?"

Misty was disoriented, her breath ragged. She was kneeling on the ground, her stockings ripped, and the contents of her purse lay scattered on the pavement of the parking deck. "Where . . . Is he here?"

Nancy was confused, picking up toiletries and dropping them into Misty's purse. "Is *who* here?"

"That horrible old man!"

"What are you talking about? What old man?"

"He was just here." Misty glanced around. They are alone in the deck. She looked into Nancy's eyes: her friend was concerned. "Oh my God. He was *just* here, I swear. We passed . . . Never mind. Just . . . never mind. I must be going koo-koo, Nance. I've got to get my act together."

Nancy smiled. "It's okay, doll. Forget it. New subject. How's the project coming?" They stood up together, smoothing their skirts and correcting their blouses in mirrored unison.

"Well," Misty said, adjusting her hair, "we're about to deliver, but I've had a few issues. Nothing serious, I hope; we'll see."

"You'll get it. I have faith in you!" She regarded Misty, touching her hand. "So . . . you all right to drive? Maybe up for a little noshing? Might make you feel better. Maybe you're just tired. I sure am! Been working my tail off."

Misty grinned. "Indeed. That music gave me quite an appetite!"

Nancy laughed. "You sure love music, I must say." She smiled at her friend. "Indian food?"

"Love it. Spicier the better!"

She hugged Misty. "My treat, doll."

The restaurant, Krishna's Dream, was decorated with pastoral Indian woodcarvings and vibrant colors; framed paintings of Indian deities hung along the walls, and the delicate aroma of saffron wafted through the air. Seated at a scrolled antique table, Misty and Nancy savored a smoky red wine as they nibbled on samosas.

"This is magical!" Misty declared, raising her glass. "A toast."

"To what?" asked Nancy.

"To the concert. And to female bonding! Who needs the boys, anyway?"

They clicked wine glasses.

"Yeah . . . I'll drink to that." Nancy sighed. "Vincent gave me a runaround, too."

Misty stared at her, her eyes reflecting shock. "*You* were involved with Vincent?"

"Long time ago. For about six months," said Nancy. "I met him when he first came to work at PDS. We were pretty serious for a while. *Any*way, it's ancient history."

"But you never told me!" Misty frowned. "I thought friends were supposed to share everything."

"Didn't want to upset you, doll. Figured you might get pissed. You know . . ."

Misty put her glass down, waving away a waiter who was about to pour more wine. "I *am* pissed . . . but not at you. At him, for claiming that I was his first 'real' relationship."

"Oh, yeah, Vince can be devious," Nancy agreed. "We're both a lot better off without that creep in our lives, he was quite the heart-breaker. Dated a few of the girls at PDS."

Misty was subdued for the remainder of the evening, disturbed by what Nancy had revealed. On the way back to her apartment, she was silent as she stared into the cold, concealing night.

The Sim-Room. Late afternoon. Misty was at her computer wearing the headset when Gabe Merced walked up to her. "You working on the exit code?"

"Yeah," she nodded. "And I think I've almost got it. Another few builds. In the meantime, we're stuck just taking the cap off or hitting the switch. I'll be glad to get it in place, too. I noticed that the jolt from reality to Meta-Reality and back not only gives me a headache at the time, but a lingering touch of vertigo even a few hours after the fact. Better when we can Transition. I feel as if doing it too quickly is giving me the mental equivalent of the bends!"

"Great!" Merced's broad smile radiated triumph. "That's a real step forward."

"One small step for woman . . . one giant leap for PDS!"

Gabe sat down next to her. "Can I try?"

"Of course." She removed the headgear and handed it to him.

"Ah," he said, "I see we're still on Mars."

"I've enjoyed prowling around the landscape in a Rover," she said.

"Maybe I'll actually get there someday."

"It's possible. Dorothy got to Oz."

"I'm working on a Moon program that should prove really popular, too. Life on a moonbase. Got inspired after seeing that scene during the other test. Done a ton of research on it."

"Wow!" Gabe said, leaning forward. "This *is* hypnotic. Been a while since I've checked it out." He removed the headset.

"All in a day's work. There's one more thing I need to see," she said, again fitting the cap over her head.

"Everything looked fine to me," Gabe said. He rubbed his eyes. "I can definitely see what you mean about transitioning, though."

Misty's face went pale and she drew in a long breath. "Oh my *God—it's back.*"

"What are you talking about?"

"That . . . that *figure* . . . Remember the storm I saw on the edge of the horizon last time we were in the Mars-sim? The black shape I talked about? Well it's been getting closer—and it's *not* a storm, Gabe. It's . . . some kind of *being.* But nothing in the databases, or in the code: I checked all that. It's . . . something else!"

"I didn't see any—"

She hastily stripped off the headset. "It's *there,* Gabe! That . . . *thing!*"

"Hey, calm down," he told her. "Probably just a ghost in the machine."

"Then why didn't *you* see it?"

"Trick of the mind. You've been going hard on this exit thing. Take a break. Go home and get some rest. We can straighten all this out tomorrow."

She stood up, shaking, her eyes haunted. "But . . . what if it's still there tomorrow? Maybe closer?"

"It won't be, I'm sure. Get a good night's sleep."

She is feeling the effects of the Scotch: I've got to stop this. Drinking only makes everything worse.

She rises from the sofa, picks up the half-empty bottle, and staggers into the kitchen. She stands over the sink for a long moment, swaying drunkenly, then pours the amber contents of the bottle down the drain.

There, it's done. Didn't help me get to sleep anyway.

She tosses the empty bottle into the recycling and returns to the living room. Sobbing under her breath, she paces back and forth, back and forth. The walls of the apartment press in around her. She holds out her hands: they are shaking again.

She is no longer sure of anything: Her reality is shattered, splintered like a broken mirror. She walks over to the computer, staring at the clunky new wireless prototype.

'Get some rest,' *they told her.* 'You're very important to us—one of our top programmers.'

And Vincent . . . Where is *he* now? Gone, like all the rest.

She grabs the headset and walks to the sliding glass door of her patio. Opening the door, she steps out onto the lanai. At the steel railing, she looks at the traffic far, far below. A slight breeze ruffles her hair. The full moon rides clear of a swollen cloudbank, fuming in the sky: a bright yellow beacon, calling to her. She stares upward, tears shining in the moonlight. Donning the headgear, she powers the mechanism up. She presses the 'Memory' button and recorded images flicker into her tipsy consciousness.

The moon . . . I'm there again—floating in the light gravity . . . exploring the craters . . . walking the rocky terrain . . .

Carefully, she steps through the rough lunar topography, balancing herself on a narrow crater edge. The solar winds are strong, licking at her like an angry animal. In the darkness of the crater, far, far below, she sees movement.

It's back . . . I knew it would be. What does it want?

She jumps from the ridge: the gravity—only an eighth of her native Earth's—buoys her for a languid moment. She smiles as a gusting windstorm blew curtained red sand across the barren landscape. The distant sun flamed from the down-pressing sky.

She was there, on Mars . . . and on the horizon, the strange dark figure was, too.

She tried to run, but the blowing sand blinded her, pelted her. Her legs felt numb.

The dark figure seemed to glide toward her over the sand, its shadow spreading like a stain before it.

Sweat pearled her skin inside the suit, her heart raced in her chest; something was wrong: the edges of reality were rippling, smearing . . . colors were separating like a faulty three-color projection image. The periphery of her vision was vignetted, as though peering into an old zoetrope. The dark figure grew larger in her line of sight . . . wavering . . . looming . . . quickening . . . converging on her in the growing storm.

She tried to scream over the howl of the terrifying winds before she lost consciousness—

"My name is Svetlana Dragonović! I am coming to you from your future."

Misty awoke with a start, breathing hard, lying in a pool of sweat in her darkened bedroom. "Jesus . . ."

That afternoon in Merced's office, Misty was distraught, her head throbbing. Gabe was concerned. "Misty, you look—"

"I'm confused. Things are mixed up. And I'm so fucking *tired*, Gabe," she interrupted. "Dreams seem *totally* real—as if I'm wearing the headset. When I wake up it feels like I'm still inside the dream. The boundaries of what's real seems hazy . . . indistinct . . . even right now, this moment."

He sat down beside her on the couch, gently touching her leg. "You're strong, Misty. I'm sure this whole thing is from the stress you've been under. Once you have the exit in place, I'll authorize more time off."

She shook her head.

Merced continued: "Your work is vital. We can't do what has to be done without your input. You're very important to us—one of our top programmers. As you said, we *need* that exit. Look, Sanjay is here tomorrow. I can stall him a day or two, but once Sanin is here as well, they'll want to sync up with all of us."

She stared at the floor. "There must be someone else who can take over for me—at least for a while. Just until I can get my head together. Maybe this woman from my dream—this Svetlana Dragonović? Her name seems . . . *familiar*. Maybe she's the woman from the other media? The one with the lunar stuff on it, remember?"

Gabe stiffened in his chair. "Svetlana Dragonović. Yes . . . she was working on an earlier version of the software. It was before the last big reorg— An outstanding programmer from what I understand; the Russians excel at this stuff! Before my time, and not my department, though. She's . . . no longer with the company. So, in answer to your question, *no*—there's no one with your experience and expertise. The whole program depends on you. Don't let PDS down . . . don't let *me* down."

She held her head in her hands. After a long pause: "All right, I'll stay . . . see what happens." She looked at him with wounded eyes. "But I don't know how long I can hang on, Gabe." She stood to leave.

He stopped her at the door. "Look, I have an idea that you'll find pretty far out."

"I'm game for anything," she told him, rubbing her temple.

Gabe paused. "Go see Vincent." He held up a hand before she could protest. "Just have lunch with the guy."

She raised an eyebrow. "Okay. Why? I told him we were finished and we *are*."

"Don't get me wrong," cautioned Gabe. "I'm not suggesting that you resume your relationship, just that you have a *talk* with him." His expression was unsettled. "Vince knew Svetlana. Well."

She was silent for a long moment, letting his words sink in. "What if he refuses to meet me?"

"Not very damn likely. At the least he'll be curious—wondering why you want to see him again. Give it a shot. Can't hurt, and it just might answer some questions."

She nodded. "Or raise even more . . ."

She met Vincent the following Friday for lunch at Krishna's Dream. He had been friendly on the phone, admitting that he never expected to hear from her again.

At the restaurant, he leaned back in his chair, regarding her with a serious expression. Always a fast eater, he had finished his entrée before she'd gone through half of hers. "I have to admit," he began, studying her, "I was pretty surprised at your phone call last week."

She smiled anxiously at him. "I hadn't intended to call you ever again, actually." She took a sip of wine.

His eyes searched her face. "Why did you call, then?"

"Curiosity, mainly. I . . . I wanted to see how you were taking our split."

He looked toward the door. "It's all okay, I guess. What do you want me to say? I've missed you? I'd like to see you? I mean, that's true, but so what? You made it pretty clear we were done."

She looked down. "I'm sorry about the breakup. I didn't mean to—"

"Hey." He shrugged. "Couples break up all the time. Relationships don't always last. I've had my share—you . . . Nancy . . ."

"Yes, she told me you two were an item at one time."

"Svetlana . . ."

"Svetlana Dragonović, right? My boss, Gabe, mentioned that you knew her. You two were involved?"

"Yeah, for a bit. She was on a project very similar to that thing you were working on."

"The one I'm *still* working on, you mean." Her voice was tense. "I'm sorry. Go on."

"Well, she started to have . . . *issues.* Sort of got delusional. She'd always suffered from insomnia, but once she was working on that VR thing, well, that was it. It's one of the reasons I left PDS. She was getting out there—claimed she was being stalked; that there was a problem with the program. Became obsessed with it, really. Then the headaches started."

Misty was feeling nervous, warm. "How long were you and Svetlana . . . together? Why didn't you ever mention her to me?"

He looked at her, his face sad and tired. "SD and I were together for about a year. I never said anything because . . ." Vincent's eyes began to water. "I never said anything because it was painful. I just had a hard time with the whole situation. The night we broke up she . . . she jumped off her patio. Ten floors down to the street." He paused, breath ragged with emotion. "She left a note. To me."

He pulled his wallet out. Inside, he rifled through the contents until he found a folded, well-worn slip of paper. "This."

Misty dabbed her eyes with her napkin and gently took the missive from his shaky fingers, reading it to herself:

> *Chuang Tzu once observed the following; may it bring you solace, as it has to me.*
>
> *'I was sleeping, dreaming that I was a butterfly flitting through the air . . . then I awoke.*
>
> *'Now, I wonder: Am I a man who dreamt of being a butterfly . . . or am I a butterfly dreaming that I am a man?'*

Goodbye, Vincent. Never forget that we are our memories. Never forget that the self is a delusion, a false construction.

And never doubt that I loved you, and still do.

— *S. D.*

DO NOT USE. SD EVIDENCE. PROOF OF CONCEPT.

She removed the SD card from Morgan's library cache and brought it closer to her face for inspection.

'SD EVIDENCE.' Of course it's SD. It's a piece of Secure Digital media. Why label the obvious? Evidence of what?

Strolling over to the recliner, she took the headset from the battery recharging station. As she sat down, she pulled the mechanism over her head, inserting the media card into the appropriate slot. She settled back into the chair before turning the cap on, then pressed the 'Memory' button:

A cool, featureless room: sterile. Waist-high, stainless steel tables.

A morgue.

She walks to a corner of the dark chamber, huddling in the shadows. She sees a pathologist working under a single intense lamp; she moves closer.

It is Vincent. He is zipping a body bag closed as she maneuvers to a better vantage point.

"Goodbye," he says, his breath fogging the air. He turns and leaves the cold room, and the door closes heavily behind him.

She walks forward into the light. A tag on the PVC bag reads 'S. Dragonović.'

As she reaches out to touch the label, the body bag ripples.

Stepping back in shock, she stares: the bag moves again. Then, slowly, the zipper peels down, pulled from the inside. The body within begins writhing more, struggling to escape the confines of the container.

The cadaver is sitting up now: her nude body is unsteady. The flesh is mottled, a veiny grey-blue, the ragged lips cyan from a lack of oxygen. The arms are covered in purple-black bruises and bloodless, gaping wounds. The feminine ribcage is compacted, knotty, and unbalanced as the body sways on the table and does not expand for breath. The ruined head tilts at a peculiar angle, the broken neck a bulging disfigurement under the delicate flesh of the throat. The face, crushed over one eye, is somewhat disguised by a matted tangle of blood-crusted hair, and the jaw, unhinged, hangs absurdly open, displaying the stumps of broken teeth and an obscenely enlarged tongue. The nose is little more than a gristled protuberance on the ghastly, unrecognizable face.

The head gimbals toward her, bone audibly grinding bone, its remaining eye fixing on her as the splintered jawbone works: "I . . . know . . . *you.*" The words are raspy, quiet, breathless in the sharp air of the room.

She stands there, muscles frozen, unable to move or scream, horror-struck by the gruesome visage of the carcass.

"You . . . *dangerous* . . ." The corpse lifts its mangled arm up and points at her with a broken-fingered hand.

The words are crackling, punctuated by static. The atmosphere of the room begins to pixelate, to flicker as she watches. The light gets dimmer and the scene is suddenly shifting, blurring. Near the horizon line, a spreading, inky shadow looms over the place, growing in size, blotting out all light.

The room plunges into darkness . . . she screams at last.

"Suddenly, everything started . . . breaking up." Misty squinted her eyes in recollection, looking from the table to Gabe. They were in his office as she explained her latest nightmare. After a beat: "Did you know Svetlana when she was at PDS?"

Gabe nodded, leaning back in his chair. "I did know her, but not very well. I remember that she was working on a project for the FBI. Pretty hush-hush stuff."

Misty nodded, listening. She rubbed the sides of her head as Gabe spoke. "What was the gist of it?"

Gabe stroked his face absentmindedly. "She was using Behavioral Sciences Profiler information and data from VICAP to create VR criminal personalities. They were going to train new FBI agents, mainly Profiler candidates, at Quantico on the use of VR for novel applications of the technology in the field. You know, like hostage negotiation, serial murder, spree killing, counter-terrorism, that type of thing."

"Interesting," Misty said. "So what happened?"

"Strange thing. She started having . . . *problems,* I guess you could say."

The tension in the room suddenly increased. Misty looked closely at her boss. "Problems? Like what? Software? Hardware?"

Gabe smiled, glancing between her and his office window. "Not sure how to explain that, as I was friends with her project manager, but didn't really know her that well."

"Who was her PM?" Her head was pulsing harder now, slow and hot.

Gabe looked away again, his face growing pale and sweaty. "Hey, Misty, after the next meeting with Sanin, maybe we *can* shelve this whole project for a while, before you crack over this figuring out this exit—"

"Who was her PM, Gabe?" She felt desperate, out of control. *"Tell me!"* The demand was more shrill than she meant it to be.

He paused, then regarded her once more, his gaze steady. "Vincent. Vincent was her PM, okay?"

She was stunned. "*My* Vincent?"

Gabe nodded. "Yeah. They were already dating when I was put in charge of this division. He said she'd been on this thing for about two years when she . . . passed away." He cleared his throat. "She was stuck on a problem. Got obsessed with trying to solve it."

"What was the problem?"

"Look, do we need to go into this? What's it going to solve?"

She looked at him, her lip curling in irritation. "It might solve a lot! Just tell me. Come on, Gabe, you *owe* me this—I've been busting my *ass* on this thing!"

Gabe was visibly agitated. He continued, toying with a pen on his desk. "Okay, okay. The hardware was good. Not as good as this new setup, mind you, but after the other one was destroyed in the fall . . . Anyway, the same old shit was happening—tight budget, politics, yada-yada-yada . . ."

"Cut to the chase, Gabe."

"As I was saying," he said, looking up for a moment, "she had a problem with the software that she'd created. An error. One of the characters she wrote. Vincent said that he took on a 'life of his own.' She claimed he was after her, stalking her."

Misty was getting frantic. "And that's why we started from scratch? That's what happened with Morgan, right? The old media . . . It *was* Svetlana in the reflection, wasn't it? I suppose she was working on that moon thing, too, right?"

Gabe raised his hand to quiet her. "Yeah, right. But . . . full confession. We *didn't* start from scratch. I . . . I just told *you* that."

Misty was startled. "*What?* Gabe, what the *fuck*—"

He continued: "I'm sorry, Misty. Anyway, I had to do something, they were all over me about budget, threatening to cut the whole project. I did what I thought was best for the team. I'm sorry."

Misty was dumbstruck. "Okay, then. So, what happened? Why did she kill herself?"

"Well," he started, "she ran into the same issues that you have. She started to get more paranoid . . . nightmares . . . headaches . . . All due to one problem: The character that she said began 'coming to life' was an amalgamation of several *real* serial murderers. He was a dangerous entity—"

"*Entity?* Oh, this is getting *weird*—"

"Just hear me out, Misty. . . . So, according to Vince, she said that she tried to get rid of the character. To erase him . . . but he wouldn't 'die.' That was an unintended consequence—a sort of side-effect that developed out of tinkering with consciousness caused by data noise and corruption. She said it was because of an error in the old Convergence chipset: the hypermerge between 'reality' and 'non-reality' had a memory leak that allowed too much 'real-time reality' into the VR environment. He became the first documented case of what she deemed 'AAS'—Artificially Aggregated Sentience. In fact, he began to *elude* her in the VR environs. At first he would change his appearance, his *aspect;* eventually, he turned the tables and started stalking her, the first *autonomous* malevolent consciousness in a VR scenario. This character *existed* to stalk, to murder. He didn't *want* an exit built in, because then the Observer was gone, and thus a potential victim . . . and audience." Gabe stopped for a moment to let his words take hold. "See, it's just as you theorized. Are these characters any less 'alive' than we are? What is the purpose of reality? Of consciousness? We learn, grow, develop in all these states. We elect to make distinctions, but those distinctions are soft, not hard delineations. Like now: Are we the Observers, or are we being Observed?"

Misty looked at him. "My *God,* Gabe. That means . . . that means *she* is 'real,' too! She's 'alive' every time someone views the data!"

"Right. In a sense. But one other thing she learned. She called it 'Engagement,' which finally resolved into 'Neurological Entanglement'

. . . Over time, with enough exposure to the VR environment, not only did her test subjects start to confuse reality with non-reality, but they stopped having a sleep interval, too. They began living in a twilight state of 'super-consciousness' . . . and it all started as a dark area on the horizon."

Misty drew her breath in sharply, eyes wide. "Oh, *no.*"

Gabe nodded, his mouth set. "She described this facet of Engagement as 'Waking R.E.M.,' and the normal sleep paralysis that happens with restorative sleep doesn't occur during this phase. Instead, her test participants described extensive sleep disruption, nightmares, hallucinations, and so on. It was a sort of *fracturing* of consciousness, not unlike schizophrenia. In the later stages, headaches. Depression. Severe anxiety. Intractable psychosis." He looked out of the window again; their room was getting dim. "Even suicide. That's when we dropped using outside research staff."

"And you didn't *tell me?*" She glared at him. Outside, the world was pitch black.

He put his hand to his mouth. "I know. I know. We should have just pulled the plug on MISTY, but—" And now the room is growing darker, darker.

Misty blinks. "Pull the plug on 'MISTY' . . . What do you mean?"

He stares at her. "Come on. You know."

"You mean," she starts, "Multiple Immersive Simultaneous Total Reality? *That* MISTY, right?"

He stands as the room grows dimmer. "Yes. That's *you,* Misty—*'MISTY'* . . . SD is writing the exit strategy." He looms over his desk, his eyes cold, lifeless, his voice low, soft. "In fact, she could be writing it right now."

Misty is confused. "I don't under—"

"Of course!" Gabe interrupts. She watches as he instantly morphs into the horrible old man from the parking deck, then into a strange, black-cloaked beast, and finally the cadaver from the morgue before changing back into her boss.

"So," she begins, slowly getting up from the couch, "what happened to this . . . *errant* character?"

He sneers, and his gaze cuts through the intensifying gloom. "Simple. SD reined him in at the lowest stack—root level . . . outwitted him by manipulating the Self-Awareness Threshold. Of course, he caught on." Gabe chuckles, his eyes narrowing. "And the exit is so obvious in hindsight: replicate sleep brain waves if a character begins acting aggressively. That allows you to escape—just go to 'sleep' and when you awaken, you'll be conscious in the 'real' world . . . thrown out of the scenario without removing the cap or cutting the switch off. You just become *aware* that you're thinking about *thinking* . . . draw total attention to the reality of non-reality . . . sort of *relax* into it. But how could you know that?"

Misty is shocked. "So that's the exit? But . . . but I haven't been able to get it working." She is rattled, her throat dry and tight. "Did . . . did this character have a *name?"*

Gabe looks at her, smiling broadly. "Just *relax,* Misty. Yeah—he *does* have a name." He suddenly reaches his hands up, grasping toward her: "It's Gabe Merced."

Before she can scream, he leaps across the table . . .

In her office, as Svetlana sits in her chair considering the headset resting on the table, Vincent stops by and peers in. "Are we on for tonight?"

She looks up and smiles, nodding. "Of course. Incidentally, I think I've fixed the glitches in MISTY. No more dark figures . . . no more out of control characters. Still have the headaches, but better Transitioning should help that. Best of all, no more jumping off of buildings to get out of the program!"

He laughs. "That's good news. So you've got the mental exit in place?"

She nods again. "I do. All it requires is a certain series of events guided by the participant's cues and emotional state. It's not perfected, but it's a start."

"What do you mean?"

"I mean if we exploit the principle behind the Observer Effect to keep the scenario in a state of 'limbo'—sort of like in the Schrödinger's Cat hypothesis—then we can insert enough ambiguity . . . uncertainty . . . *into the Probability Module to disrupt the narrative logic. A little nod to Heisenberg, I suppose. I'm calling it 'Overt Awareness.'" She arches her brow. "So, if you are forcibly entered into another conceptual mindframe, it disturbs the anticipated storyline, which then kicks you out of the scenario. Just a little simple coding and a twist of Eastern thought. Don't know why I didn't come up with this before. I predict once you see how elegant this solution is, you'll be pleased."*

He crosses his arms. "Yeah? How'd you figure it out?"

She rubs her hands together, smiling evilly. "Let's put it this way—there's more than one way to skin the cat. But if I tell you my way, I'll have to kill you."

They both laugh.

Fitting the cap over her head, she continues: "You know how I am; I hate divulging secrets." She punches up the Moonbase session and reclines into the cushion of the chair. "As I always say—there are many entrances, but only one exit . . ."

Author's Note:

What is a ghost, exactly? Are they bundles of ectoplasmic ooze, or the projections of a paranoid mind? Perhaps they are the cosmic awareness of past events, or reverberations of electromagnetic energy. Maybe they are the by-product of consciousness. Do they exist without humans to comprehend what they are? Or are they clues to an alternate realm? And what are they trying to convey: warnings? information? comfort?

Acknowledgments

"Black Box" was first published in *Dark Discoveries* No. 14 (July 2009).

"'By Any Other Name . . .'" originally appeared online in *Horror Bound Magazine* (http://www.HorrorBound.com/; October 2008).

"The Central Coast" was first published in *The Bleeding Edge: Dark Barriers, Dark Frontiers,* edited by William F. Nolan and Jason V Brock (Cycatrix Press, 2009).

"The Hex Factor" was first published in *Ethereal Tales* (November 2008).

"The History of a Letter" was first published in *Black Wings II: New Tales of Lovecraftian Horror,* edited by S. T. Joshi (PS Publishing, 2012).

"Milton's Children" was first published as a standalone novelette (Bad Moon Books, 2014).

"Object Lesson" was first published in *The Devil's Coattails: More Dispatches from the Dark Frontier,* edited by Jason V Brock and William F. Nolan (Cycatrix Press, 2011).

"One for the Road" was first published in *Night Terrors II,* edited by Theresa Dillon and Marc Ciccarone (Blood Bound Books, 2012).

"P.O.V." was first published in *Dark Discoveries* No. 19 (March 2012).

"Pathologist's Roulette" originally appeared online in *Everyday Weirdness* (http://www.EverydayWeirdness.com/; May 2009).

"Poem from the Future" was first published in *Calliope* (Fall 2008).

"Red-Wat-Shod" originally appeared online in *Paul Kane's Shadow Writer* (http://www.shadow-writer.co.uk/guest1.htm; September 2011).

"The Underground" originally appeared online in *SNM Horror Magazine* (http://www.snmhorrormag.com/; August 2009).

"Valor: A Fable" was first published in *Ethereal Tales* (July 2009); this version is revised.

"Van Helsing: His True Story" was first published in *Slices of Flesh,* edited by Stan Swanson (Dark Moon Books, 2012).

"What the Dead's Eyes Behold" was first published in *Dark Discoveries* No. 18 (April 2010).

"Where Everything That Is Lost Goes" was first published in *Like Water for Quarks,* edited by Elton Elliot and Bruce Taylor (MVP Publishing, 2011).

All other works in this volume are published here for the first time.

About the Author

Jason V Brock has been widely published in magazines, comics, and anthologies such as *Butcher Knives & Body Counts, Animal Magnetism, Fangoria,* the *Weird Fiction Review,* S. T. Joshi's *Black Wings* anthology series, *Like Water for Quarks,* and many others. He also served as managing editor/art director/contributor for more than three years at *Dark Discoveries* magazine. Brock runs the well-regarded biannual genre print digest/e-book and website *[NameL3ss],* online at *http://www.NamelessMag.com.*

Brock served as coeditor/contributor to the award-winning, critically acclaimed Cycatrix Press anthologies *The Bleeding Edge: Dark Barriers, Dark Frontiers* and *The Devil's Coattails: More Dispatches from the Dark Frontier,* with William F. Nolan. Brock's latest anthology is titled *'A Darke Phantastique'—Encounters with the Uncanny and Other Magical Things.*

Brock has also assisted Nolan on other projects, including the Bluewater Productions comics *Logan's Run: Last Day* (as story consultant and lead costume designer) and the graphic novel *Tales from William F. Nolan's Dark Universe* (as co-writer), and as co-author for an addition to the Logan saga entitled *Logan Falls.*

Brock's films include the highly regarded documentaries *Charles Beaumont: The Short Life of Twilight Zone's Magic Man, The AckerMonster Chronicles!* (about legendary agent and *Famous Monsters of Filmland* editor Forrest J Ackerman), and *Image, Reflection, Shadow: Artists of the Fantastic* (featuring H. R. Giger, Roger Dean, Ernst Fuchs, and many more artists from all over the world). An accomplished artist and musician himself, Brock has had multiple showings of his artwork and illustrated his own books in addition to creating posters and packaging for his films and his former progressive rock band ChiaroscurO.

A health nut and gadget freak, Brock lives in the Vancouver, WA, area and loves his wife Sunni, their family of reptiles/amphibians, and practicing vegan/vegetarianism.

Visit his website at http://www.JaSunni.com.

www.ingramcontent.com/pod-product-compliance
Lightning Source LLC
Chambersburg PA
CBHW061426030726
47503CB00005B/1319

9781614980551